THEM BONES

THEM BONES

David Housewright

MINOTAUR
BOOKS
NEW YORK

FOR RENÉE
AND RENÉE AND RENÉE
SOME MORE

First published in the United States by Minotaur Books, an imprint of St. Martin's Publishing Group

THEM BONES. Copyright © 2025 by David Housewright. All rights reserved. Printed in the United States of America. For information, address St. Martin's Publishing Group, 120 Broadway, New York, NY 10271.

www.minotaurbooks.com

The Library of Congress Cataloging-in-Publication Data is available upon request.

ISBN 978-1-250-36051-9 (hardcover)
ISBN 978-1-250-36052-6 (ebook)

Our books may be purchased in bulk for promotional, educational, or business use. Please contact your local bookseller or the Macmillan Corporate and Premium Sales Department at 1-800-221-7945, extension 5442, or by email at MacmillanSpecialMarkets@macmillan.com.

First Edition: 2025

10 9 8 7 6 5 4 3 2 1

ACKNOWLEDGMENTS

Allow me to acknowledge my debt to Grace Gay, Kayla Janas, Keith Kahla, Eric Pfeifer, Alison J. Picard, Emily Polachek, Sabrina Soares Roberts, and Renée Valois for their assistance in writing this book.

ONE

Angela Bjork had first appeared to me like, well, an angel—an angel riding a white horse.

What happened, I had been drugged and left to die on the Great American Desert, what some people called the 475,000 square miles of barely populated land known as the Great Plains, by miscreants from Libbie, SD, who thought it would be fun if I disappeared without a trace; my body consumed by animals and insects. It's a long story; I'll have to tell it to you someday.

I nearly perished the way they had planned, too. There was no water where I had been dumped, no rivers or lakes. There wasn't a single tree anywhere. I saw no power or telephone lines, no silos, no fences, no roads; no high towers with blinking red lights, no wind turbines spinning in the distance. Only a limitless horizon in every direction.

I began walking east because that was the direction home. Despite what you might have heard, the Great Plains are not flat. There were plenty of low, rolling hills and ravines to contend with. Sandstone and shale. Plus, the damned vegetation. Along with the wheatgrass, other prairie grasses grabbed my shoes, pulled at my legs and slowed my pace. I started hiking at about four miles an hour. It wasn't long before my speed began to diminish. After a while I was lucky if I was doing one mile an hour. I began to feel as if I were on a gigantic conveyor belt and the earth was rotating at walking speed beneath my feet so that I gained no ground. I was merely putting one foot in front of the other and trusting, hoping, that eventually I would get somewhere worth going. Instead, I got nowhere very, very slowly.

Hours passed. Then days.

The unrelenting sun, wind that never stopped blowing, dehydration, hunger, physical and mental exhaustion—they all pounded me like a hammer on an anvil. The symptoms became too pronounced to ignore—dizziness, headache, stomach pain, nausea, and an unpleasant taste in my mouth that I would have been unable to swallow or spit away if I could swallow or spit. I fell and got up, fell, and got up again. Only it was becoming more and more difficult each time.

It was when I was convinced that I was slipping away, that I first saw it; something white moving on the horizon. It came and it went and for a few moments I was convinced I was hallucinating. Then I saw it again. Since it seemed to be heading toward me, I started moving toward it. After a while, I saw that the something white was a horse. There was a rider on the back of the horse.

Angela's hair was the color of wheat and neatly tucked beneath her wide-brimmed cowboy hat, the hat tied beneath her chin to keep it from falling off. She wore a blue cotton short-sleeve shirt tucked inside worn blue jeans; the legs of the jeans tucked inside boots. Her eyes were also blue. Her soft face and arms glistened with sunscreen.

Did I mention the dizziness? I simply did not believe that she was anything more than an optical illusion until I reached out and patted the side of the horse's neck.

"You're real," I said.

Angela quickly slid out of the saddle and dropped to the ground. She unwound the strap of a canteen from the pommel of her saddle. She unscrewed the cap and offered the canteen to me. I took the canteen and drank. I tried to drink slowly.

She asked if I needed help.

"Why yes," I told her. "Yes, I do."

That was over seven years ago. Now she was standing in front of me just inside the entrance to Rickie's, the jazz joint owned by my wife. There was a lot of gushing, and hugging, mostly by me. I was so very, very glad to see Angela after all those years.

Rickie's was divided into two sections, a casual bar on the ground floor with a small stage for happy hour entertainment, and a full restaurant and performance hall upstairs. I led Angela to a table in the downstairs section where we could talk with the expectation that I would eventually take her upstairs for dinner. Nina Truhler saw us and made her way to the table. She was smiling and shaking her head at the same time. I introduced her as my wife, something I was always proud to do, and she and Angela shook hands. Nina kept shaking her head.

"I knew you'd be pretty," Nina said. "When McKenzie told me the story of being saved from certain death by a girl on a white horse, there was no doubt in my mind that you'd be pretty. That's just the way things happen in his life."

Angela blushed at the remark, yet honestly, I'm sure she's heard it many times before. Nina sat with us and there was some chitchat until Angela explained why she had wanted to meet me again.

"McKenzie, I'm a little embarrassed to ask because you've already done so much for me," she said, "only I need a favor."

"You have an unlimited supply coming," I told her.

"I'm at the University of Minnesota now."

"Really? I thought you were at Penn State."

"That's where I earned my bachelors in geology, thank you very much for helping with that."

"You're welcome."

"My dad has always accused me of taking advantage of you the way you paid for so much of my education."

"Like I told you at the time; consider it a finder's fee from an eccentric millionaire. Besides, I would have paid a great deal more if you didn't have all that scholarship money pouring in."

Angela blushed again.

"How are your parents?" I asked.

"You're going to laugh."

"Not even if I thought it was funny."

"They moved to Las Vegas."

"What?"

"Remember when I brought you to the ranch after I found you on the prairie?"

"Vividly."

"My dad told you about working the land, working with horses, working dawn to dusk; all that 'real man' stuff."

"Yes."

"That's what I grew up with," Angela said. "Every day. He didn't want me to go to Penn State. He wanted me to go to the University of Montana because he said the people who went there were 'our kind of people.' After I left for school, my parents—they didn't even call me. Instead, they sent me an email. I couldn't get back for Thanksgiving, so they sent me an email explaining that they were selling the ranch, all the horses, selling Flipper . . ."

"Flipper?" Nina asked.

"That was the name of my horse."

"You called your white horse Flipper?"

Angela looked at Nina as if that was the silliest question she had ever heard.

"Anyway," she said, "they sold everything and retired to Las Vegas. I had Christmas dinner that year at the Bellagio. Talk about culture shock."

Angela laughed but I didn't. A promise is a promise.

"Partly it was because of me, I know that," she added. "Dad and Mom knew I didn't want to live on the ranch. They knew I had plans that didn't include residing in a hamlet that had fewer people than there were in my geochemistry class, so when they received an offer—I thought the old man would be bored out of his mind. This is a guy who worked from sunup to sundown nearly every day of his life. I thought he loved it; couldn't live without it. Goes to show—I mean, the man plays pickleball, now."

"Oh my God."

"Plus, he has season tickets for the Raiders and the Golden Knights hockey team."

"The Aces, too?"

"Women's basketball? Please, McKenzie. You met my father. Anyway, my parents made a lot of money, and they seem pretty happy in their retirement, so . . . The windfall helped pay for my master's, too."

"Your master's?" Nina said.

"In paleontology from the College of Earth and Mineral Sciences at Penn State. I'm working on my doctorate now."

"You said you were at the University of Minnesota," I reminded her.

"The man I was working with, my mentor, Dr. Hegarty, Weston Hegarty, he took a position as head of the U's Department of Earth and Environmental Sciences. I followed him here. I'm a member of the research faculty plus I occasionally work as an adjunct professor."

"Paleontology," Nina said. "That's the study of dinosaurs, isn't it?"

"Yes. In my case I'm studying vertebrate fossils from primitive mammals."

"I didn't know there were any dinosaurs in Minnesota," I said.

"There aren't many. That's because during the Paleozoic, Mesozoic, and Cenozoic eras most of the state was underwater. But in Montana—McKenzie, that's why I'm here."

"Tell me," I said.

The dinosaur fossil was revealed one inch at a time. It was many inches before Angela appreciated what she had found and many more inches after that before she announced her discovery of the dinosaur remains to anyone else including her colleagues. She had been walking along what appeared to her to be an ancient riverbed about two miles from the dig. That's how you prospect for fossils, Angela told Nina and me. You walk around and look.

Some scientists have employed ground-penetrating radar, she said. The problem is that the density of fossil bones is very similar to the density of the rocks where they sit so there are many false negatives. You could dig and dig in the rocks only to find even more rocks. Some bones have been found with Geiger counters, except that's hit and miss, too. Also, the machines were expensive and unwieldy, and they required electricity, needed skilled technicians to operate them and interpret data, and could survey only a small area at a time. An expert fossil hunter could cover far more ground on foot; she could get to areas that machines could not.

Angela was an expert. I know because she told me so. The fact that she did it with a wink and a smile . . .

"Truth is, anyone can find a specimen," she said. "Most fossil hunts are conducted in areas of high erosion. As rocks and soils wear down, wear away, you'll find buried bones slowly coming to the surface where they can be found. That's why researchers keep going back to the same sites. Searching in areas where there is little or no erosion, like Minnesota, will rarely reveal anything new. Yet in high erosion regions there are new fossils to discover on every trip.

"The trick is to know what to look for. In some cases, the bones will have a distinctive texture and color compared to the surrounding rocks. Usually, though, they look very similar. In others—pattern recognition can be crucial. You need to remember that fossils on the surface are eroding themselves, so what you're searching for are the bits of bones that are partially buried, that have broken edges or are resting at odd angles; bones that look a little out of place. What I found—the bone appeared to have a slightly curved surface like the side of a bowl. That's why it looked to me as if it didn't belong."

Angela went to her knees and used a two-inch paintbrush to clear the area around the bowl. The more dirt and rock she brushed away; the more curved surface was revealed. She began using a dental pick and blunt trowel to scrape the dirt along the edges while being careful not to damage the fossil in any way. Dinosaur bones may be huge, yet they are also very fragile, and many have cracks, which means they need meticulous handling, Angela said.

"You'd be amazed at how much Krazy Glue we use," she told us.

Angela kept scraping and brushing and the curved surface grew in size. Finally, she bent down and licked it.

"You licked a dinosaur bone?" Nina asked.

Angela chuckled as she answered, "Yes."

"Why would you do that?"

"Rocks and fossils might look alike, but fossils still have the structure of living bone tissue. They'll still have a pattern of microscopic, honeycomb-like tubes running through them. If you lick them, the tubes on the fossil will draw moisture out of your tongue. If it sticks, it's probably bone. If it doesn't, it's probably rock."

Convinced that she found a fossil of some significance, Angela began a careful survey of the area around it. She was searching for float, isolated fragments of bones that might belong to the fossil she found and discovered nothing.

Angela marked the spot, took a few photographs with her phone, and sat down to write notes in her journal. That's what scientists do, she told us; they document everything. She knew she didn't have much time. The sun set on the Great Plains like someone pulling down a heavy shade. She finished, placed the notebook in the prospecting kit that held all her tools, and marched back to camp.

There are a surprising number of dinosaur digs scattered across Montana, North and South Dakota, Missouri, Colorado, Wyoming, Utah, New Mexico and even unlikely spots like Maryland and Florida—at least I was surprised when Angela told us about them. Many were sprawling affairs that had been operating as tourist attractions for decades. Others were supported by museums and universities, yet open to the public. For a fee, amateur paleontologists were welcome to spend a day, a weekend, a week or even longer digging alongside professional paleontologists in established quarries for a perfectly formed tooth from a brontosaurus or a fragment of a rib from a stegosaurus. The fees from these citizen scientists helped cover the expense of the digs and their assistance was invaluable, I was told.

The U's dig—that's what Angela called it—was located "in the middle of nowhere and that's coming from a girl who was raised on a ranch in the middle of nowhere." It was situated on private land in southeastern Montana more or less midway between the towns of Ekalaka, population 399, and Broadus, population 456, and just south of an unincorporated community called Powderville that was little more than a small cluster of buildings erected at a little-used crossroad. It wasn't open to the public, at least not yet, and was financed by the University of Minnesota, Macalester College in St. Paul, and the Science Museum of Minnesota.

"Minnesota has a vibrant paleontology community," Angela said.

Who knew? my inner voice replied.

'Course, paleontologists don't just pitch a tent in the middle of nowhere and start digging. They first look for rocks from the Mesozoic era that are approximately sixty million years old. One of the places that have those rocks in abundance is the Hell Creek Formation. The formation begins along Hell Creek near Jordan, in eastern Montana, and stretches over portions of that state as well as North and South Dakota and Wyoming. A lot of fossils have been unearthed there including prehistoric fish such as sharks and rays, crocodiles, lizards, snakes, turtles, frogs, and salamanders. A few birds have also been discovered as well as an impressive assemblage of plants and trees. And then there were the dinosaurs, lots of dinosaurs—*Tyrannosaurus* and *Triceratops* to name just a couple.

The reason the Minnesota crew picked that particular site was because a kid riding a horse—Angela had no idea if it was white—found a bone that he gave to his older brother. His brother gave it to his girlfriend who promptly gave it to her other boyfriend who brought it to his professor at Macalester and asked, "Is this anything?" The professor was shocked, first that the bone had somehow remained intact, especially after all the careless handling, and second, that it came from an *Anzu*, a birdlike dinosaur one paleontologist labeled the "chicken from hell."

One thing led to another and now there was a large multi-layered hole in the ground that had been expanding slowly outward over the past five years. Plenty of fossils had been unearthed, too—more remains from the *Anzu*, teeth from a *Tyrannosaurus*, bones from an *Edmontosaurus*, and the nearly complete skeleton of an *Acheroraptor*, described as a feathered lizard, that the Science Museum of Minnesota was anxious to put on exhibit.

Angela strolled past the now vacant quarry toward the encampment as the heavy gray dusk turned to night. She could hear the tarps that had been erected over the quarry to protect the team and its fragile specimens from the sun flapping in the ever-present wind. There was a pole barn about the size of a two-car garage standing between the quarry and the encampment. The doors had been swung open and the lights were on. Angela could see members of the team cleaning and examining fossils on the tables inside and she wondered if someone had made a discovery. The lights were also burning inside a long mobile home that hadn't been mobile since it was anchored near the barn half a decade earlier. It was used as an office and residence for the PhDs who managed the site, rank having its privileges. A couple of small RVs were parked at sharp angles near the mobile home as if the owners were afraid they would be attacked by Native Americans who, let's face it, had a legitimate gripe.

There was no running water, of course. That and other provisions were periodically brought in from Ekalaka. A 320-gallon propane tank fueled an outdoor generator that provided the camp with light and powered the coolers and grills that served as a field kitchen. The bathroom was a pair of his and hers porta potties.

Angela lived in one of the dozen tents erected across from the RVs. There was a Black man sitting on a stool in front of the tent next to hers wearing a khaki-colored hat with a brim the size of a small umbrella, a battery-operated lantern at his feet. In southeastern Montana in May the daytime temperature averaged in the low seventies, yet the sun was unrelenting; there was no protection from it. In fact, an ongoing debate in the camp concerned exactly where the nearest shade tree could be found.

The man was eating. When Angela approached, he lifted his plate toward her.

"Macaroni and cheese," he said. "I have plenty."

"Thank you, Gary," Angela said.

Gary scooped out a plate for her while Angela deposited her prospecting kit and dragged a folding beach chair from her tent to his. Angela took the plate and fork and started eating.

"I love this stuff, I don't know why," she said.

"Did you know that macaroni and cheese dated back to fourteenth-century Italy? Thomas Jefferson discovered it in Paris and had James Hemings, the classically trained French chef that he had enslaved, cook it for him in Monticello."

That caused Angela to tilt her head so she could watch Gary's face beneath his hat.

"Kraft Foods introduced mac and cheese to mainstream America during the Great Depression claiming you could 'make a meal for four in nine minutes.' Huge hit, partly because it was so cheap. It became even more popular during World War II because you could get two boxes for one food rationing stamp."

Angela ate and watched some more.

"My mother made it for us once a week."

"My mother made it, too," Angela said. "Only she would chop up a tomato and mix it in."

"Owoo," the man said beneath his hat. "Gourmet mac and cheese."

Gary and Angela reached toward each other, clinking their plates as if they were wineglasses.

"Tell me something," Angela said. "Do Black people get sunburned?"

"Sure, just not as badly you lily-white folks."

"I didn't know."

"Hmm."

"You're the only Black paleontologist I've ever met," Angela said.

"We are a unique and exceptional species, this is true."

"Seriously, you're also one of the very few Black people I've ever spoken to. Growing up out here"—Angela waved as if she meant the Hell Creek Formation—"I never actually saw a Black person up close until I went to Penn State except on TV and in the movies."

"There are no Black cowboys in Montana?"

"None that I am acquainted with."

"Something you don't see in the old western movies and on TV, one in four cowboys were Black."

"Another one in four were Mexican. I know my cowboys, Gary."

"Yet you're not racist at all."

"How does the song go? *You have to be carefully taught?* No one bothered to teach me. Well, that's not entirely true. The politics in Montana are ultra-conservative and so is the media. It just never stuck."

They clinked plates again.

"I haven't seen you most of the day," Gary said. "It makes me nervous when you wander the prairie by yourself."

"I'm a lot more comfortable on the prairie than I am in some neighborhoods in Minneapolis."

"Me, too. Only tell me—did you find anything?"

Angela showed him the flat of her hand and gave it a little wave.

"Angieeeeeeee," Gary hissed.

"I don't know. I—I don't know, yet."

"Do you want me to go out with you tomorrow?"

"No. And Gary, please, until I'm sure . . ."

Angela placed an index finger against her lips in the universal sign of silence.

"What's this?"

The question was asked in a loud voice, causing Angela and Gary to lift their heads and glance at the young man walking toward them.

"Secrets?" he asked just as loudly. "We're keeping secrets now?"

"Only from you," Angela said.

"I thought we were one big happy family here at the dig."

"Every family has a hierarchy. There're Mom and Dad. Then there're the older siblings." Angela waved a thumb at Gary and herself. "Then there's the kid who lives across the street and hangs out with the youngest child. That would be you."

"Here I told everyone we were Bronco buddies."

"I wish you wouldn't."

"Bronco buddies?" Gary asked.

"Jordan and I both rode out here in Dr. Larsen's Ford Bronco," Angela said. "Nearly eight hundred miles, plus an overnight in Bismarck, North Dakota. Now he thinks we're pals. More than pals."

"That's somewhat presumptuous."

Jordan squatted down in front of their chairs and turned his head toward Gary.

"Professor Phillips, this is clearly an example of the discrimination rampant in this camp," he said.

Gary Phillips pushed the rim of his hat up with one finger, revealing his entire face.

"Discrimination?" he asked.

"Against undergrads."

"Only against undergrads who don't know their place," Angela said.

Jordan pointed at Angela while staring at Phillips.

"See."

"What are you?" Phillips asked. "A sophomore?"

"I start my junior year in the fall."

"A junior then. You're out here to fulfill one of the two field-camp requirements you need to get your bachelor's degree in geology from the University of Minnesota, correct?"

"Yes, sir."

"Meanwhile, Professor Bjork is a member of the university's research faculty and fills in as an adjunct professor while she pursues her PhD. You see the problem?"

"She's already explained it to me."

"On several occasions," Angela added.

"Yet you don't seem to get it," Phillips said.

"I found a claw," Jordan said.

"Whoa, what?"

"A claw."

"Where?" Angela asked.

"At the quarry, the north end of the quarry." Jordan curled his hand and bent his index finger so that it resembled a hook. "It's about three inches long. Completely intact. It just slid out of the formation into my hand. Dr. Seeley said it looked like an *Anzu wyliei* toe claw, but he wanted to examine it more closely before saying for sure."

"That's great," Angela said. "Congratulations."

"It's why I came over. Us undergrads are going to celebrate, and I thought you might like to join us. Herschel is breaking out his guitar and Simon has had some beer on ice for just such an occasion, he said."

"Are you old enough to drink?" Phillips asked.

Angela set down the now empty plate and rose to her feet.

"Don't tease him," she said. "This is a wonderful discovery, Jordan. Is that what they're working on in the pole barn?"

"I think so."

"Show me," Angela said even though she led the way.

Jordan followed closely behind. He turned his head to glance at Phillips. The smile on his face caused the Black paleontologist to laugh out loud.

Dr. David Seeley and a woman not much older than Angela were standing at a wooden table beneath a fluorescent light. He was gently scrubbing the *Anzu* claw he held in the palm of his hand with a toothbrush while she trickled water from a clear plastic bottle over the top of it; the water splashing into a metal bowl beneath their hands. Movement caused them to glance upward, and they both watched Angela and Jordan entering the barn.

"Ah, Mr. Wall and the elusive Professor Bjork," he said. "Come see."

Angela noticed that the woman flinched at the title "professor" yet kept pouring the water.

Jordan and Angela were approaching the table when Seeley said, "Enough." His assistant ceased pouring the water and set down the bottle. Seeley carefully dried the fossil in a small white towel and offered it to Jordan.

"This is as fine a specimen as I've ever seen," he said.

Jordan took the claw as if he was afraid it would break. The thorough scrubbing revealed that it had once been white, although it was now streaked with brown. Finally, he held it above his head as if the claw was part of his own hand. He repeated what he had said when he had first discovered the fossil in the quarry.

"Wow, look at this."

"I look forward to adding it to our exhibit," Seeley said. "We might have to include your name."

"You would do that?" Jordan asked.

"In the brochure at least, certainly."

"Wow."

Jordan handed the claw back to Seeley and turned toward Angela.

"Immortalized in the Science Museum of Minnesota," he said.

"Now aren't you glad you chose this field trip instead of studying rocks in Ely, Minnesota?" she asked.

Jordan smiled brightly and Angela was afraid that he might attempt to hug her. She turned away from him and addressed the assistant.

"Ashley, we haven't chatted for a while," Angela said. "How are you?"

"Fine," Ashley answered. "Dr. Seeley, should I wrap it?"

"Photos first."

The woman took several of them with a digital camera while Seeley cataloged the fossil both on a laptop and in longhand on a paper ledger. It included all available information associated with the find such as what, where, when, how, and who did the finding.

"In case you're wondering, Mr. Wall, the catalog number is SMM202451C," Seeley said.

Jordan repeated the number to himself while Ashley set down the camera and gathered materials that she had already prepared for the task. First, she covered the claw in paper towels. Afterward, she wrapped it in strips of burlap that had been soaked in liquid plaster. Seeley explained it to Jordan.

"It's called plaster jacketing," he told the student. "It's like using a cast on broken bones. When the plaster hardens, it acts almost like armor. After the fossil has been safely transported and is ready to be studied or put on display at a place like the Science Museum, we can cut away the plaster without damaging the fossil inside."

"This is so fucking cool," Jordan said. "Excuse me, Doctor."

"No, no, that pretty much describes it."

After she was finished, Ashley washed her hands in the bowl that had caught the water they had used to clean the fossil. She then placed the specimen along with documentation on a shelf that already held a dozen plaster casts of various sizes.

"Are we done for this evening?" she asked.

"I don't know," Seeley replied. "I heard something about a party."

"Please, Doc," Jordan said. "Doctor. It would be great if you dropped in. You, too, Professor DeLuca. It's no big thing. We're just going to hoist a few in honor of my claw."

"Your claw?" Ashley DeLuca asked.

"I know everything that we find will be divided between the U and Macalester College for study and eventually"—Jordan gestured at Dr. Seeley—"you guys get to put it all on exhibit, but yeah, I think of it as my claw. My *Anzu wyliei* toe claw."

"Honestly," DeLuca said.

"When I was an undergrad, I was a member of a team that discovered a *Quetzalcoatlus* . . ." Angela said.

Jordan attempted to repeat the name yet failed.

"It's a flying dinosaur," Angela added. "The largest ever found; has about a thirty-six-foot wingspan. It's now on display at the North Museum in Lancaster, Pennsylvania, and you know what? I still think of it as mine, too. Especially the beak."

"You excavated the beak?" DeLuca asked.

"In a manner of speaking. I tripped over it during a dig in West Texas."

"No. You tripped over it?"

"Ended up face down in a gully."

DeLuca thought that was funny.

"The guys on the team laughed, too," Angela added. "Dr. Hegarty, though, was not amused."

Angela noticed the smile leave DeLuca's face at the mention of her mentor's name.

"I guess I'll see you later, then," Angela said and moved toward the door.

"We should go, too," Angela said.

She and Jordan were heading toward the exit when Seeley called to her.

"Professor Bjork, a moment, please."

Angela returned to the table. Seeley waited until Jordan left the barn before speaking to her.

"Professor Bjork . . ."

"You know that technically I'm not a professor . . ."

"Adopt the title, at least while you're at the dig, especially when interacting with the undergraduates. Angela, it's a small community; an intimate community. Students and teachers working side by side day after day and living side by side night after night and there's not much to do at night is there? It would be clever to say that what happens in Montana stays in Montana, yet that's not true. What you do here will follow you home."

"I understand."

"So did I when I was a younger man, yet mistakes were made."

Seeley stared at Angela as if daring her to ask what mistakes. She didn't. Instead, she flashed on the fact that the man held a PhD in paleontology yet worked as a curator for a museum and wondered briefly if that was a career choice.

"I understand," she said.

"Remember, you have enemies."

"I do?"

"Too harsh a characterization, perhaps. But rivals, certainly. Professor DeLuca for one. She's an assistant professor in your school's Department of Earth and Environmental Sciences who wishes to become an associate professor, followed by full professor and, no doubt, distinguished professor—you know how the road to tenure twists and turns. Her future looked bright, too. Then you arrived, a protégé of her new boss with, no doubt, the same ambitions as her. Let's just say she doesn't necessarily wish you well, and gossip—gossip, my dear, is her friend."

Angela's shoulders sagged and she found herself leaning against the table.

"I understand," she repeated.

"So, you keep saying, yet I'm not entirely sure that you do."

"But I do, David, I do indeed. I was given a crash course when I arrived at Penn State. Going to high school out here—there were thirty-two students in my senior class, and we all grew up together. We were like brothers and sisters, sometimes kissing cousins; we looked out for each other. My freshman year at State—somehow it became common knowledge that I was a small-town girl. Hannah from Montana they called me. Naïve or easy, probably both. A senior insisted—emphasis on the word 'insisted'—that I let him show me the constellations, which turned out to be a good thing because he was the one who ended up seeing stars and a lot of people found out about it. There was some name-calling after that yet guys started backing off."

"I bet."

"The undergraduates, I could deal with them, but a couple of the professors—not so much while I was an undergrad; yet after I started pursuing my master's it was like suddenly I was legal, you know what I mean?"

"I do."

"Dr. Hegarty looked out for me."

"The University of Minnesota has a code of conduct," Seeley said.

"That's the assumption, isn't it? That I'm a walking violation."

"What I'm saying is that the code works both ways. Don't let anyone push you around."

Angela thought it over for a few beats before she replied.

"Thank you, David," she said. "I won't."

The fire was burning brightly in the metal fire bowl and Angela's first thought as she approached the group that had gathered in a circle around it—where did the firewood come from? Certainly, it wasn't gathered in the treeless area where the dig was located. A quick glance at the wood stacked near the bowl told her it was store bought; someone had paid seven-eight bucks for a bundle at a gas station or grocery store. She was wondering what her father would say about that when she heard her name.

A young woman that Angela knew as Winter Billock had hopped up from where she was sitting and waved Angela over. Winter had been sitting next to DeLuca who didn't seem happy about the invitation yet said nothing. As Angela made her way around the circle Jordan stood, opened the cooler he had been sitting on, and withdrew a can of Tumbleweed IPA with the logo of the Lewis and Clark Brewing Company.

"Here you go, Professor," he said.

The words caused Angela to flinch. Jordan had never called her that before—it was always Angela or Ms. Bjork—and she wondered if he had been listening at the pull barn door when she was speaking with Dr. Seeley.

Angela accepted the beer and moved to where Winter and DeLuca were sitting on a narrow bench. Winter immediately rose and offered her seat.

"No, no," Angela said.

"Please," Winter replied.

Angela smiled and patted the woman's shoulder as Winter sat cross-legged in front of the bench. Winter was petite with short red hair; Angela wagered that she would be carded in every bar and club she walked into until she was at least forty-five. What's more, she seemed to have adopted Angela as a role model. Angela told Nina and me that she couldn't imagine anything more daunting than being someone's role model.

Angela gave DeLuca a nod as she sat. She was gratified that DeLuca gave her a nod in return.

From there Angela was able to make out the entire team. There were seven undergraduates from the University of Minnesota, including Winter, Jordan, Herschel, and Simon Stevens, and two more from Macalester College named Luke Peterson and Derek Weiland who were sitting next to Professor Phillips, who was also from that prestigious private school.

There was a bit of a rivalry between the two groups.

"I would much rather be a Scot than a Gopher," one of the Macalester contingent had insisted when the two groups began to mingle.

"Make that a *Golden* Gopher," a representative of the U had replied.

Yet for the most part they all got along fine.

Next to them were Dr. Seeley from the science museum and Dr. Nicholas Larsen, also from the U. Then there were DeLuca and Angela.

"That makes eleven men," she told herself. "And three women."

Angela had seen lopsided numbers like that before, especially when she was an undergrad participating in the field trips required for her own degree. As much as Jordan's attentions annoyed her, she knew that DeLuca and Winter were probably getting the same treatment. Especially Winter. She didn't have a title to frighten away aggressive suitors.

While Angela was surveying the team, she noticed that Larsen was watching her. When their eyes met, he looked away. Angela let it slide with little thought. It wasn't something that hadn't happened to her many times before, she told us.

As promised, Herschel had indeed broken out his guitar, a six-string Gibson acoustic, and he was playing it hot to wild applause when he finished.

"I had never heard that before," Simon said. "That was terrific."

"It's called 'Classical Gas,'" Herschel said. "It was written by a guy named Mason Williams in, I don't know, 1968."

"So, old music," Jordan said. "Like Rachmaninoff."

"What?"

"I thought the only music geologists knew was rock and roll," Winter said.

"Is your favorite band the Rolling Stones?" Simon asked.

"Swear to God, you guys are as dumb as a bag of rocks," Herschel said.

"Be patient, Herschel," DeLuca said. "You know geology students all have their faults."

Angela gave her a nudge with an elbow.

"Good one, Ashley," she said.

"I never liked being called a geologist," Weiland said. "I prefer rock star. But that's just the way I roll."

"Please stop it," Phillips said.

"Just so you know," Angela said, "I'll never take you people for granite."

This time DeLuca nudged Angela.

"Nice," she said.

"I'm begging you," Phillips said. "For the love of all that is good and kind in the world, please stop."

"On a more serious note," Larsen said.

The entire assembly grew quiet and turned its attention to him. Larsen was more or less in charge of the dig, although there wasn't a formal declaration as far as Angela knew.

"First, congratulations to Jordan Wall for his find."

The group applauded and cheered while Jordan behaved as if he had scored a touchdown in the big game.

"Something else," Larsen added. "We have rules at this dig. One of them is that no one—no one—is allowed to leave the encampment alone. No one is allowed to go prospecting without a partner. I'm speaking to you, Ms. Bjork."

A collective "Owoo" came from the undergraduates.

"Someone's in trouble," one of them said behind his hand.

"It's not funny," Larsen assured them. "It is easy to get lost; there are few landmarks to guide us out here. What's more, injury is a real possibility given the terrain we're dealing with. If anyone gets hurt—how far away is the nearest medical facility, would you estimate, Dr. Seeley?"

"At least a ninety-minute drive."

"That's assuming we can even locate you on the prairie."

"I assure you, Doctor"—Angela gestured at the Minnesota state flag flying above the mobile home that was invisible in the dark—"I could see the flag at all times."

"Nonetheless. The rules are there for a reason and they will be obeyed."

"Of course, Doctor," Angela said.

After a few silent moments it became clear that no one had anything more to say, so Herschel began playing his guitar again. This time he selected a song that everyone seemed to know, "Sweet Caroline." It was during the chorus that DeLuca nudged Angela again.

"I can't believe Larsen called you out like that in front of everyone," she whispered.

"He wanted to make a point," Angela whispered back.

"That no one is above the law?"

"It would be pretty to think so. Listen, Ashley . . ." Angela tapped DeLuca on her knee. "I found something; I think. Come out with me tomorrow."

"Why?"

"Because us girls need to stick together."

That caused me to raise an eyebrow.

"Really?" I asked.

"I never thought of Ashley as a rival and certainly not an enemy until Dr. Seeley brought it up," Angela told Nina and me. "But what is it they say? Keep your friends close and your enemies closer?"

TWO

The two women met on the edge of the encampment shortly after breakfast. They were dressed for the environment. Both wore hiking boots and jeans. Angela had on a peach-colored long-sleeve gardening shirt and a Stetson cowboy hat that she had worn since she was seventeen. DeLuca also wore a long-sleeve shirt, only hers was a heather-colored lightweight crew top that hung loosely on her, plus an olive sun hat. They both carried bright orange buckets like the kind you get at Home Depot. Inside the buckets they carried their prospecting tools and lunch.

"Where are we going?" DeLuca asked.

Angela glanced over her shoulder at Gary Phillips, who gave her a wave like he was Queen Victoria and Angela was one of the minions she was passing in her carriage.

"This way," she said.

DeLuca followed her out onto the prairie; shortgrass crunched beneath their hiking boots. They followed their own shadows, walking directly west, their backs to the rising sun. They walked for about forty minutes, mostly over grayish sandstone and shale, while dodging the occasional tuft of wheatgrass and purple prairie clover, junipers, nodding onions, and bitterroot. Occasionally, DeLuca would glance behind her, shielding her eyes against the sun while she searched the horizon for the flag flying on the high pole next to the mobile home. If she was anxious about getting lost, though, she didn't show it. At least not to Angela. Finally, they came upon the ancient riverbed that Angela had discovered the day before. A small pile of rocks marked the spot. Angela knelt next to it. DeLuca knelt across from her.

Angela bent down and blew the dirt off the fossil and brushed it with her fingers. DeLuca caressed it with her fingertips, too.

"Do you think . . ." she said.

"I don't know."

"A skull?"

"I don't know," Angela repeated.

DeLuca twisted her body and examined the dirt and rocks strewn around them. She rose to her feet and walked in a circle. She bent and picked up a few of the rocks and tossed them away. She bent and picked up another, licked it, and tossed that one, too.

"I don't see any float," she said.

"Neither did I."

"How did you find this?"

Angela smiled at her.

"I tripped over it," she said.

DeLuca smiled in return.

"You seem to have lucky feet," she said.

A moment later, the two women were emptying their buckets. DeLuca had a thick foam mat that she knelt on. Angela put on a pair of knee pads. They carefully set their tools close at hand like a surgeon might and placed water bottles just within reach. Without a word, they began to patiently dig and chip and brush away the layers of earth covering and surrounding the fossil, depositing it into the buckets. Occasionally, Angela would stop working to take a photograph or record a measurement. DeLuca began to hum quietly. Angela attempted to identify the tune and decided it was just something her rival was creating as she went along.

"It sounds baroque," Angela said.

DeLuca paused for a moment before saying, "I'm sorry."

"No, no, no, I like it."

Still, it was a good forty-five minutes before DeLuca began humming again.

Their painstaking work exposed several more inches of the fossil; the surface area was the size of a dinner plate by the time they broke for lunch. The women were impressed by the diamond-shaped scales they found on top of the fossil. There was a Latin word for it that they had both learned while studying for their master's years earlier—*caputegulae*, meaning "skull tiles."

"This could be"—DeLuca paused as if carefully considering her next word—"important."

"I'd like to keep it to ourselves until we're sure."

"Why?"

"Because it's ours."

"You mean yours."

"I mean ours, Ashley. I can't do this alone and if they're going to list someone's name next to mine at the Science Museum of Minnesota, I'd rather it be yours than one of the guys."

DeLuca continued to eat her PB&J while Angela ate leftover macaroni and cheese from a plastic container that she had kept in an insulated lunch bag.

"Some people think that you're receiving preferential treatment from Dr. Hegarty," DeLuca said. "They call you teacher's pet."

"Hegarty is aware of that. That's why he insists I need to work twice as hard as everyone else. Is that fair?"

DeLuca didn't answer. Instead, she took another bite of her sandwich and sipped from her water bottle to wash it down.

"There are only so many spots available at the U," she said.

"Enough for both of us," Angela told her.

Good for you, sweetie, my inner voice said. Yet I remained quiet while Angela continued telling her story.

The two women finished lunch and resumed digging. Hours later, DeLuca announced, "I have an edge."

Angela stopped digging and watched as DeLuca gently slid her fingers back and forth about an inch and a half between the fossil and the wall of dirt and rock. As she did, her fingers slipped deeper and deeper still until they curled beneath the fossil.

They smiled at each other as if they had just discovered gold.

"We need to get back," Angela said. "If we come into camp after dark, Larsen will freak."

The women documented the work they had done, covered the fossil with a tarp that they anchored with dirt and rocks from their buckets, took up their possessions, and walked directly east. Once again, their shadows led the way.

"Angela?"

"Angie."

"Angie. Most people call me Ash."

"Ash."

"Listen, I know you like roughing it in your tent," DeLuca said. "But my RV—it's small, only sleeps two, but I have a satellite dish attached to the roof so, if you want to come over later and watch the Twins game . . ."

"Sounds like fun," Angela said.

"Twins," I said. "Minnesota Twins? I like this woman."

Nina gave me an elbow to the ribs.

"Don't interrupt," she said.

The two women returned to their dig early the next morning. They were followed there by the curiosity and unanswered questions of the other members of the team. Winter Billock had asked if she could go with them and Angela and DeLuca were both tempted to allow it, especially when she repeated what Angela had claimed—"Us girls need to stick together."

"Tomorrow, I think," Angela said. "All will be revealed tomorrow. I hope."

The work seemed to go more quickly the second day, although that might have been because of the heightened excitement both women felt. They did not stop for lunch.

Their task was made easier partly because they didn't need to dig very deep. The fossil was only buried a couple of inches below the surface. Finally, all of the edges of the top of the fossil were exposed. They had dug, in fact, a two-inch deep trench all around it. Angela knelt to take measurements. The skull was triangular and wider than it was long—twenty-five and a quarter inches by an even twenty inches—and it had pyramidal shaped horns. Yet it was the pattern that covered the top of the skull that excited them the most, the *caputegulae*.

"It's an *Ankylosaurus*," Angela said. "We found the skull of an *Ankylosaurus*."

"Oh. My. God. Angela, oh my God. Do you know how many *Ankylosaurus* there are in the world?"

"I don't know. A handful. But Ash, Ash, Ash, no one has ever discovered a complete skeleton."

"Oh my God!"

The two women embraced and started hopping up and down. Angela began to cry. DeLuca said, "Don't you dare," and then she started crying, too.

"Pictures, pictures, we need pictures," DeLuca said.

Angela waved at the fossil.

"Get on the ground, get on the ground," she said.

DeLuca did, lying next to the *Ankylosaurus,* like it was a lover. Angela took several photos and then laid on the other side of the fossil. She held the cell phone at arm's length and took several selfies of the three of them together.

Despite their revels, Angela and DeLuca were scientists and they soon began acting like it, albeit with dazzling smiles on their faces. They dutifully documented everything they had done and even took a few more photographs of the *Ankylosaurus* without posing in any of them. Afterward, they carefully covered their find with the blue tarp and anchored it with heavy stones.

The sun was several hours from setting when they started walking back to the encampment.

"Do you think the skull is intact?" DeLuca said.

"I don't know."

"Do you think we actually have a complete skeleton?"

"I don't know, but I'm more than willing to spend the rest of the summer trying to find out."

"You and me both. Oh Angie, this is . . ."

She couldn't think of an adequate adjective to complete the sentence.

Angela took DeLuca's hand and gave it a squeeze.

"I know what I'm going to write my dissertation on," she said. "What about you?"

"Oh, Angie, the papers we're going to publish."

Angela released DeLuca's hand, pulled her cell phone from her pocket, and held it up.

"Do you get coverage out here?" DeLuca asked.

"It's iffy."

Nonetheless, Angela attempted to make a call. To her great joy, it went through.

"Dr. Hegarty," a deep male voice answered.

"Good afternoon, Doctor, I hope I'm not disturbing you."

"Angela?"

"I'm strolling out here on the Great Plains of Montana with Professor Ashley DeLuca. I have you on speakerphone. Say hello to Dr. Hegarty, Ash."

"Hello, Doctor. I hope things are going well back at the big U."

"What's going on?" Hegarty asked. "Have you two been drinking?"

DeLuca thought that was terribly funny.

"You could say we're both high on life," Angela said.

"Angela," Hegarty repeated.

"Weston."

"Angela."

Angela stopped moving and held the cell just inches from her mouth. DeLuca moved in close.

"Weston, Ashley and I just unearthed the top of the skull of an *Ankylosaurus*."

Dr. Hegarty took a long time before he replied.

"Are you serious?" he asked.

"I'm calling my boss by his first name, you're damn right I'm serious. We have an *Ankylosaurus,* we have an *Ankylosaurus*." DeLuca joined in. "We have an *Ankylosaurus*."

They began jumping up and down again.

Even before they reached it, the two women could sense that their colleagues in camp were all agog over their discovery—that's the word Angela used when she told Nina and me about it. People seemed to be moving around quickly and noisily without any particular purpose. Winter dashed toward them as they were passing the quarry.

"Magnificent," she jumped into Angela's arms, forcing the woman to drop her bucket.

"Magnificent, magnificent," Winter repeated.

Angela glanced at DeLuca.

"We're magnificent," she said.

"Yes, you are," Winter said. She released Angela and hugged DeLuca. The professor seemed both surprised and appreciative by the gesture.

"You're both magnificent." Winter released DeLuca. "Can I see it? Will you show it to me? Can you do it now?"

"How did you know . . . ?"

"Dr. Hegarty called Dr. Larsen to congratulate him on the find. Larsen took the call in the quarry and people heard what was said. I heard him, too. Hegarty said that whatever Larsen needed to excavate and preserve the *Ankylosaurus* he would get no questions asked. He said he was already making arrangements."

Angela and DeLuca glanced at each other, a look of dismay on their faces. They knew that Larsen would not be happy to learn about the find from his superior; that he most certainly would have wanted it to be the other way around. He said so when he ushered the two women into his makeshift office inside the mobile home.

"You should have told me first," Larsen said.

"We were a couple miles from camp, and we just had to tell somebody," Angela said.

"I have a cell phone, too." Larsen pointed a finger at Angela. "Ms. Bjork, you seem to think this entire dig has been undertaken and financed for your personal aggrandizement."

Angela's hands curled into fists. She told Nina and me that she came *this*close to going off on her supervisor. Whether or not DeLuca could read her intentions, she intervened just in time.

"As Professor Bjork suggested, we were both pretty excited," DeLuca said.

Larsen spun toward her as if he was surprised that she was standing there, much less had the audacity to speak.

"I was so excited that I attempted to send a text to my mother telling her that *I* found the *Ankylosaurus* which is not true, of course," DeLuca continued. "As Professor Bjork made it abundantly clear to Dr. Hegarty, *we* found the remains. We as in she and I and the team. I'm quite certain that by the time this affair is concluded, there will be more than enough credit to go around."

Larsen responded by glaring at her. Angela had no idea what kind of personal relationship he and DeLuca had, yet she was convinced that in that moment it had been irrevocably altered. Especially after Larsen replied.

"From this moment forward, I expect you both to behave as professionals and not giddy schoolgirls," he said.

"Yes, of course, Doctor," DeLuca said.

Angela continued to clench her fists.

"Shall we all take a look at this historic find of yours?" Larsen said.

They opened the door of the mobile home to discover that the entire population of the encampment was waiting outside. Angela and DeLuca stepped back so that Larsen stood in front of them and picked up the buckets they had left at the door. Larsen glanced toward the west. There was less than two hours of sunlight left. He calculated at least an hour there and back, plus who knew how long they would linger at the find.

"Make sure you're wearing the proper footwear," he said. "Everyone carries a working flashlight."

Larsen's announcement was met with cheers. The group quickly dispersed, and Larsen stepped back inside the mobile home. That gave the two women a brief moment alone.

"Now I know why you invited me on this adventure," DeLuca said. "Yesterday, Larsen was on my side, now he's not."

"Don't blame me, Ash. You're the one who decided to stick up for your friend and colleague."

"Friend and colleague—that's something else I'll have to text Mom about if I ever get coverage again."

It was an excited group of fourteen that trudged two miles across the Montana prairie, Angela and DeLuca leading the way. At about the one-mile mark Larsen stopped and looked back toward the camp.

"I thought you said you could see the flag from here," he said.

"I can still see the flag," Angela said. "Can't you?"

Larsen glared at her, yet she was getting used to it.

"Tomorrow we will mark the trail with posts topped with red ribbons interspersed no less than fifty yards part," he said. "Dr. Seeley, will you see to it?"

"Sure," Seeley said.

Behind them, Jordan said, "I don't even know what an *Ankylosaurus* is."

"It's a dinosaur," Weiland replied.

"I got that part."

"*Ankylosaurus* is a member of the family *Ankylosauridae*, not be confused with *Ankylosuchus . . .*" Phillips said.

"Professor, please explain it to me like I'm a geology major and all I know about dinosaurs is what I saw in *Jurassic Park*."

"It's an armored dinosaur. Its armor consists of knobs and plates of bone called ostederms or scutes that are embedded in its skin. Estimates suggest that it's anywhere from four-to-six feet tall and twenty to thirty feet long. It has four legs and a tail; the tail has a club on the end that it uses to protect itself from predators. It feeds on fibrous and woody plants such as ferns and shrubs and it also eats pulpy fruits . . ."

"We don't know that," Larsen said.

"Doctor, I would argue that its cusp-like teeth and the shape of its beak would seem well adapted for that task, plus the requirements for nutrition . . ."

"Nonetheless . . ."

"Anyway, because it has such a low center of gravity, an *Ankylosaurus* would be able to knock down trees like elephants do. Only a few specimens have ever been discovered and none have been completely intact."

"Wasn't there an *Ankylosaurus* called Bumpy in an animated *Jurassic World* movie on Netflix?" Weiland asked.

"You're killing me, kid. You're killing me."

Finally, they were there. Both Angela and DeLuca knelt, removed the rocks from the tarp, and lifted it away. Angela told me later that for a moment, she was actually afraid that the fossil might have disappeared. She didn't know why.

The group crowded around the exposed remains. There were plenty of oohs and aahs; photographs were taken. Even Larsen was visibly impressed although he tried not to show it.

"Given what we can see of the fossil—late Cretaceous period?" he said.

"Yes, sir," Angela told him.

"I recommend that we dig a trench around the fossil, a hole, so that it essentially sits on a pedestal. Attack it that way."

"Yes, yes," Seeley said. "However, we must remember, the fossil isn't the only thing of importance. The rock around it is also valuable. It may hold clues to the life and death of the creature—plants, tracks, and fossilized feces as well."

"We could, we should take the buckets of excavated pieces and wash them," Phillips said. "Sift through it looking for teeth, invertebrates, fossilized plants—what else?"

"I don't want to give up on the existing quarry, but this find . . ." Larsen glanced at his watch, which Angela found inexplicable. "It was our original plan to shut down the dig during the first week of September. We all have daytime jobs after all. Then there's the weather. Out here it can be—volatile."

"You mean like Minnesota?" Seeley asked.

"That would give us the remainder of May, June, July, and August," Larsen continued.

"One hundred and eight days," Phillips said.

"Let's see how much progress we can make by then." Larsen turned toward Angela and DeLuca. "What do you think?"

"Works for me," Angela said.

"Works for me," Larsen muttered in reply.

While Larsen's expression suggested that he was annoyed with Angela, the smile on Phillips's face announced that he was anything but. Yet, while the group was following the beams of their flashlights back to the camp he gave her a nudge.

"So, you and Ash as opposed to, I don't know, you and me," he said. "Last time I share my macaroni and cheese with you."

"Something that Seeley said the other night convinced me that I should . . ."

Angela stopped walking when she realized what Phillips was telling her.

"Oh, no," she said.

Phillips took another three strides before he also halted and turned to face her.

"Oh, Gary, I'm so sorry," Angela said. "I didn't think."

Phillips didn't respond at first, yet after a few beats he smiled brightly across the distance that separated them.

"It's fine," he said. "We learn as we go."

Yeah, my inner voice said. *That's what you always say when you hear news that you don't like.*

On day one hundred and seven, if you were counting backward, the entire crew gathered around the dinosaur. Because of the pyramidal shaped horns, the scientists knew which direction the *Ankylosaurus* was facing. While there was a continuing debate over the actual length of the dinosaur, they decided to err on the side of caution and go with the longest estimate of thirty feet by six feet wide. Dr. Larsen made the measurements and drew the rectangle around the fossil himself and faced his team, shielding his eyes against the morning sun.

"We cannot underestimate the value of what Ms. Bjork and Professor DeLuca have discovered here," he said.

Behind her, Angela could hear Jordan mutter, "*Professor* Bjork."

"We'll dig outside this line, being careful as Dr. Seeley suggested, to preserve fossilized plants, tracks, feces, whatever we unearth that that might provide insights into the life and death of the animal," Larsen said. "The tendency will be to work hard and fast; dig an adequate size ditch around the fossil and then move toward it. I beseech you, slow and steady. We're not prospectors digging for gold. We're scientists searching for knowledge that has been hidden from us for more than sixty-seven million years. Patience."

He did something then that surprised Angela and made everyone else applaud. He handed her a shovel and said, "Shall we begin?"

Angela moved to the edge of the circle directly in front of the fossil and scraped off the top layer of rock and dirt and carefully dropped it into her plastic bucket. She did this a few more times before everyone else found a spot and started doing the same thing. Herschel started singing.

"*We dig dig dig dig dig dig dig from early morn till night. We dig dig dig dig dig dig dig up everything in sight.*"

"What the hell is that?" Jordan asked.

"'Heigh-Ho.'"

"What?"

"'Heigh-Ho.' From *Snow White and the Seven Dwarfs. Heigh-ho, heigh-ho . . .*"

"Are you kidding me?"

"You can be Grumpy."

"Hey guys," Phillips said. "Dig, dig, dig . . ."

Winter had positioned herself close to Angela. She started giggling. Angela looked up at her.

"Kids," she said.

By the end of May, the dig had advanced nicely. The group had even unearthed a few fossils of value. Weiland discovered what appeared to be a tooth from an ancient shark and Professor Phillips found a fossilized palm fruit with spines on its outer wall. The fruit resembled previous finds that had been nicknamed *Spinifructus antiquus* which, Phillips claimed, helped support the theory that the *Ankylosaurus* ate pulpy fruit. To which Dr. Larsen smiled broadly and said, "Isn't this great?"

Also by the end of month, the geology students had fulfilled their summer field course requirements and were preparing to abandon the dig; their places to be filled by a second group of students arriving from Minnesota. Only Winter Billock and Simon Stevens chose to remain. They were pursuing geology degrees like the others, except that in their cases it was in anticipation of eventually gaining a master's in paleontology. It was the same track that Angela had taken—paleontologists usually have undergraduate degrees in geology or biology. Both wanted the experience of being part of the find and they knew it would look good on their applications.

Larsen had remained in camp to meet and greet the large van containing the new students. He was surprised that Dr. Weston Hegarty was among them. Hegarty told him that at the last minute he decided to hitch a ride so he could evaluate the find firsthand.

"Don't worry, Nick," he said. "I won't be in your hair for long. I'll be leaving tomorrow morning with the departing students."

By then, the camp had acquired a utility vehicle with a cargo box and a heavy trailer. Using all available space, Larsen was able to transport Dr. Hegarty and the students to the dig, driving slowly past the posts that marked the route over the uneven terrain. Hegarty was met with enthusiasm by the senior staff. He received hugs from both DeLuca and Professor Phillips. Angela deliberately picked up a plastic bucket and held it in front of her when he approached so that he was forced to shake her outstretched hand instead of embracing her.

"This man was my very good friend and mentor," Angela told Nina and me. "He was also my boss, the boss of nearly everyone there, and I just didn't think a public display of affection would go over very well with the rest of the staff, especially Larsen and Ashley."

Hegarty was effusive in his praise of the team and the progress they had made. They had made good progress, too. The "trench" as they called it, was more like a shallow bowl, the sides of the bowl surrounding the fossil, and dropping about two feet from the lip to where it was stretched out.

Angela and DeLuca had managed to expose enough of the *Ankylosaurus* skull that its eyes were visible, or at least the slightly oval sockets that, everyone was excited to note, faced forward instead of sideways like most plant-eating dinosaurs. Effusive or not, though, Angela knew the man well enough to recognize that he was disappointed.

"Sitting in his office at Tate Hall reviewing our reports, I just knew Weston was hoping to see the damn thing mounted on a pedestal like Sue," Angela told us.

"Sue?" Nina asked.

"The *T. Rex* they have on exhibit at the Field Museum in Chicago."

While Hegarty might have been disappointed, he demanded photos be taken and plenty of them. Him and Larsen. Him and

Seeley. And Phillips. And DeLuca. He did not take a single pic of himself and Angela, though, unless others were posing with them. He also took a video of the specimen, moving in a slow circle from the skull all around the fossil and back to the skull again.

The new set of geology students was also taking pics.

"I heard rumors," one said, "but I didn't believe them."

"Rumors?" Larsen asked.

"At school. When I signed up for this instead of one of the other field trips, I was told I might see a real live dinosaur. This isn't alive, but geez man. What the heck is it, anyway?"

"Class will be in session soon," Larsen said.

According to Angela, after the students were settled in, they all received a crash course on how to dig for fossils along with a lecture on what the University of Minnesota, Macalester College, and the Science Museum of Minnesota expected of them. Larsen, Phillips and Seeley also combined to give them a brief sermon on the current state of paleontology.

Seeley started with an explanation of how science works.

"People get excited about dinosaurs starting usually when they're children because someone gave them a stuffed *Tyrannosaurus Rex* or because they read a book or saw a movie. Well, all that came from science. We know about dinosaurs because a scientist carefully excavated a fossil, and reconstructed the skeleton, and placed the skeleton in a public repository such as a museum for everyone to see and study." Seeley raised his hand. "How many of you have seen a dinosaur in a museum? Could have been St. Paul. Or Chicago. Somewhere else."

Everyone raised a hand.

"That's science," Seeley said. "The kind of science we do here."

"Unfortunately, not all dinosaur fossils are studied by scientists; they don't all end up in a museum," Larsen added. "Instead, a lot of them are now being sold to private owners like they were works of art."

"You guys know who Nicholas Cage is?" Phillips asked. "The actor? Won an Oscar; did the *National Treasure* movies? He found himself in a bidding war with Leonardo DiCaprio and Russell Crowe over the skull of a *Tyrannosaurus*; eventually he bought it for $276,000. Later, it was discovered that the skull had been looted from Mongolia and he was forced to return it."

"I don't think he got his money back, either," Seeley said.

"The point is, more and more fossils are falling into the hands of private investors," Larsen said. "In most of Europe and here in the States, specimens discovered on private land belong to the landowner and can be sold to the highest bidder. You get auction houses selling fossils like they were paintings by Van Gogh or Rembrandt. The SVP—the Society of Vertebrate Paleontology, of which we are all members here—begs them not to sell dinosaur bones. Our fear is that when they go into private collections they'll disappear from view, and we might not get to study them. Or they won't be properly maintained. Instead, we believe fossils should be held in a public trust where anyone can study them instead of ending up in the hands of mega-rich people looking for trophies. Unfortunately, the auction houses refuse to listen."

"Institutions like the Science Museum of Minnesota simply can't afford to compete with these guys, either," Seeley said. "We don't have the resources. The only reason the Field Museum in Chicago has Sue, which cost over eight million dollars, is because corporate partners like Walt Disney World Resorts and Ronald McDonald House Charities were willing to help foot the bill."

"We realize that most of you guys are geology majors," Phillips said. "Well, from a geological standpoint, the rock in which the fossil is found is just as important as the fossil itself. To figure out how old a specimen is or what its environment looked like, we need to know exactly where it came from. Private fossil-buyers might be unable to provide that information."

"Long story short, for the next—what is it?" Larsen asked. "Twenty-four days? For the next twenty-four days we expect all of you to behave like scientists and not college kids on a camping trip. Having said that, do any of you like s'mores?"

Once again, the entire group circled the fire bowl, this time accompanied by the new students. Jordan was sitting next to Winter across from Angela. She noticed that they were holding hands. She liked that they were holding hands; it was a relief to her, she told Nina and me. Herschel brought out his Gibson.

"Professor DeLuca?" he asked. "What's your favorite piece of music?"

"You'll think I'm joking."

"No, I won't."

"Rachmaninoff."

"Here we go again," Phillips said.

"No, seriously," DeLuca said. "The third movement of Sergei Rachmaninoff's *Second Symphony*, the adagio—I just love that."

Herschel strummed a few bars on his guitar, looked up and said, "I don't know that one. But I promise, Professor, just for you, I'm going to learn it."

"You can always come back next year," she told him. "We'll be here."

"Professor Bjork, what's your favorite song?"

Angela bowed her head and took a deep breath; she told us she didn't know what came over her. It felt to her at that moment as if all of her dreams were coming true; as if her future was so close that all she had to do was reach out her hand. She lifted her head, yet instead of naming the song she loved, she began to sing it slowly, softly, as if she were afraid that someone would stop her.

"Moon River, wider than a mile, I'm crossing you in style someday."

Herschel let her sing the first verse a cappella before joining in for the rest of the tune, letting her voice dictate the rhythm. When Angela started singing about her huckleberry friend, she began to choke up yet managed a strong finish.

The camp was quiet for a long moment before Phillips raised his beer can.

"To them bones," he said. "And those who hunt them."

Morning came early to eastern Montana as it always did, bringing with it the promise of heat and wind. Once again Angela dressed in jeans and a long-sleeved shirt, her hair hanging down under her Stetson. Only her face and hands, all protected by sun lotion, were exposed to the sun. She stepped outside her tent. Movement to her right made her turn her head and she watched the geology students packing the van for their long journey home. Movement to her left caused her to turn her head again. Jordan Wall was standing in front of her, a backpack slung over his shoulder.

"Professor Bjork," he said. "I was hoping to see you before we left."

"I hope you had fun out here, Jordan. I hope you learned something."

"I learned a great deal. Professor, you know I'm in love with you, right?"

"Jordan . . ."

"No, listen, please. I owe you an apology. I'm sorry if I have ever made you feel uncomfortable for as much as five seconds. I'm sorry if I caused people to gossip about you. That was never my intention. I only wanted—well, you know what I wanted."

"Thank you, Jordan. You're a good kid."

"I'm twenty and you're twenty-four and you call me kid."

"I'm a teacher and you're a student, so yes, I call you kid."

"I graduate in a couple of years."

Angela did something then that she said was unprofessional as hell. She hugged Jordan close and whispered into his ear.

"Come see me after you graduate, and we'll talk."

"Count on it," he said, and they broke their embrace.

Jordan adjusted his backpack and walked toward the van.

More movement caused Angela to turn her head yet again. Winter Billock was standing five tents away and watching them both. Angela couldn't read her expression from that distance. All she saw was the young woman bending to pick up her orange bucket and moving toward the trail leading to the *Ankylosaurus*.

"Dammit," Angela said aloud.

THREE

May became June and June became July and the weather began to take its toll. The high temperatures were dancing in the nineties, actually hitting triple digits on several days, while the lows dropped into the low sixties at night, sometimes fifties. Most of the group was shocked that it could shift from so hot to so cold merely with the rising and setting of the sun. Meanwhile, the wind never ceased blowing. Never. The scientists began to think of ten miles per hour as a slight summer breeze, barely strong enough to lift a loose-fitting hat from your head. That's because it would also gust as high as twenty, thirty, forty, and even fifty miles per hour. On one memorable occasion it reached sixty miles. The joke was on that day it was also cooler—a comfortable eighty-five degrees Fahrenheit.

"Who the hell would live out here?" one of the geology students demanded.

"I don't know, but they gotta be nuts," Angela replied.

Dehydration became an issue and with it fatigue. The crew was putting in ten-hour days, sometimes longer.

"It's not like we had anything else to do," Angela told us.

Under those conditions, you'd think tempers would become short and jokes become insults. Yet Angela assured Nina and me that the opposite occurred. The core group of scientists grew even chummier; everyone looking out for everyone else. At one point, DeLuca accidently chipped off a piece of the *Ankylosaurus* skull, threw her dental pick to the ground and screamed "Fuck!" to the high heavens. A moment later, Phillips appeared with his cell phone, tapped a couple of links, and set it next to her; the phone playing Rachmaninoff's *Second Symphony*. Next, he handed her a tube of Krazy Glue to repair the damage.

Not a word was spoken except by Winter who asked, "Professor DeLuca, could you turn up the volume?"

Angela celebrated her twenty-fifth birthday at the dig. Baking a cake seemed impossible, so her colleagues gave her ice cream wrapped in a waffle and topped with sprinkles and a candle along with a lecture from Professor Phillips about how the ice cream cone was invented at the 1904 World's Fair. Angela said she loved them both.

Simon Stevens celebrated a birthday, too, turning twenty-one. He also received an ice cream cone, plus "Your first can of legal beer" from Phillips, and a kiss on the cheek from Winter. Later, Angela overheard him speaking of it to Phillips.

"She's so pretty and so smart," Simon said.

"Apparently, she likes you."

"Nah. She only has eyes for Jordan Wall."

"In case you haven't noticed, son," Phillips said. "Jordan isn't here."

During this time, Angela and Winter became close, often sitting in front of the fire bowl that now had a battery-operated lantern shining out of it—what idiot would start a fire in that heat?—and chatting about this, that, and other things. That's how Angela learned the origin of Winter's name. It turned out that she had three sisters. The first was born in July so her parents called her Summer. The second was born in May so they named her Spring. She, the third, was born in January, so, keeping with what was now a family tradition, they christened her Winter. To top it off, a fourth sister was born in October and became Autumn.

"What if one of you had been a boy?" Angela asked.

"They would have named him Michael after my father."

Several times Angela felt the urge to talk to Winter about Jordan yet, she told us, she always chickened out.

'Course, the entire crew didn't remain at the dig throughout the summer. They all returned home at one time or another to see their families and take care of personal business, especially during the long Fourth of July weekend. Everyone except Angela.

"Truth was," she told Nina and me, "there was no place that I would rather have been."

It was during the week following the Fourth that a special visitor arrived at the encampment. Angela knew who he was long before he was driven to the dig in a maroon SUV because she and the rest of the crew had been warned to treat the man with the utmost respect. His name was Andrew Cooke, and he owned the ground that they were standing on.

The crew applauded when he . . .

"Wait, wait," I said. "He owns the property where you discovered the *Ankylosaurus*?"

"Yes."

"All the other fossils, too? Where the main dig is? The quarry, pole barn; all of that?"

"Yes."

"Who is this guy?"

By then I had acquired a notepad—it had the name and logo of Rickie's on the top and the street address, phone number, and website address on the bottom. I wrote down everything Angela told me.

"Andrew Cooke was originally from eastern Montana, not

far from Billings," she said. "He attended the Carlson School of Management at the University of Minnesota. Class of 1960. I know because he told me that he was there when the Gophers won the national college football championship, the school's last football championship. Murray Warmath was coach. None of that's important. What's important is that Cooke became seriously wealthy in the hospitality industry. Not running hotels but supplying products to hotels. Towels, soaps, shower rods and curtains—that sort of thing. He also invested in real estate that he would later sell to hotels, motels, and restaurants. The land in Montana—should I tell you the story?"

"Yes, please," I said.

The crew applauded when Andrew Cooke was helped from the backseat of the SUV by a middle-aged woman who held him by the arm as if she were afraid the old man would fall. Cooke smiled while he waved dismissively at the crew with his free arm.

"You don't need to butter me up," he said. "I'm buttered, I'm buttered; believe me."

Dr. David Seeley moved quickly to his side.

"Andrew," he said. "I am so very glad to see you here."

"Oh, I wouldn't have missed this," Cooke said. "I wouldn't have missed it if it was the very last thing I ever did."

By then the driver of the SUV had emerged from the vehicle and moved to stand next to the woman who was still supporting Cooke. He glanced at the people and the dig as if he was wondering what he was doing there.

"I don't think you've met," Cooke said. "David, this is my granddaughter, Megan. Megan Cooke-Jackson . . ."

"Oh, but we have met." Dr. Seeley shook hands with her. "So very nice to see you again, Meg."

"Nice to see you, too, David," Megan replied.

They both smiled brightly at each other.

"This is her husband, Kevin Jackson," Cooke said.

Dr. Seeley shook hands with him, too. He kept smiling, but Angela thought he was only being polite.

"David," Cooke said, "is actually Dr. David Seeley from the Science Museum of Minnesota where they're going to put my dinosaurs on display."

Your dinosaurs? my inner voice asked.

Dr. Larsen quickly approached the trio from the trench where the *Ankylosaurus* was located.

"Nick," Cooke exclaimed. "There he is."

"Andrew," Larsen said.

Instead, of shaking hands, the two men embraced.

"Where is it?" Cooke asked. "You said it was even better than that lizard you found. Oh, hey, about that. David, when are they going to put it up, the *Acheroraptor*?"

"Hopefully by Christmas," Seeley said. "The museum is going to throw a 'gala'"—he quoted the word with his fingers—"and invite the public, the media. We've been talking to Twin Cities Public Television about covering it. You'll be the guest of honor, of course."

"I am so looking forward to it. The best Christmas gift."

"You're going to like this one, too," Larsen said.

He relieved the granddaughter of Cooke's arm and slowly spun him toward the trench. Angela said that Cooke didn't appear frail, yet he moved as if he was. She and DeLuca were standing in the trench, watching and listening, their tools in their hands. They both stepped back as Larsen and Cooke approached, revealing the skull of the *Ankylosaurus*.

"Oh, look at her, look at her," Cooke repeated.

The entire crew stood by and watched as the old man was led into the trench; smiled as his eyes grew wider and wider. Dr. Larsen walked Cooke right up to the dinosaur. By then Angela and DeLuca had exposed the beast's snout and much of its pre-maxillae, the very tip of the upper jaw baring teeth. The old man gently set his hand against the jaw; stroked it as if it was the cheek of his granddaughter.

"This is wonderful," Cooke said. "This is everything I have ever wanted—since I was a kid I wanted this and you and you—you're making my dream come true, aren't you? All of you. I'm so grateful. You probably don't know it, but back in the forties, early fifties, when I was still a child—they were digging for dinosaurs on the formation even then. I would meet 'em, the paleontologists; talk to them; wanted to grow up to be just like them. Do what they did. Only life had other plans and I, well . . . When I heard some land had become available; this was in the eighties—I had some money by then, so I bought it, thinking that one day I'd retire. I'd retire early and come out here and dig for dinosaurs just like those guys. Only I never did, never did, and then you came along saying how you found a bone out here and asking if you could keep prospecting and I said . . . Oh, man."

Cooke kept stroking the jaw and the snout and the top of the skull as if he was attempting to memorize it by touch.

"You're not going to sell this, are you?" he asked.

"Of course not," Larsen said.

"I mean we have a contract. Anything you find you get to keep; you get to study, you get to put on exhibit. If you sell it, though, I get half. Only I don't want you to sell it. I don't."

"We absolutely are not going to sell it," said Seeley. "We hope to eventually make the *Ankylosaurus* the first thing that visitors see when they step through the door of the science museum."

"And my name's going to go on it?" Cooke said.

"On a plaque just like the *Acheroraptor*," Seeley said. "The discovery, analysis, and exhibition of this dinosaur were all made possible by the generosity of Andrew Cooke."

"Hell, we'll probably name it after you," Larsen said.

"No," Cooke said.

Megan Cooke-Jackson was standing at the edge of the trench.

"Why not?" she said. "Andy the *Ankylosaurus*."

"No," Cooke repeated.

"You have to admit, it does have a nice ring to it," Angela said. "Sue the *T. Rex*. Andy the *Ankylosaurus*."

"Andrew," Seeley said, "this is Professor Angela Bjork. She's the one who actually found the dinosaur."

"Me and Professor Ashley DeLuca," Angela said, gesturing toward the woman standing behind her.

"Then they should name it after you," Cooke said. "I mean Sue; she was named after the woman who found her, Sue Henderson."

"I don't think so," Angela said.

"Oh, yes," Cooke said. "Think about it, David, Nick. Angie the *Ankylosaurus*. And if you want, you can name the other dinosaur after me."

"Andy the *Acheroraptor*?" Angela said.

Cooke waved a finger at her.

"Angie and Andy," he said. "Sounds like a match to me."

Most of the crew chuckled at the suggestion while Kevin Jackson, standing behind his wife, shook his head and rolled his eyes.

"What?" Cooke asked him. "You don't approve?"

"If you want people to remember you as being a giant lizard, a lizard with feathers, sure, why not?"

Angela said she and the others didn't know if they should laugh until Megan drove her elbow into her husband's stomach, forcing him to grimace. Then everyone laughed including Cooke.

"Andy the lizard," Cooke chanted. "By all means, let history think of me as a lizard. God knows I have it coming."

Only Angela didn't believe that was true. She and Andrew Cooke spent a great deal of time chatting around the fire bowl that evening after he discovered that she was also a Montanan. "A dying breed," Cooke labeled the two of them. He told her a little bit of his life that seemed to be filled with both success and generosity. He married a woman he had met at the U, which is why he remained in Minnesota, and eventually had five children, eleven grandchildren, and six great-grandchildren.

"That's what matters most," Cooke told her. "Family. If I learned nothing over the decades, I've learned that."

Even as he spoke the words, Angela noticed that Megan Cooke-Jackson was sitting next to Dr. Seeley. She told us that suddenly Megan seemed younger than she thought when they met. "Maybe because of the way the light reflected off of her face and hair," she said. At first, Megan and Seeley seemed to be enjoying each other's company, smiling and laughing and occasionally reaching out to tap a thigh or caress a wrist or squeeze a hand. Only now they were sitting quietly next to each other and staring at the lantern as if they had run out of the words that they were allowed to speak to each other.

Cooke asked Angela about her own family and gave her a "tut, tut," when she announced that she was twenty-five and unmarried with no intention of changing her marital status in the immediate future. He was impressed, however, when she told Cooke about her parents who were now living the good life in Vegas.

"Good for them." He slapped his hands together three times. "Spend your money. Have fun. You—you're an only child you say?"

"'Fraid so," Angela told him.

Cooke said that her parents were lucky in that regard. They didn't have to worry about trusts and wills; about dividing their estate when they passed. He had worried about it ever since his dear wife passed "Going on ten years now," he said. "I miss her every day." Finally, Cooke said he decided to hell with it, he'd divide his estate equally among all his descendants which, he admitted, annoyed a couple of his children.

"They believe I should leave all my money to them, and they

should be allowed to disperse it to their children and so on down through the years," Cooke said. "Only I want everyone to know where the money came from. Is that selfish? Giving every member of my family, even the one-year-old, two million bucks each?"

Angela said she didn't think so.

"Oh, and in case you're wondering," Cooke said, "I have already put all of my Montana property into a trust to be shared by the University of Minnesota, Macalester College, and the Science Museum of Minnesota, so you can keep finding dinosaurs that you can name after me."

While they chatted, Angela noticed that Kevin Cooke was holding court with Gary Phillips, Simon Stevens, Ashley De-Luca, and Winter Billock. While he kept his distance from Phillips and Simon, Kevin had no problem with placing a hand on Ashley's back or wrapping an arm around Winter's shoulder. Phillips seemed oblivious to Jackson's efforts while Simon gave him a side-eye every time he made a gesture toward Winter.

"He was flirting with them," Angela told Nina and me. "He was trying to find out which one of them was the most responsive and then make his move."

"Are you sure?" I asked. "His wife sitting there?"

"McKenzie, you don't think I know when a man is flirting?"

"Did either Winter or Ashley give in?"

Eventually, Phillips and Simon moved on, Angela told me, followed a short time later by DeLuca, leaving Kevin alone with Winter, although everyone sitting or standing around the fire bowl could easily see them together including Megan.

"I doubt anything came of it," Angela said. "Only I was distracted by a conversation with Cooke and Dr. Larsen about the future of the dig and I lost track."

It was in early August that yet another plan was formulated. Once again, Dr. Hegarty had arrived at the camp—this time he called ahead—with another flight of geology majors. Larsen, Seeley, and he, with input from Phillips, decided that they would concentrate their remaining time on excavating the *Ankylosaurus* skull, which they believed was intact. Much of the lower jaw was still underground and the rest was covered with rock and dirt. They didn't care. The plan was to dig beneath it and then plaster jacket the hell out of it— those are my words, not Angela's—and ship it to the science museum where it would be cleaned and prepared for study and display.

That left the skeleton of the *Ankylosaurus* to consider. Efforts, most of it provided by Phillips, Winter, and Simon, had exposed much of the top of the skeleton and the scientists believed that it, too, was largely intact which, by itself, would be a spectacular find. Nothing close to a complete skeleton had ever been unearthed.

"I worry about the weather," Larsen said.

"So do I," Hegarty replied.

"Digging the ditch around it has made it more vulnerable to the Montana winter."

"We could build a shelter to enclose it."

"Or we could plaster jacket the entire block and ship it to the science museum, too," Seeley said.

"Have you any idea how huge a block of sandstone that would be?" Hegarty asked. "Thirty feet by seven by six at least. And the weight? I can't even guess the weight. The amount of plaster alone . . ."

"We'd have to get a flatbed truck back here."

"And a crane," Phillips added.

"It's just not practical," Hegarty said.

For some reason that remark caused Dr. Larsen to start laughing. Soon the other scientists joined in as if they were all at a Chris Rock show. Finally, they turned to Angela and DeLuca.

"Well, ladies," Hegarty said. "What do you think?"

"You're asking us?" DeLuca asked.

"It's your dinosaur."

On Tuesday afternoon of the last week of August, Day Five according to Professor Phillips's backwards calendar, with the temperature at ninety-two degrees and the wind gusting to forty miles per hour, a crane using a web sling cautiously lifted the *Ankylosaurus* skull out of the bowl of sandstone and gently deposited it in the bed of a bronze-colored 2016 Ford F-150 pickup truck with the name Doyle Trucking painted on the door. By then it had been encased in plaster; the plaster supported by a wooden frame. The skull was covered with a tarp and carefully strapped down while everyone watched. Angela told Nina and me that she didn't realize that she had been holding her breath until she started sucking in oxygen like she had been underwater for three minutes.

The truck was slowly driven over the rough terrain to the camp and parked next to the pole barn so that it was facing the makeshift road connecting the camp to the highway. The crane remained at the dig, along with a flatbed truck that would eventually carry the immense rectangle of rock containing the *Ankylosaurus* skeleton. The trucks had come from the Twin Cities with Dr. Hegarty leading the way; the crane was brought in from a construction site near Broadus, Montana.

Along with securing the *Ankylosaurus*, everyone was busy packing and cleaning up. By the end of the week, the dig would be effectively abandoned for the winter, and a caravan of RVs and SUVs carrying the entire staff, plus Winter and Simon—the other geology majors had all been sent home the week prior—would accompany the trucks on their long journey to downtown St. Paul and the Science Museum of Minnesota.

That evening, though, the staff plus the drivers spent a lot of time sitting around the lantern in the fire bowl. Not a lot was spoken. Yet at the same time, no one wanted to go to sleep, although eventually they all did.

"I was so happy," Angela told us. "And then . . ."

FOUR

A scream woke her up. At first Angela didn't know that it was a scream; didn't know that she was awakened by anything more than a bad dream. Then she heard a second scream. She quickly rolled off the collapsible cot that had been her bed for the past one hundred days and immediately put on her shoes; she was already wearing gym shorts and a T-shirt. A glance at her smartwatch told her it was 3:08 A.M. The witching hour.

She stepped outside her tent and found Professor Phillips already standing outside his; he was dressed in shorts and holding his shoes in his hands. The only light came from a nearly full moon and the lamp hanging above the door of the pole barn.

"Gary, did you hear . . ."

A third scream.

It came from near the barn so that's what Angela began sprinting toward. Phillips took three painful steps on the rocky ground and paused to slip on his shoes. He had nearly reached Angela's side when they heard a gunshot.

Phillips halted immediately. He had heard gunshots before.

Angela continued running.

In front of her, she could hear the engine of the pickup truck carrying the *Ankylosaurus* skull as it was started; she could see its headlights snap on. It started moving quickly down the dirt road. Angela slowed as she watched; she told us she couldn't believe what she was seeing.

"*Noooooo!*" she shouted and began picking up speed again, altering her route so that she was now chasing the pickup.

"Stay where you are!" someone else shouted; a male voice that Angela said she didn't recognize.

Angela kept running after the truck.

She heard a second gunshot.

And a third.

Someone yelled, "Get down."

Angela felt the full weight of a large body slamming into hers. She lost her footing, fell, and slid across the rock and dirt and wheatgrass.

Another shot was fired.

Angela rolled onto her stomach. Her head came up and in that moment, she could see the taillights of a second car. In the next moment, she saw it pick up speed and follow the truck down the road, although she couldn't hear it.

Electric, my inner voice said. *That's how they snuck into camp without being heard.*

Completely ignoring the fact that she had just been tackled, Angela pushed herself to her feet.

"I wanted to go after the truck," Angela told Nina and me. "I was desperate to go after it. I saw Larsen's Ford Bronco parked near the mobile home. I ran toward it. Opened the door. Jumped in. Only there were no keys in the ignition. I started screaming, 'Where are the keys, where are the keys?'"

By then nearly everybody in the camp had gathered at the barn. That's when Angela saw Dr. Hegarty. He was lying on his back on the ground; Dr. Seeley checking his pulse, checking his pupils; Dr. Larsen hovering above them both. She climbed out of the SUV and dashed to Hegarty's side. There was a wound on his forehead above his left eye and a stream of blood seemed to be flowing over the eye, down his check and chin and neck. The sight made Angela cover her mouth in fear and horror. Larsen was demanding that they get Hegarty to a hospital. Now. Right now. Out where they were, there was no waiting for an ambulance. Yet, Angela told us that she froze, "Just standing there like an idiot," while Larsen, Seeley, and Phillips lifted and carried her friend and mentor to Larsen's SUV and laid him across the backseat.

"Everyone stay here," Larsen said. "Everyone stay calm."

He climbed into the vehicle and drove off; Seeley in the backseat with Hegarty.

"The driver, one of the drivers from the Cities, his name was Ralph, Peter Ralph; he was standing behind me," Angela said. "He was yelling, 'Where's my truck? Where the hell is my truck?'"

I wrote on my notepad—*Did Ralph still have his keys?*

Angela glanced around her. Professor Phillips, dressed only in shorts, was standing near the drivers, both of whom also appeared as if they had just rolled out of bed. The eldest of the two—his name was Patrick Bittle—had rested a hand on Ralph's shoulder. "Take it easy," he said. Ralph appeared to Angela as if his child had just wandered off into a shopping mall somewhere.

Simon was standing in the middle of the barn and looking around as if he didn't know where he was. Unlike the others, he was fully dressed.

Winter appeared in the entrance of the pole barn attired only in panties and a T-shirt. She was shaking like a leaf in a hard wind and Angela didn't know if it was because of the cold or because she was frightened. Winter began talking.

"I was walking to the porta potty," she said. "I heard voices. I looked toward the barn. The light above the barn—I saw a man hit Dr. Hegarty with something. Something black that he held in his hand. Dr. Hegarty fell and I screamed. The man saw me. He pointed at me, and I screamed again. Another man, I think he was a man, he was—I didn't see him at first. He was dressed in black and standing—I couldn't see him in the shadows. Suddenly, he started running toward me. I screamed again, only this time; this time I didn't just stand there. I started running. I don't even know where I was running to. I just started—he shot at me. Oh my God."

"No." DeLuca wrapped her arms around the girl. "No. I saw it. After I heard you scream, I went to the window of the RV. I saw him. He was pointing his gun into the air when he fired. He was just trying to frighten you."

"Well, guess what?"

"He frightened me, too," DeLuca said.

"Did you see his face?" Angela asked. "Did you see who it was?"

Both DeLuca and Winter shook their heads.

"Right after that, I saw the truck start moving down the road and then I heard you shouting," DeLuca said. "Only I didn't see you. I saw the taillights of a car . . ."

"I saw it, too," Winter said. "But I didn't hear a thing."

Definitely an EV.

Winter was still shivering despite the embrace of the older woman.

"C'mon," DeLuca said. "Let's get you inside, let's get you warm."

She slowly spun the young woman around and walked her toward the RV.

"How 'bout you?" The question came from Phillips. "Are you okay?"

"What?" Angela asked.

He gestured first at Angela's forehead and then at the cuts and abrasions on her shoulder, elbow, thigh, and knee where the rocks had scraped away layers of her skin.

"I didn't know I was hurt," Angela told Nina and me. "I didn't feel any pain until Gary mentioned it."

"I'm sorry," Phillips said. "I'm the one who tackled you."

"Why?" Angela asked.

"Honey, one of the first things you learn where I come from, you hear gunshots, you run in the opposite direction."

Angela gave it a moment's thought before she replied—"You didn't, though. You ran after me."

The Black man shrugged.

Behind her, Angela could hear Ralph speaking again. This time he was holding his cell phone to his ear.

"Where am I?" he asked. "I have no idea where the fuck I am. Don't you have GPS or something?"

Phillips reached out his hand and made a gimme gesture with his fingers.

"I got this," he said.

Ralph reluctantly passed him the cell phone.

"This is Professor Gary Phillips," he said. "To whom am I speaking?"

He paused while he listened to the reply.

"Ms. Curry, our camp is located approximately twenty miles straight south of Powderville . . ."

Every member of the crew save for Angela had grown up in the city and they were shocked that the Powder River County sheriff hadn't responded in what they thought was a timely fashion. I wasn't. I looked it up later. The sheriff's department had a staff of five overseeing 3,298 square miles. Its office was located in Broadus, nearly an hour's drive from Powderville, plus another half hour over an iffy makeshift road to where the camp was to be found. To receive a call in the dead of night, gather a team, and head to what Angela herself labeled as the middle of nowhere in less than one hundred minutes, yeah, I would call that a decent response time.

The crew had all dressed while they waited except, I learned later, for Winter who was barely holding herself together inside DeLuca's two-person RV. Coffee was brewed and poured, and they were all sitting or standing inside the pole barn while they drank it. Someone had attempted to call both Dr. Seeley and Dr. Larsen, yet couldn't get through.

It was a full hour before sunrise when they saw the headlights of the sheriff's SUV moving toward them. Angela wasn't surprised that the first thing the sheriff did after he parked his vehicle and stepped out was to adjust his cowboy hat and the gun belt that held his semi-automatic. Yet she was surprised by his deputy. He was Black. She found herself looking from him to Professor Phillips and back again. She had never seen two Black men together in Montana; the state had fewer than six thousand African Americans out of a population of over a million.

The deputy seemed surprised as well. He was staring at Phillips when the sheriff asked, "You call it in?"

The driver answered for Phillips.

"Someone stole my truck," Ralph said.

"I'm afraid it's more complicated than that," Phillips said. "A man was attacked."

"I know," the sheriff said. "I've been in contact with the Dahl Memorial Hospital in Ekalaka."

"Can you help us?" Angela asked. "We haven't been able to get through to them."

The sheriff removed a notebook from his pocket and read what he wrote there before speaking.

"Your Dr. Weston Hegarty is still unconscious," he said. "I don't know the extent of his injuries. I'm sorry I can't be more helpful."

No one had anything to say to that.

"What happened?" the sheriff asked.

"My truck was stolen," Ralph repeated.

Apparently, the sheriff preferred to handle what was simple, first. He beckoned the driver forward and began asking questions, starting with the make, model, and license plate number of his pickup; the name of the company Ralph worked for was painted on the side—Doyle Trucking. The sheriff wrote everything down. So did I.

After he finished taking notes, the sheriff activated the microphone on his shoulder and spoke to whomever was listening, issuing a BOLO for a bronze-colored 2016 Ford F-150 pickup truck with a Minnesota license plate that was carrying a large cargo beneath a blue tarp in its truck bed to all law enforcement agencies within reach, especially the Montana Highway Patrol.

I jotted a note on my pad—*At least a two-hour head start. How far could they get? North Dakota? South Dakota? Wyoming? Nebraska? Canada?*

"Tell me about the cargo," the sheriff said.

Professor Phillips did while the crew listened intently. Apparently, the fact that the thieves made off with a priceless *Ankylosaurus* skull didn't seem to faze the sheriff one little bit. He began to ask more questions, starting with one I would have asked the moment I arrived—"Is everyone accounted for?"

"Accounted for?" Phillips asked.

"Is everyone here who's supposed to be here?"

Phillips started counting heads; it hadn't occurred to him to do it before. Winter and DeLuca were in DeLuca's RV. Angela was standing next to him; Simon was sitting next to the two drivers. Hegarty, Seeley, and Larsen were in Ekalaka. The crane operator had departed for his home in Broadus long before sundown. He mentioned that to the sheriff.

"George Hankin?" the sheriff said. "We know him."

He nodded at his deputy who quickly returned to the SUV. I learned later that the deputy made a phone call, waking first Hankin's wife and then Hankin who claimed that he had been home all night, just ask his wife and kids if you don't believe him. He also admitted that he knew exactly what was in the plaster jacket that he lowered onto the bed of the Ford F-150 because he was told about it when he arrived with his crane that afternoon.

"Those scientist guys insisted on telling me," he said. "'Be careful, be careful' they kept yelling."

The sheriff began interviewing the witnesses one at a time beginning with Winter. She was sitting wrapped in a blanket on a chair in DeLuca's RV. The blanket didn't stop her from trembling. The sheriff wanted to speak to her privately, only DeLuca refused to leave her side. That's how Angela learned that the sheriff asked a lot of the same blunt questions in several different ways as if he expected Winter to give different answers—DeLuca had told her so. Winter's responses remained consistent, though, and when the sheriff finished, he rested a hand on the young woman's shoulder and thanked her for her time and patience. He also said that he admired her courage, which caused Winter to tear up. Except, along with the tears came a bright smile. The trembling ceased.

He asked a lot of blunt questions when it became Angela's turn, too. At first, she thought he was deliberately trying to confuse her, yet soon realized that he was seeking more specific details.

"I was told that you ran after the pickup," the sheriff asked.

"Yes."

"I was told that the suspect ordered you to stop and when you didn't, he shot at you."

"I don't know if he shot at me or not. Professor DeLuca said he fired in the air when he encountered Winter Billock."

"Why did you run after the truck?"

"The *Ankylosaurus* skull was important to me. *Is* important to me."

"You shouldn't have done it."

"What would you have done?"

"I would have called the police."

"We did. Hours ago."

If the sheriff was offended by the dig, he didn't show it.

While he asked his questions, Angela took note of the sheriff's clothes. He was wearing beige cargo pants, a tan shirt and a tan vest with the word SHERIFF printed above his right pocket and FLOR above his left. The vest held a taser, magazines for the semi-automatic handgun, a pouch for handcuffs, and a walkie-talkie that apparently complemented the radio attached to the epaulet on his left shoulder. What caught Angela's eye, though, were the four different colored ink pens strapped to the pocket below his nametag.

"Why would he need four pens?" Angela asked.

I told her that I didn't know.

Something else, Angela told us—the sheriff wasn't wearing a badge. Only a patch on his right shoulder that was emblazoned by a seven-point star superimposed over a background consisting of mountains and clouds. In the center of the star was a black silhouette of a cowboy riding a bucking bronco.

Maybe in the rush to get to the scene he forgot to put on his badge, my inner voice suggested.

Finally, Sheriff Flor asked her the same questions that he had asked everyone in the camp—"Who do you think is responsible for this? Who do you suspect?"

Angela didn't have an answer.

No one in the camp had an answer, although the questions would keep repeating in their minds like an old vinyl record, the needle caught in a groove.

It was bright sunshine when Sheriff Flor and his deputy finally left the camp after first promising the group that they would keep in touch. No one felt like breakfast, yet Professor Phillips insisted that everyone eat. He made scrambled eggs with diced tomatoes and shredded cheese on the field stove. According to Angela, the only one who ate like she was hungry was Winter, who was now dressed for the day.

At about ten A.M., Dr. Larsen returned to the camp with news concerning Dr. Hegarty.

"He's going to be fine," he told the group that huddled around him. "He suffered a concussion, and he has a gash on his forehead above his right eye that required stitches. But he's conscious, all his vitals are normal; he's talkative. The medical staff claims he's going to be fine. I left him chatting happily with Dr. Seeley."

"Happily?" Simon asked.

"The doctor on duty felt the need to explain to us that a blow hard enough to cause unconsciousness, cause a concussion, was also hard enough to kill him so, yes, Dr. Hegarty was happy. Professor DeLuca, if I may impose on you, I'd like for you to relieve Dr. Seeley later this afternoon. I don't want to leave Dr. Hegarty alone."

"Yes, certainly."

Satisfied and relived that Hegarty was going to recover, several people asked the next question simultaneously—"Does he know who hit him?"

"He told the Carter County sheriff that he didn't recognize his attacker."

I looked that up later, too. The Carter County Sheriff's Department had four deputies covering 3,348 square miles. The Dahl Memorial Hospital was located in Ekalaka, the county seat.

"Dr. Hegarty reported that he heard a noise and stepped outside the mobile home to investigate," Larsen said. "I wish he would have wakened Dr. Seeley and me, first, but . . . He heard a noise and stepped outside and saw two men who were—what was the term he used? He said he saw them hot-wiring the pickup truck."

"Geezus," Peter Ralph said.

"Weston yelled at them to stop and one of the men turned and hit him in the head. The next thing he knew, he was in the emergency room at the hospital. Dr. Seeley and I were unaware that this was happening, of course. We didn't know what was happening until we heard the scream that woke us up. Ms. Billock, how are you doing?"

"Better," Winter said.

"Are you sure?"

"Yes, Doctor. I'm fine."

"The rest of you?"

He was told that everyone else was fine, too.

"I'm not going to pretend that this isn't a catastrophic event," Larsen said. "Losing the skull like this . . . I was assured that the authorities will soon locate the skull"—Larsen gestured at Ralph—"along with the truck, but I don't know. The theft seems so well thought out, doesn't it? However, in the meantime, we must not forget who we are and why we're here. There's still the matter of the *Ankylosaurus* skeleton, which some might argue is of greater importance than the skull. Ladies and gentlemen, we still have much work to do and a very short time to do it."

Off to work they went. The crane operator was lured back to the camp on Thursday and the *Ankylosaurus* skeleton that was embedded in its massive plaster-jacketed block of sandstone was loaded onto the back of the flatbed truck and secured.

Dr. Hegarty was released from the hospital the same day. This time when he appeared at the camp, Angela did hug him and kept hugging him until he pushed her away.

"It's okay," he told her, "I'm okay," although Angela said that the bandage and bruises above his eye suggested that he was not. Yet, despite everything that had happened, Hegarty appeared to be in fine spirits. He thanked everyone at the camp for their concern and for their hard work. He gestured at the tarp-covered plaster block on the back of the remaining flatbed truck.

"We're guarding this, right?" Hegarty asked.

Sheriff Flor did not keep in touch as promised. On Friday, however, an investigator working out of the Major Case Section of the Investigations Bureau of the Montana Department of Justice's Division of Criminal Investigation—yes, I know it's redundant—drove the two hundred miles from his office in Billings to ask the same questions that Flor did, plus a few more of his own, specifically—"What is this *Ankylosaurus* skull worth, anyway?"

"From a purely scientific viewpoint it's priceless," Dr. Hegarty told him.

"Let's pretend the people who took it aren't scientists."

"A skull of a *Tyrannosaurus Rex* was excavated from the Hell Creek Formation in Harding County, South Dakota, about a hundred miles from here," Dr. Seeley said. "It sold at auction two years ago for six million dollars. I imagine that this skull, because of its scarcity, would be worth at least that much."

"Well, shit," the investigator said.

Peter Ralph asked about his truck. The investigator said that it hadn't been recovered as far as he knew. He said he hoped the pickup was insured.

I wrote a single word on my notepad—*Insurance.*

Like the sheriff, the investigator also said that he'd keep in touch. No one believed him.

On Saturday, the camp was shut down and abandoned for the coming winter. All the tents, chairs, cots, coolers, and grills were stored in the pole barn; the propane tank was secured, and the porta potties were collected and driven off. The scientists seemed ambivalent about it, their mood swinging from festive to distressed as they repeated the same questions both silently and out loud—"Where is the *Ankylosaurus* skull? Will we ever get it back? Who did this?"

The entire party made the eleven-hour drive to the Minnesota Science Museum in downtown St. Paul without stopping except for fuel and restroom breaks. DeLuca, Winter, and Angela rode together in Ashley's small RV. They didn't speak much; a shroud of depression seemed to envelop them. It was when they were nearing the Cities that DeLuca began to vent.

"I can't believe this is happening," she said. "We worked so hard. I don't mean just at the dig, but our education, our careers and this, and this . . . No one's going to help us, either. Dr. Seeley even called the FBI, and they said it wasn't their problem. Not their problem! Are you kidding me? The *Ankylosaurus* is going to end up on the black market somewhere and some rich prick is going to buy it and there's nothing we can do about it. Nothing."

Neither Winter nor Angela replied. What were they going to do? Disagree with her? Yet as they approached St. Paul, my hometown, Angela had a thought.

"I know a guy," she said.

That was nearly a month ago and I asked Angela why she hadn't contacted her guy sooner.

She leaned back in her chair and used both hands to fluff the golden hair off her neck. By then we had moved to a table inside Nina's office because we agreed that Maud Hixson would be greatly annoyed to have us constantly talking in the back of the performance hall while she crooned "Close Your Eyes" from the stage. Nina and I had finished our meals, yet Angela's sea bass remained half eaten. I knew from experience that it was a very good sea bass, so I blamed her loss of appetite on the story she told us.

"Every time I think about what happened, talk about what happened, my emotions swing all around," Angela said. "Anger and depression, I get that. Yet I also feel shame. As if all this happened because of me. Like it was my fault because I wasn't—because I wasn't worthy enough to bring home the *Ankylosaurus*. Does that make sense?"

"It's not an uncommon feeling," I told her. "Victims often blame themselves. They tell themselves that they were in the wrong place at the wrong time as if that's what caused the crime. It's not."

"Something else. Just going to work or walking across campus; having a cup of coffee at Coffman Union, I'll feel—I don't know. 'Anxious' isn't the right word."

"Vulnerable," I said.

"Yes. Like I'm not safe. Like anything could happen."

"That's not uncommon, either."

"McKenzie, can you help me?"

Nina reached across the table and took Angela's hand.

"Of course he can," she said. Only the glance I gave her made her reassess her declaration. "Can't you?"

"Angela," I said. "What happened after you came home?"

"McKenzie . . ."

"I need more information."

"We moved the sandstone block containing the *Ankylosaurus* skeleton, what was left of it, anyway, into the basement of the Minnesota Science Museum. We've been chipping away at it ever since."

"I mean with law enforcement."

"I don't understand."

"Have you been questioned by anyone in law enforcement since the theft?"

"No, and that's—that's one of the reasons why I'm here. I kept thinking the FBI or those people in Montana . . ."

"The DCI."

"DC . . . ?"

"Division of Criminal Investigations."

"Yes. I kept thinking that somebody would be trying to solve the crime; that somebody would be looking for the *Ankylosaurus*. That's one of the reasons I waited so long before calling you. I thought, I don't know, that someone else should be doing this; was doing this—let them do their jobs, I told myself. Only nobody has. At least not as far as I know. I asked Weston, Dr. Hegarty, about it and Gary Phillips, too, and they haven't heard anything, either. Like you said, it's been almost a month."

"What about the media?" I asked.

"The newspapers, the St. Paul and Minneapolis papers— they each ran a story and so did the local TV stations. I know that Dr. Hegarty and Dr. Seeley were interviewed and so was Professor Phillips. I wasn't, though. *The Journal of Paleontology* did a piece and so did *The Journal of Vertebrate Paleontology* that's published by the SVP. Only I wasn't interviewed for any of them, either."

"Okay."

"Okay?"

I had the notepad in front of me and I started leafing through the many pages that I had filled.

"Something that your Dr. Larsen said . . . Here it is. He said, after he came back from the hospital where they took Dr. Hegarty, he said 'The theft seems so well thought out.' Well, he was right. It was well thought out, well planned, by people who knew exactly what they were doing."

"So?"

"I equate this to art theft . . ."

"Yes," Angela said. "Art theft. We've been thinking that ourselves."

"Which means that one of three things is going to happen or has already happened. First, the theft was commissioned by someone who wanted that specific skull, who hired a crew to take it. That means the thieves have probably already delivered the goods and were paid off; it means the skull is locked up in someone's vault somewhere.

"Second, the thieves and/or the fence that employed them have put the skull on ice and are now patiently waiting until they find a buyer to take it off their hands. I say patiently because this could take years.

"Finally, the thieves and/or fence are waiting for things to cool down a bit; waiting for law enforcement to move on to more pressing matters which, based on what you've told me, it might already have done. When that happens, they'll attempt to sell the skull back to the University of Minnesota or to the insurance company. Who is the insurance company, do you know?"

Please, please, please, my inner voice chanted.

"I think Midwest Farmers Insurance Group," Angela said.

Thank you, thank you, thank you.

I wrote the name on my notepad.

"I know people over there," I said aloud.

"Would that happen, though?" Angela asked. "The university, the Minnesota Science Museum, they're public institutions. They receive state funding. Would they buy stolen property?"

"Not directly," I said. "And certainly not openly. Yet they both have rich alumni, rich benefactors, don't they? People who might be induced to kick in a few bucks on the down-low, who might be persuaded to act as go-betweens. It happens all the time in sports."

Andrew Cooke is a university alumnus, my inner voice reminded me. *And he's involved with the science museum.*

I wrote his name on my notepad, too.

"Will you help me, McKenzie?"

Angela was leaning forward when she asked that question again. I set my pen down and leaned back in my own chair. Nina watched me do it. The expression on her face suggested that she genuinely didn't know how I was going to answer.

"Of course I will," I said. "I'll try, anyway."

The two women both smiled as if they were relieved.

"Only Angela, you might not like what I find out. I know you're not going to like what I'm about to tell you now."

"What?"

"I'd bet the ranch that it was an inside job. Someone at the dig was helping the thieves."

"I don't believe it," Angela said.

"Think about it . . ."

Angela's voice rose three octaves and I was sure Maud Hixson could hear her even though we were on the floor beneath the stage where she was crooning.

"I don't believe it," she said.

Nina rested her hand on the young woman's again, only Angela flicked it away and stood up.

"These are my friends," Angela said.

"You dug the skull out of the sandstone, wrapped it in plaster, set it in the bed of a pickup truck and parked the truck next to the pole barn. That same evening, at least two thieves infiltrated the camp and stole the truck."

"I know what happened, McKenzie. I was there, remember?"

"How did they know the skull was ready for the taking? How did they know it would be sitting in the back of the pickup? Angela, how did they know the skull was even at the dig? Someone must have told them."

"No."

"They couldn't have stolen it while it was in the ground. They had to wait . . ."

"It was the driver. Ralph whatshisname. Or the other one. They must have done it."

"It's certainly possible," I said. "We'll check them out, first. Only Angela—"

"I can't believe this. I won't believe that one of my friends at the dig is responsible."

"Possibly I'm wrong."

Angela gave it a few seconds of hard thought. Her voice was barely above a whisper when she spoke.

"Only you're not, are you?" she said.

"No, I don't think so."

Angela slowly sat back down.

"Dammit," she muttered.

We chatted some more after that. I gathered all the contact information for her and everyone else at the dig that she could give me. At the same time, I tried to find out where everyone was and what they had been doing since the theft. It turned out that Angela had kept at least a nodding contact with all of them except the two truck drivers. They were all still in the Cities.

Afterward, there was more hugging but less gushing. I promised Angela that I would keep in touch and that she should contact me if she had any additional thoughts.

"Text before calling," I told her. "In case I'm involved in something."

She looked at me as if she couldn't imagine contacting me any other way.

Once Angela left, a member of Nina's waitstaff appeared to clear the table.

"Do you want to go upstairs?" Nina asked. "Maud should be starting her second set by now."

"In a minute," I said.

I rested my head against the back of the chair and closed my eyes.

"Dinosaurs," I said. "Do you believe it?"

"Remember when you went after that Stradivarius violin that was stolen?" Nina asked me. "This at least should be easier to find."

"You think so?"

"It's bigger."

"Very true."

"You're going to let me help, right? Like Nick and Nora Charles in *The Thin Man*?"

"I should never have made you watch that movie. What do you have in mind?"

"First, we need a list of suspects, starting with the people who were at the dig when the skull was stolen. Here."

Nina grabbed my pad of notes, tore off a blank page, and started writing. I watched her do it, feeling a little like Victor Frankenstein; thinking that I had created a monster. When she finished, Nina turned the page toward me and I read the names she had listed there.

Angela Bjork—UM
Dr. Weston Hegarty—UM
Dr. Nicholas Larsen—UM
Professor Ashley DeLuca—UM
Professor Gary Phillips—Mac
Dr. David Seeley—SMM
Winter Billock—Student UM
Simon Stevens—Student UM
Peter Ralph—Truck driver
Patrick Bittle—Truck driver
Something Hankin—Crane operator*
Jordan Wall—Student UM*
Andrew Cooke*
Megan Cooke-Jackson*
Kevin Jackson*

I asked her why the asterisks for the last five names.

"They weren't there when the theft took place," Nina said. "That doesn't mean they weren't involved."

"Okay."

"Should I tell you who I think did it?"

"By all means."

"Dr. Nicholas Larsen."

"You think that why?"

"Bear with me."

I settled back into my chair to listen.

"Why did Angela involve Ashley DeLuca in her find?" Nina asked. "It was because Dr. Seeley from the science museum told her that they were rivals for the same jobs at the U of M. Now, think about Larsen and Dr. Hegarty. Hegarty was at Penn State. He was hired by the U to take over the department— what do they call it?"

"The Department of Earth and Environmental Sciences."

"Larsen is the number two man."

"We're not exactly sure what his position is yet."

"I bet, though, that he thinks he should have the top job, that the U should have put him in charge instead of hiring some guy from off campus. And now he wants revenge."

"You think Dr. Larsen arranged to have the *Ankylosaurus* skull stolen for revenge?"

"That and the money it'll fetch."

"Okay."

"You don't agree?"

"No, no, you might be right. The thing to do, though, is gather all the information, all the facts, and then figure out what happened instead of coming up with a theory first and searching for the facts that prove it. Doing it the other way around is why so many innocent people go to jail."

"What are we going to do first?"

We?

"If I had overseen the investigation, the first thing I would have done was request a search warrant so I could examine every phone call, text, and email sent by every one of the ten people at the dig from the moment the trucks arrived until after the skull was taken. Only I wasn't. We might be able to get around that, though. I know people."

"Well then, what are we going to do second?"

I knew exactly what "we" were going to do second, only I decided not to tell Nina; I wanted it to be a surprise. Instead, I said, "Let me think about it." The moment she left her office, though, I sent a text. An hour later, I received a phone call that I took where Nina couldn't eavesdrop on the conversation. After exchanging pleasantries, the caller asked, "What can I do for you?"

"You're not going to believe this," I said.

FIVE

Special Agent Brian Wilson invited me to meet him at Caribou Coffee in Brooklyn Center because, he said, he didn't want riff-raff like me hanging out at FBI headquarters. It would give the place a bad name, he said.

The invitation came at the end of a phone call I made to him early in the morning after meeting with Angela Bjork.

"Brian," I said when he answered the phone.

"What do you want, McKenzie?"

"Why should I want anything?"

"You called me Brian."

"Isn't that your name?"

"You nearly always called me Harry."

"You keep telling me that you don't like that nickname even though you bear an uncanny resemblance to Harry Dean Stanton, the actor."

"No one else believes that, least of all my wife."

"Brian . . ."

"What do you want, McKenzie?" he repeated.

"I just received my season tickets to the Wild. I know how much you like your Original Six hockey teams if you want a few games."

"In return I'm supposed to do what exactly?"

"Geez, you have a suspicious nature."

"I've known you for a long time, McKenzie . . ."

"There was a major theft in southeastern Montana . . ."

"We don't do Montana. That's the Salt Lake City Field Office, although I think they have an office in Billings. Why don't you call them?"

"Because I don't have a friend over there that I've actually helped out once or twice over the years who might now feel, I don't know, beholden."

Brian sighed heavily.

"What was stolen?" he asked.

"The skull of an *Ankylosaurus*."

"That's a dinosaur, isn't it?"

"Yes, sir."

"How did you—wait. The University of Minnesota just lost a dinosaur. Is that what we're talking about?"

"How did you know they lost a dinosaur?"

"I read the newspapers."

"That makes you a member of a shrinking minority."

He paused long enough after that that I thought I might have lost the connection.

"Brian?" I asked.

That's when he told me to meet him at the Caribou.

"Oh, and I'd like to see the Montreal Canadiens and the Boston Bruins if you have them."

Ninety minutes later I stepped inside the Caribou Coffee off Lake Breeze Avenue. Brian was sitting at a table. He was not alone. A woman with dark brown hair sat across from him. She was wearing blue jeans and a blue shirt. Her shoes were designed for running; she wore a black sports jacket despite the eighty-degree temperature to hide her weapon.

I walked up to the table.

"Brian," I said.

"McKenzie." He gestured toward the woman. "Linda Ambrose."

I offered my hand.

"Special Agent—"

I stopped speaking the instant that her hard eyes met mine. Her mouth twisted into an expression of surprise and anger.

"Why don't you say that louder so they can hear you in the parking lot?" she said.

Is she undercover? my inner voice wondered.

I withdrew my hand.

"I apologize, Ms. Ambrose," I said. "Can I get you guys anything from the counter?"

Ambrose used her fingertips to flick the edge of an empty white plate that was set in front of her.

"Another raspberry white chocolate scone," she said.

I turned my back and moved to the counter. Swear to God I thought I heard snickering behind me.

One raspberry white chocolate scone and an Americano later, I sat at the table, setting a new plate on top of the old one in front of Ambrose.

"So, you're McKenzie," she said. "I thought you'd be taller."

"Excuse me?"

"Your reputation precedes you."

I glanced at Brian, who was trying hard to keep a straight face.

"I have a reputation?"

Brian started chuckling.

Are they messing with you?

"I'm told you like to get involved in affairs that are none of your business," Ambrose said. "One or two of them might even have involved the Bureau."

"I occasionally do favors for friends."

"Do you have a lot of friends?"

I was looking at Brian when I answered, "Not as many as I thought."

His chuckle suggested that he thought I was being funny.

"Brian tells me that you recently lost an *Ankylosaurus*," Ambrose said.

"It wasn't lost. It was stolen."

Brian began to spin his index finger in a tight circle in the air.

"Tell us about it," he said.

I did, repeating to the special agents what Angela Bjork had told me only more quickly and with considerably less detail. While I spoke, Ambrose ate her scone. We both finished at about the same time.

"A year ago, a federal grand jury in Salt Lake City returned a thirteen-count indictment against four people accused of shipping $1 million in stolen dinosaur fossils to China," Ambrose told me. "In addition, the crew was accused of causing more than $3 million in property damage including the loss of the scientific value of the bones as well as the cost of restoring and repairing them."

"That's what the scientists seemed to be most concerned with, the damage and loss of scientific knowledge," I said.

"Here's the thing, though—McKenzie, the fossils were excavated from public land; from federal and state land and then transported out of the country. That's why the Bureau was involved, the U.S. attorney. Your *Ankylosaurus* was found on privately owned property; it was taken from private citizens. See the difference?"

"Yes."

"Do you have evidence that the skull was transported across state lines?"

"No."

"It's a state crime, then, not federal; it's not the Bureau's jurisdiction. But you already knew that, didn't you? You knew it before you called."

"Were you involved in the Salt Lake City investigation?" I asked.

Ambrose was looking at Brian when she answered by repeating her question—"Do you have any evidence that the skull was transported across state lines?"

"Not yet," I said.

Ambrose kept watching Brian.

"Why am I here?" she asked.

"Linda," Brian said. "McKenzie isn't asking for help. He's asking for permission."

Ambrose gave it a few beats before she rose dramatically from the table.

"Do not think for a moment, McKenzie, that the Bureau supports much less condones your activities in this matter," she said. "Do not for a moment believe that anything you do is at our direction or with our permission. Understood?"

"Yes," I said.

Ambrose turned to look at Brian.

"Did that sound stern enough?" she asked.

"I'm sure there'll be no confusion," Brian answered. "Right, McKenzie?"

"None," I said.

Ambrose rested a hand on my shoulder; then gave it a pat.

"You have a plan, don't you?" she said.

"It's a work in progress."

"Thanks for the scone. Brian knows how to get in touch with me if you have a reason to get in touch with me."

"Thank you."

Brian smiled at me as Ambrose walked out of the coffee shop.

"Any questions?" he asked.

"What hockey games do you want now?"

I didn't bother to call, but instead drove directly to the head-quarters of Midwest Farmers Insurance Group in downtown St. Paul after meeting with Brian. I managed to finagle my way to the tenth floor yet was stopped by an officious woman who demanded to know what I was doing there. I told her who I came to see. She told me not to move. I didn't, not even to sit in one of the chairs in a lobby while she disappeared down a corridor. A few moments later, she returned and escorted me to an office. There was a nameplate mounted at eye level next to the door frame that read MARYANNE ALTAVILLA. I stepped inside. There was a desk in the office. On the desk was another nameplate that read MARYANNE ALTAVILLA. I figured there was a joke in there somewhere only I let it slide.

Maryanne sat behind the desk. She was dressed in her uniform of severe black jacket and skirt and white dress shirt. Her hair was nearly the same color as the jacket and skirt. It was pulled back in a ponytail.

"Thank you, Eveleth," she said.

She waited for my escort to depart before Maryanne left her chair, circled the desk, and gave me a hug.

"McKenzie," she said. "How are you?"

"Couldn't be better. You?"

"The same." Maryanne returned to her chair. "How's Nina?"

"Spectacular."

I glanced around her office. Maryanne once explained to me why she kept so few personal items there. "I'm a minimalist," she had said. "I like to keep it simple." I found something, though, that had not been there the last time I visited—a framed photograph of a woman with long hair; green eyes peeking out from under schoolgirl bangs. Her name was Genevieve

Katherine Bonalay, aka G. K., the woman who had been acting as my personal attorney ever since she helped me dodge an obstruction charge and I helped her client escape a murder conviction nearly eight years ago. I picked up the photograph to get a closer look.

"So, how's it going?" I asked.

"G. K. and I made a promise to each other," Maryanne said. "We promised we would never discuss our relationship with you."

I returned the photograph to her desk.

"That hurts," I said. "Especially since I'm the one who introduced you two."

"I appreciate it, too. I really do. Still . . ." Maryanne sighed. "What do you want, McKenzie?"

"Must I want something? Can't I just drop in to say hi?"

"The last time you just dropped in to say 'Hi' you were trying to track down $654,321 that was stolen from an armored truck that we insured."

I wasn't surprised that she remembered the exact amount. Maryanne Altavilla was always the smartest person in the room no matter what room she happened to be in. That's why she was promoted to chief investigator in the Midwest Farmers Insurance Group's Special Investigative Unit at the tender age of twenty-seven.

And yet three years later, the only personal item in her office is a pic of your lawyer, who is how many years older?

"I've been told that Midwest Farmers insured a dig in southeastern Montana sponsored by the University of Minnesota, Macalester College, and the Science Museum of Minnesota," I said.

"You're talking about the *Ankylosaurus* skull." Maryanne leaned back in her chair and clasped her hands on top of her head. "How did you get involved in this?"

"I owe a favor to a woman who was involved in the dig, a big one."

"Of course." Maryanne gestured at the chair in front of her desk. "What do you want from me?" she asked.

I sat.

"My life would be so much easier if you guys had already made a deal to buy the skull from the thieves," I said.

"Why would we do that?"

I deliberately made my answer sound like a question—"To minimize your company's losses?"

"What losses?"

The question caught me by surprise.

"Am I mistaken?" I asked. "Farmers didn't insure the dig?"

"We did, yet only to a point. We insured the material aspects of the dig, the buildings, the equipment; the people, although we insisted that everyone present at the dig have their own health insurance. However, we did not insure what came out of the ground."

"Why not?"

"In order to insure an exhibit against theft or damage, the company needs a reasonable estimate of the monetary value of the exhibit. A scientist screaming his *Ankylosaurus* skull is worth in excess of six million dollars doesn't qualify."

"Who did the screaming?"

"I don't know. I wasn't at the meeting. McKenzie, think of it as a work of art . . ."

Which is what you've been doing.

"The Minneapolis Institute of Art buys a painting at auction. Its value is determined when the auction hammer drops. Let's say ten million dollars. That's what we insure it for; premiums are calculated accordingly. A dinosaur bone dug out of the ground, though? What is that worth?"

"What people are willing to pay for it, I guess."

"How much is that?"

"You're asking me?"

"Your opinion would be just as valid as the next guy's. The

interesting thing—one of the interesting things, according to my research—is that while the sponsors of the dig would certainly like to be compensated for their loss, if most scientists had their way, dinosaur bones would be considered worthless. Apparently, they're afraid that by creating a set value for a *Tyrannosaurus* toe or a *Triceratops* horn—or an *Ankylosaurus* skull—treasure hunters and poachers will be encouraged to scavenge for them on public land; that it would assist the black market in determining scarcity and value."

"Farmers didn't insure the skull?" I asked.

"Not for six million. I'm sure that before the matter ends up in court, though, the company will agree to pay a token sum."

"So, you're not interested in getting it back?"

"Did I say that, McKenzie? I don't think I said that."

I stared at her from across her desk. She stared back. If we were playing poker I would have folded my hand, but then I'm a lousy poker player. Chess, on the other hand . . .

"You mentioned that you did research," I said.

"Did I? Yes, I guess I did."

"What research?"

"Nothing that you couldn't do yourself."

"That's not necessarily true. For example, I can't access the Montana DCI and the Powder River County Sheriff Department's incident reports. I can't lobby either of them to contact a judge and request a search warrant to determine which of the ten people at the dig made a phone call or sent a text or email the day the skull was stolen."

Maryanne looked up and away, a habit she had when she was recalling something.

"Oh, but McKenzie," she said. "You haven't established a nexus between the individuals and the crime—the crime being the disappearance of the skull. You can connect them to the existence of the skull, yes, but not the actual theft."

"Excuse me?"

"What's more, we're talking about ten individuals, all innocent until proven guilty. To request a search warrant seeking all the call, text, and email information from such a broad group of people, why that's nothing but a glorified fishing expedition. A witch hunt. They don't allow that in Montana. They don't invade people's privacy without cause; their judges don't, anyway. At least, that's what I've been told."

"You can't be serious."

The expression on her face told me that she was. It also told me that she wasn't happy about it.

"Tell me, McKenzie—if you were to recover the *Ankylosaurus*, what would you do with it?"

"I would see that it was returned to its rightful owners."

"Would you demand fifty cents on the dollar like you did when you captured that embezzler ten years ago? The deal that made you a multimillionaire; the reason you quit the cops?"

"Not this time."

"Still, I wonder why I should help you."

"Because I introduced you to the love of your life?"

"How do you know she's the love of my life? We could just be—never mind."

We stared at each other some more.

"Check your email, later," Maryanne said.

"Thank you."

"McKenzie, understand that this doesn't mean that you're acting as a representative of the Midwest Farmers Insurance Group. We will take no responsibility for your actions."

"You sound just like the FBI."

"Oh God."

Andrew Cooke lived in an area of St. Paul called Macalester-Groveland, the neighborhood taking its name from the prestigious college situated at the eastern border and the park and community center on the western. His house was located in that part of the neighborhood known as Tangletown because of its winding streets and was only a block away from the house where Ma Barker and her murderous brood used to live back in the early thirties. It was a modest two-story Victorian, something you might move up to after leaving your starter home, yet not at all where you might expect a multimillionaire to live. There was a plaque attached to the front porch, though, proclaiming the house to be a member of the community's Century Building Project, meaning it was at least one hundred years old. I wondered if that had something to do with it.

I parked my Mustang, walked up the concrete path to the front door, and knocked. A woman dressed in a light sweater and jeans, her hair pulled back, opened the door.

"Yes," she said. "Can I help you?"

She was a full decade younger than I was, yet I flashed on what Angela had told me about the "middle-aged woman" who had accompanied Cooke to the dig and decided to take a chance.

"Ms. Cooke-Jackson?" I asked.

"Yes?"

If she's middle-aged, what are you?

"My name is McKenzie. If it's possible, I'd like to speak to your grandfather."

"Who are you?"

"I'm an investigator looking into the disappearance of the *Ankylosaurus* skull."

"Why do you need to talk to him about that? He wasn't there when it was stolen."

"Well, for one thing, it's his dinosaur."

"My grandfather is very upset about this as it is. I don't want you making it worse."

"Ms. Cooke-Jackson . . ."

"Just Jackson. My husband doesn't like the hyphen."

Interesting.

"Ms. Jackson . . ."

A voice called to her from inside the house.

"Who is it, darlin'?" it asked.

"No one," Megan said.

"Please," I said.

She shook her head and sighed before opening the door further.

"It's an investigator, Grandfather," she said. "He would like to talk to you about Andy."

Andy?

Megan stepped aside to give me room and I entered the house. On the other side of the foyer stood a tall, slender man with a full head of gray hair that was rumpled as if he spent a lot of time running his hand through it. From what Angela told me, I knew that he had to be at least eighty-five. The hair made him appear younger.

"Mr. Cooke." I extended my hand and he shook it; his grip was not strong. "My name is McKenzie."

"Call me Andrew."

"Thank you, sir."

"You're an investigator?"

"In a manner of speaking."

"Who do you work for?"

"That's where it gets complicated."

"I'm too old for complicated. We better sit down."

Cooke moved slowly to the living room, his hands using the furniture he passed for support. He led us to a half circle of chairs and sofas facing an ancient fireplace. He sat in a chair with thick red cushions and carved arms. It reminded me of a throne. Megan followed us to the living room and sat in the chair nearest her grandfather. I sat across from them on a sofa that appeared to be as old as Cooke was.

"You're looking for my dinosaur," he said. "Glad to hear that somebody is. Who are you working for? Not the police or you would have said so, flashed me a badge and acted oh so superior. Not the insurance company, either, which refuses to pay up. I'm thinking of suing, by the way."

"A friend asked me to look into the theft."

"What friend?"

"Angela Bjork."

Cooke tilted his head and squinted. His hand came off his lap, his fingers splayed. The memory seemed to return to him as his fingers slowly closed into a fist.

"Yes, yes, yes," he said. "Angela. Angie from Montana."

Cooke turned toward his granddaughter.

"She's very pretty," he said.

"I remember," Megan told him.

"Angie hired you to find my dinosaur? Whatever she's paying, I'll double it. I want Andy back."

"Andy?" I asked.

"Andy the *Ankylosaurus*. Originally, the scientists wanted to name it after me but I said they should name it after Angela instead because she's the one who actually found it but now I'm thinking—McKenzie, why are you here?"

People keep asking you that.

"To learn if the thieves have contacted you," I said. "To ask if they offered to sell the skull back to you. I'm guessing no."

"I haven't heard anything from anybody. Sell it back to me, you say? For how much?"

"That depends on how desperate the thieves are to make a profit. Midwest Farmers Insurance Group claims it's not liable to compensate the victims for the loss of their property, so it's highly unlikely that they would pay. The University of Minnesota as well as the Science Museum of Minnesota are partially funded by the state, so it would be difficult, although not impossible, for them to pony up the dough. Which leaves multi-millionaire entrepreneur Andrew Cooke, who actually owns the dinosaur . . ."

"Technically, I don't."

"Who is connected to both the university and the museum. With each step, the price should drop."

"By how much?"

"If you believe the skull is worth six million dollars . . ."

"Who says that?"

"David," Megan said.

Cooke and I both looked at her.

"I'm sorry," she said. "I didn't mean to interrupt."

Cooke reached over and patted her hand.

"Darlin', you can interrupt anytime you want," he said.

"Dr. David Seeley at the Science Museum of Minnesota, he believes that the skull is worth six million."

"He told you that? When?"

"A while ago. I don't know how he came up with that figure."

"You've been seeing a lot of him."

"Have I?"

Cooke spoke to me.

"Megan here, my granddaughter; she's been acting as my private assistant ever since I moved in with her. A few years after my wife passed, I retired and gave my business to the kids. I was going to buy into one of those high-priced assisted-living condominiums, except the family said no. Said they would look after me. What they meant was that Meg would do it. At least she's the one who lost the vote."

"I voted for myself, remember," Megan said. "So stop it."

"Your husband didn't."

Megan could only shrug at that.

"Anyway, six million smackeroos is a little pricy, even for—what did you call me? A multimillionaire entrepreneur?"

"Like I said, the price will go down. By the time it reaches you, I'd bet it would be ten percent or less. You could probably get it for less. An *Ankylosaurus* skull would be awfully hard to sell on the down-low. I know of a guy who stole a four-million-dollar Stradivarius violin. He ended up trying to sell it back to the insurance company for one hundred and fifty thousand. 'Course, he was sent to prison for a very long time."

"Doesn't matter," Cooke said. "No way I'm gonna reward a bunch of crooks for stealing from me. Well, not just me. You know what I mean."

I gave him a dramatic shrug.

"You think I should?" Cooke asked.

It'll certainly help with what you have in mind, my inner voice said.

"It might be smart to at least go along with them until you can contact the right people," I said aloud.

"Are you the right people, McKenzie? How did you get involved with Angie from Montana, anyway?"

I gave him a very condensed version of how Angela and I met; of what I was doing in Libbie, South Dakota, in the first place.

"I'll be damned," Cooke said. "You're the Lone Ranger." He turned to Megan. "He's the Lone Ranger."

Megan shook her head as if she didn't know what her grandfather was talking about. Cooke sighed deeply.

"I am so old," he said. "The Lone Ranger, he wore a black mask and rode around the Old West righting wrongs and bringing bad guys to justice with his faithful Indian companion, Tonto. You don't know who the Lone Ranger was?"

Megan shook her head, although I had the impression that she did know but was content to let her grandfather rant.

"I always wondered how he did that," Cooke continued. "How he could afford it."

"He had a silver mine," I told him. "That's where all the silver bullets came from that he would leave with the people he helped; his calling card."

"I didn't know that."

"I heard his character was based on a real-life Black deputy U.S. marshal named Bass Reeves."

"I heard that, too. Probably why they made the Lone Ranger a white man dressed in white who rode a white horse. Black men weren't allowed to be heroes to white children in those days. That didn't change until Jackie Robinson."

"Are you a baseball fan, Mr. Cooke?"

"I've had season tickets to the Twins ever since Rod Carew won the MVP in seventy-seven."

Megan tilted her head back and rolled her eyes, giving me the feeling that she had heard all these stories before.

"Are you a fan, McKenzie?" Cooke asked.

"Very much."

"You say Angie from Montana isn't paying you, so I won't insult you by offering money, either."

Please, insult away.

"But if you can find my *Ankylosaurus*, man, I'll give you half my tickets. They're real good seats, too. Right behind home plate."

"Which is another reason I'm here," I said. "I have no official standing. It'll be easy for the folks at the university and the science museum to slam their doors in my face."

"Ah," he hummed. "But if you had a letter stating that you were acting on my behalf . . ."

"That should keep those doors open."

"I'll dictate one, have it printed on letterhead, and have Meg deliver it first thing. I'll have to think about the other thing, though—paying to get my skull back."

I rose from the sofa and offered Cooke my hand.

"Deal," I said. "You're going to go to a couple of those ball games with me, right?"

"Are you going to buy the beer?"

"Andrew, where I come from, the man who pays for the tickets never buys the beer."

Cooke gestured at his granddaughter.

"Now this is the kind of guy you should have married," he said.

She didn't say if she agreed with him or not.

Eventually, we made our way to the front door. Cooke walked slowly. He brushed her hands away when Megan tried to help him, although Megan remained close by his side in case he needed help. Along the way, we agreed to keep in touch. Cooke said he would call me if anyone contacted him about buying Andy. I gave them both a business card printed with my name and cell phone number. Cooke waved it at me.

"Not exactly a silver bullet, is it?" he said.

According to its website, Doyle Trucking—the Flatbed and Heavy Hauling Experts—was an owner-operator trucking firm that provided services to meet the specific freight and commercial needs of any company or individual including emergency delivery services. It claimed that it would pick up freight any time day or night and deliver it directly to its destination. From its list of clients, it seemed quite large:

3M-Cargill-General Mills-Ford-US Military-Ritchie Bros. Auctioneers-ExxonMobil-eBay-Schlumberger-Caterpillar-Jackson Janitorial-Lund Boats-John Deere & Company-Best Buy-Bemidji Airlines-Dairy Queen

Yet, from the size of its yard in South St. Paul, it also seemed small. I saw only one truck in its lot and its office was the size of a drug store. When I entered, I found a man standing behind a counter and working a computer. He didn't bother to look up at me.

"Help ya?" he asked.

"I'm looking for Peter Ralph," I answered.

"Ralphie," the man shouted, again without looking away from his computer screen.

A moment later, a second man appeared through a door that I assumed led to the garage. Angela had not described anyone when she told us her story and while Andrew Cooke and his granddaughter looked the way I had pictured them, Peter Ralph did not. For some reason, I expected the kid in the holiday classic *A Christmas Story*, glasses and all. Instead, I got a humanized version of *Wreck-It Ralph* with unruly brown hair, thick eyebrows, and a body built for professional wrestling.

He glanced at the man behind the counter, who pointed at me and said "Visitor."

"Yeah?" Ralph said.

"My name is McKenzie. If you have a sec, I'd like to ask you a few questions about the *Ankylosaurus* that was stolen along with your truck."

"Are you from the insurance company?"

"No."

"Dammit, man. C'mon. The truck was stolen on August 29. It's now September 27. That's thirty days by my count. They said they would pay to replace my truck after thirty days."

"I take it the F-150 hasn't been recovered."

"Not by anyone who decided to give it back, it hasn't."

"I'm sorry to hear that."

"No, you're not," Ralph said. "You only care about that dinosaur thing."

"That's partly true," I admitted. "On the other hand, if we could find your Ford pickup, we might be able to find the *Ankylosaurus* skull. And vice versa. At least we'd know where to start looking."

"Yeah, well—what do you want to ask me, anyway? You know, you're the first person to talk to me about this since we got back from Montana, except, well, for the insurance guy, but that was over the phone. I had to sign some documents, but that was done electronically, too. No one ever does business face-to-face anymore."

"Who's your insurance company?"

He told me. It was a competitor of the Midwest Farmers Insurance Group called People's Financial. Ralph also told me that there was a lawsuit brewing between the two of them.

"What happened, the university, I think it was the university; they decided to sue me, sue Doyle. They say we're liable cuz the dinosaur was on my truck when it was stolen. They say that I took possession of the skull, so that makes it my responsibility. My insurance company says, oh, no, no, no, it's all on the U because my truck was parked at their facility; that they're responsible for securing their facility so their insurance company should be paying me. Meanwhile, I'm standing in between 'em goin' what the hell, man? Right now, all I want is for someone to replace my truck, 'kay?"

Funny Maryanne didn't tell you about this, my inner voice said. *I wonder why.*

"No one has asked you about the actual theft?" I asked. "I mean no one from law enforcement."

"Not since Montana. You'd think someone would have by now."

You would, wouldn't you?

"How'd you get the gig in the first place?" I asked.

"If you're not from the insurance company, why are you asking? Are you a cop?"

"I'm investigating the theft on behalf of the University of Minnesota," I answered, which wasn't exactly untrue.

"Then you know that professor guy . . ."

"Dr. Hegarty?"

"Yeah, yeah Dr. Hegarty. Had a funny first name. Weston. Yeah, yeah. From the U. He comes in and says, hey, I need a couple of guys to pick up some shit in Montana and bring it back here and I'm like, yeah, we can do that. See, we get a dollar and eight cents per mile for a long-haul door-to-door delivery job like that. Montana—it turned out to be 1,482 miles round trip. That's sixteen hundred bucks, a pretty good week for me. Bittle, too. Patrick Bittle."

"Is Bittle here?"

"Nah, he's on the road. A short job to Eau Claire, Wisconsin, and back. He'll be in tomorrow."

I made a mental note of that.

"Tell me about Dr. Hegarty," I said.

"He comes in and says he needs to rent a couple of trucks to pick up something in Montana. We're like sure, what do you have in mind? He tells us the size of the loads, only after that he starts getting vague. Says he's not at liberty to say. We're like, what is it, a secret? He says, yeah, it's a secret. Well, we don't do secrets. This one time a guy wanted me—this is right after they made marijuana legal in Minnesota. He wanted me to drive to Oregon, load up a truck with a ton of grass, and drive it back to Minnesota. But I'm supposed to do it in secret. You know why? Because growin' and sellin' grass in Oregon and Minnesota might be legal, but it ain't everywhere else in the country and if the Feds catch you takin' it 'cross state lines they're gonna throw your ass in jail until the year two thousand and twenty-five million. So, this professor says what we're gonna be hauling is secret and I'm like, yeah, you're gonna have to do a little better than that, buddy. But he promises that the freight's not illegal and it's not dangerous and he's from the U, right? Not some guy off the street. So we're like, me and Bittle are like, a job's a job, man."

"You knew it was valuable, though."

"Everything we haul is valuable. But what it was that needed two trucks, one big and one small? I had no idea until—so, we're on the road and we stop in Bismarck to gas up and grab something to eat and that's when he tells us what we're gonna haul back home and I'm like, wow, is this really a thing? And he's like yeah, but we're forbidden to tell anyone because it's valuable and the fewer people who know it's on the road the better. And I'm like, that's fine with me. Who am I gonna call, anyway? My brother-in-law? He's a shady character but what is he going to do with a dinosaur? Sell it on eBay? People do that, you know; sell shit on the internet that they steal; that they shoplift. I'd bet my brother-in-law's done that plenty of times. But a dinosaur? You'd think the cops would catch on to that pretty quick."

"You'd think," I agreed. "When did Dr. Hegarty schedule the job?"

"He came in on Monday afternoon and we left on Tuesday morning."

"Short notice," I said.

"I guess he didn't want us thinkin' or talkin' too much about it. Anyway, sixteen hundred bucks, man, I would have left right then and there. Only we waited until first thing Tuesday. I had the doctor in my pickup and Bittle followed behind."

Ralph admitted that he was impressed when they reached the dig and saw what the scientists were doing. He said that he and Patrick Bittle took a lot of pics that they were going to post on their website and use for ads and brochures. They were convinced that they could only help business later, the business they and their two buddies shared.

"Not so much now," Ralph added.

"Tell me about the robbery," I said.

"Man, I didn't see anything; what I told the sheriff and what I told the insurance guy when he called. I was in a tent the whole time. Nice tent. It had cots."

"What did you think when you heard the screams?" I asked.

"I thought it was a bear."

"A bear?"

"Yeah, yeah. I thought a bear had wandered into camp and people were like freakin' out."

"And the gunshots?"

"I figured someone shot the bear or at least was trying to scare it off. It wasn't 'til later and I saw my truck was gone that I called the cops. No one else thought to call the cops, lot of good it did, anyway. We were in the middle of bum-fuck Egypt. And now—I had to rent a truck to keep up my end of the business until the insurance company gives me the money to buy a replacement."

I thanked Ralph for his time and offered my card, asking him to call me if he thought of anything else. "Sure," he said as he took my card. That's when I hit Ralph with my theory just to see how he'd react.

"Someone inside the camp was working with the thieves," I said. "Someone let them know that the skull was sitting on the back of your truck and that both were there for the taking."

I was surprised by how calmly Ralph answered.

"Hell yeah, I believe it," he said. "I mean it's not like someone drivin' by saw an Amazon box sittin' on the front steps of a house, you know? I'm surprised the sheriff didn't ask tougher questions than he did; surprised he didn't make us all give up our phones. 'Course, if it was me, I would've had one of them burner phones that you see in cop shows on TV and as soon as I was done usin' it, I'da tossed it into a hole or whatever."

SIX

Nina was kneeling on the cushions of our sofa and waving her hands. She reminded me of a little girl explaining to anyone who would listen exactly what she wanted for Christmas that year.

"Do you think he did it?" she asked.

We had just finished dinner—we actually have dinner together at home from time to time. I was sitting in a chair across from her in the living room area of the high-rise condominium we shared in downtown Minneapolis. Except for a master bedroom and guest room with en suites, plus a bathroom for visitors, we didn't have rooms so much as areas—dining area, music area where Nina's Steinway stood, office area with a desk and computer, and a kitchen area that was elevated three steps above the rest. The south wall was lined almost to the ceiling with books. The entire north wall consisted of tinted floor-to-ceiling glass with a dramatic view of the Mississippi River where it tumbled down St. Anthony Falls. The chair and sofa were located between them and arranged in front of a fireplace that we rarely used, although given the uncommon chill in the October air that might change.

"I'm not leaning that way, right now," I said. "I'll confirm what Ralph told me when I interview the scientists and later I'll try to interview his partner . . ."

"Bittle."

"Yes, Patrick Bittle. Right now, though—it's the timing. Ralph claimed he didn't know what he was transporting back to the Cities until around noon on Tuesday. If he was telling the truth—Nina, the theft took place thirteen hours later at three-oh-eight A.M. on Wednesday. It takes eleven hours to drive from the Cities to Powderville in Montana—yes, I looked it up. That doesn't count driving from Powderville to the camp, either. That's assuming the thieves could find the place in the dark. I just can't see Ralph and his partners putting it together in such a short amount of time. Plus, he was riding with Dr. Hegarty. How could he have made a call? I suppose he might have ducked into a restroom while they were having lunch in Bismarck, still . . ."

"Bittle," Nina repeated.

"He had the luxury of being able to call whomever he wanted while on the road, that's true. But again, it's the timing. Thirteen hours. Besides, how could they have known that the skull would be carefully wrapped and placed in the truck that very day?"

"Wouldn't timing be an issue for everyone else at the camp, too?"

"Not necessarily. With the others—whoever planned this out knew exactly what they were going to steal and approximately when they were going to steal it. After that, it was just a matter of stationing people in the area and waiting for the perfect opportunity."

"What if, what if . . ." Nina started waving her hands some more. "What if they had camped out somewhere, the hijackers, with the plan of hijacking the load as soon as the truckers tried to take it home. You know, stop the trucks on the highway, pretend to beat up the drivers, then drive away but, but, but instead they called them, they meaning Bittle or Ralph or maybe even someone else in the camp, and they decided to change their plans."

"Why would they do that?" I asked.

"It would have been easier than stopping a truck on the highway, wouldn't it?"

"I suppose."

"I'm just saying it's possible. Isn't it possible?"

"Anything is possible."

Nina smiled at me.

"You're having way too much fun," I told her. "I remember when you hated it when I agreed to do these favors for people."

"I only hate it when you get shot or clubbed or blown up. What are we going to do next?"

There's that "we" again.

"I'm waiting for the email Maryanne promised," I said. "Listen, don't you need to go back to the club?" I asked.

"I don't *need* to go back. I have a competent staff, you know. Why? Are you trying to get rid of me?"

"Never."

I had a thought that involved blankets and cushions in front of the fireplace, but before I could give it voice, Judy Garland started singing, "Clang, clang, clang went the trolley, ding, ding, ding went the bell." It was my new ringtone, replacing Louis Armstrong. I had lost a bet to Nina's daughter Erica, the result being that she was allowed to pick my ringtone for a month. Trust me when I tell you that it could have been much, much worse than "The Trolley Song."

There was no name attached to the number that flashed on my screen. I answered anyway.

"McKenzie," I said.

"McKenzie, this is Megan Jackson."

"Ms. Jackson . . ."

"It's okay, you can call me Megan. McKenzie . . ."

"Yes, Megan."

"I have the letter that my grandfather promised to give you."

"That's great. I could swing by your place if it's convenient."

"No. If it's okay"—Megan's voice dropped in volume—"I would like to talk to you somewhere private."

"Talk?"

"There are things you should know."

"You're welcome to come to my condominium."

"I think it would be better if we met in a public place."

She wants to talk privately in a public place?

"Of course." I was watching Nina who was watching me. "There's a jazz club not too far from where you live called Rickie's. On Cathedral Hill."

"Oh, I know Rickie's. I love that place."

"Say"—I glanced at my smartwatch—"in an hour?"

"Thank you, McKenzie."

"Thank you."

I ended the call.

"What?" Nina asked.

"I guess we're going to the club after all."

I was sitting at the bar when Megan Jackson walked in. She had changed clothes. Gone were the jeans and sweater, replaced by a black sleeveless sheath dress that clung to her curves. Her hair fell to her shoulders, and she was wearing makeup that gave her face an autumn glow. My first thought—*This is the woman Angela considered middle-aged?*—was followed quickly by one that was more pertinent—*Did she change clothes for you?*

Megan stood by the door and glanced around, clearly looking for someone. She was approached by a woman with short black hair and the most stunning silver-blue eyes I had ever seen. The woman smiled and asked Megan a question. Megan answered. The woman smiled some more and led Megan directly to where I was sitting.

"Mr. McKenzie," the woman said. "Your guest has arrived. Would you like a table or would you prefer to remain at the bar?"

"A table, please, if one is available," I said.

The woman smiled again and led us to the table that she had carefully selected twenty minutes earlier because its location allowed her to watch us from a spot behind the bar without being easily seen herself.

"Your server will be with you momentarily," Nina said and retreated to her spot.

Megan and I sat across from each other, yet only after she very deliberately chose the side of the table that would allow her to look out on the rest of the downstairs area of Rickie's including the entrance, an act that made my inner voice go, *Hmm* . . .

"You look very nice," I said.

"Thank you."

A moment later, our server appeared. She handed Megan a menu. Megan gave it back.

"Only a drink," she said before looking at me. "I hope you don't mind. I'm meeting someone, later."

"Not at all," I said.

So, she didn't dress up for you. Oh, well.

Megan ordered a mojito and I chose Maker's Mark on the rocks. The server left. Megan set her purse on her lap and reached inside. She pulled out a white number ten envelope with the name and logo of Andrew Cooke's company printed in the return address field and set it in the center of the table.

"Grandfather hopes this is what you need," she said.

I dragged it toward me, opened it, and took out a folded sheet of paper. Printed under the company's letterhead and above Cooke's signature were the words:

To Whom It May Concern:

Mr. McKenzie is acting on my behalf to locate and recover the *Ankylosaurus* skull I now refer to as "Andy" that had been stolen from my property in Montana. I will consider it a personal favor if you cooperate with his investigation and assist him in any way that he requests.

Sincerely,

Andrew Cooke

"Yes, this will do nicely," I told Megan.

"My grandfather prefers subtly. He told me when he dictated the letter that referring to the skull as Andy and calling his request a personal favor is so much more effective than writing 'do what I want or I'll be really pissed off.' He also said keeping it short makes the letter read more like an order than a request."

"He's a smart man," I agreed.

I refolded the letter and slipped it back into the envelope as the server delivered our drinks. Megan took a sip of hers and I took a sip of mine. We kept quiet for a few long moments before I became bored.

"You said you wanted to speak in private," I reminded her. "You said that there were things I should know."

"Now that I'm here, I'm not sure that was such a good idea after all."

I retrieved the envelope and held it up for her to see before setting it back on the table. Megan laughed, leaned back in her chair, and covered her face with her hands.

"I walked into that one, didn't I?" she said. "McKenzie, I don't mean to drag you into a family drama . . ."

"Drag away."

"My marriage is in trouble. I'm convinced my husband is going to divorce me. He's going to do it five minutes after my grandfather dies because that way he can pocket half of my inheritance. Probably, Kevin would have left me by now but

Grandfather, in his infinite wisdom, announced on Christmas Eve last year that he was going to divide his wealth equally among all of his relations, including his great-grandchildren. My share would be two million dollars. Approximately, two million. Most of his wealth is in index funds so it'll depend on where the stock market is."

"You could always beat your husband to it," I said.

"Don't think I haven't thought about it. It's been in my mind ever since I discovered—Kevin's been cheating on me. He's been cheating for years. At first, I thought it might be just a phase, a midlife crisis . . ."

She's too young to have a midlife crisis. Hell, you're too young to have a midlife crisis.

"I confronted him about it and Kevin was apologetic as hell. 'It will never happen again,' he promised me. For the longest time it didn't. At least I wasn't aware of it happening. Only I now know for a fact that he's cheating again. It started after we invited—after I invited my grandfather to live with us. Naturally, I blamed myself. Only now I'm tired of blaming myself."

"I know a good lawyer," I said.

"I might take you up on that, but for now—McKenzie, I think there's a chance that Kevin was involved in the theft of Andy."

Wait. What?

"What makes you say that?" I asked.

"I don't know if you're aware of it, but we visited the dig, the site where they uncovered the *Ankylosaurus*, right after the Fourth of July. It was the happiest I've seen my grandfather since, God, years. His health hasn't been the best lately, hasn't been good at all, but seeing the skull and talking to the scientists seemed to have a terrific therapeutic effect on him. While we were driving home, Kevin asked how much an *Ankylosaurus* skull would be worth. My grandfather said he didn't know, and he didn't care; there was no way they were going to sell it. I said—it's on me, McKenzie. I said that the scientists told me, David Seeley told me, that a *Tyrannosaurus Rex* skeleton called Trinity, which was actually made up of the bones from three different *T-Rexes*, sold for six-point-one million dollars at auction in Switzerland and the *Ankylosaurus* would be worth at least that much. Kevin didn't say a word after that. Never brought up the subject again. Then, when was it—two months later?—we received news that Andy had been stolen. Both Dr. Larsen and Dr. Hegarty came over to the house to tell us and all Kevin could say was 'That's too bad.' McKenzie, how could he be so nonchalant unless he already knew what was happening?"

"I don't know, but Megan, that's hardly an admission of guilt."

"McKenzie, this is a guy who gave me a fifteen-minute lecture on the quality of the lasagna I served at dinner last night."

"Megan, what does your husband do?"

"For a living? He runs a company called Jackson Janitorial."

Where have you seen that name before?

"He provides cleaning and janitorial supplies for the hospitality industry—hotels, motels, bed-and-breakfasts. He's been affiliated with my grandfather's company for, I don't know, ten years. That's how we met."

"Does he do okay?"

"If it wasn't for my grandfather, well, my father and uncles who run Granddad's company now, Kevin would probably be out of business."

"Divorcing you would be very costly, then."

"I'm sure a million dollars would help ease the pain. And if he actually did steal Andy—I've been hanging on so I can keep an eye on him, watch his movements."

"That's probably not a good idea," I said. "And something else—an inheritance is not considered community property, at least not in Minnesota. It's not considered marital assets to split for divorce, so he wouldn't be able take your money."

The information seemed to catch Megan by surprise.

"But then why is he still . . . ?"

Before she could complete the question, Megan's eyes caught something over my left shoulder; they widened in recognition. At the same time, she shook her head. Its movement was nearly imperceptible, and I probably wouldn't have noticed if I wasn't watching carefully. I fought the impulse to turn to see what Megan was looking at.

Let's hope Nina is paying attention.

"Besides your husband seeming not to care that the *Ankylosaurus* skull was stolen," I said, "what else has he done or not done that caused you to become suspicious?"

Megan took a sip of her drink before answering.

"Furtive phone calls," she said.

Furtive? my inner voice asked.

"Furtive?" I asked aloud.

"Sneaky. Sly. Umm . . ."

"I know what the word means."

"He'll get a phone call or a text and he'll excuse himself to take it. He never used to do that; he didn't care how inconsiderate he was being. He started doing it—McKenzie, he started doing it right before Andy was stolen."

"You said you thought he was cheating on you," I reminded her.

"Shit."

"Excuse me?"

"Shit, shit, shit . . ."

The shit that Megan was referring to walked right up to our table like he owned it.

"There you are." The man spoke in a loud enough voice that customers sitting at nearby tables stopped what they were doing to look. "What the hell are you doing here?" He threw a thumb in my direction. "With this asshole?"

"And you are?" I asked.

"McKenzie, this is my husband, Kevin Jackson," Megan said.

"Mr. Jackson," I said.

He was about six feet tall with matinee idol good looks. He ignored my greeting. I offered my hand. He ignored that, as well. His voice increased in volume; nearly all the customers were now watching us.

"What the hell are you doing here, you bitch?" he asked.

Megan was on her feet.

"What did you call me?" she wanted to know.

"Whoa, pal," I said.

"Don't fucking 'pal' me," Jackson said.

This is what comes from conducting business meetings in a bar.

He jerked a thumb at his wife.

"You think I don't know that she's been stepping out on me?" he said.

Stepping out, is that a thing people still say? Along with matinee idol good looks?

"That's a laugh," Megan said. "Me stepping out on you."

I guess it is.

"Why are you even here?" Megan asked. "I thought you had a"—she quoted the air—"'business meeting.'"

"I did, right up until your grandfather told me that you had"—he also quoted the air—"'a business meeting here.'"

I was surprised that Nina or one of her people hadn't intervened by now; she absolutely will not accept disturbances in her place. I decided I best move quickly to dispel the riot.

"Just so you know, Ms. Jackson did have a business meeting." I spoke softly. "With me. Also, just so you know, Rickie's is owned by my wife. That's why I'm here; that's why I asked your wife to meet me here. You should also know I'm taking it very personally that you're making a scene in my wife's place. Now, Jackson, you can either lower your voice and sit down or you can leave."

"You don't fuckin' talk to me; I'll kick your ass."

I rose slowly, deliberately, and spoke in the same manner. Nina's daughter, Erica, called it my "cop voice."

"No, you won't," I said. "You might try, but you will be unsuccessful."

Megan snickered. I wish she hadn't. My experience, a woman snickers with derision at a husband or boyfriend, the husband or boyfriend will usually react impulsively. Jackson did not disappoint. He looked away, yet at the same time he clenched his right hand into a fist, took a half step forward, and slowly turned his head toward me, a look of determination on his face.

Geez, could he possibly be more obvious?

He threw a hard jab at my face. I used both my right and left hands to push it away; the punch went off target by about four inches. I used both hands up to grab his wrist as his fist slipped past my head. At the same time, I raised my left elbow, twisted my body, and drove my elbow against his mouth. The blow seemed to catch Jackson by surprise. I hit him a second time just because. The blows staggered him. I didn't hit him hard enough to knock him down, though. But then I didn't mean to.

Jackson seemed flabbergasted. So did Nina's customers. There were a few oohs and aahs and a woman asked, "Did you see that?"

"Do you really want to do this, Jackson?" I asked. "Here? Now?"

I let him wrestle his arm out of my grasp. He took a long step backward.

"I didn't come here to start a fight," he said.

"Yes you did, just not with me. Still . . ." I gestured at an empty chair. "We can talk."

I thought Jackson was going to accept my invitation. Instead, he turned on his wife.

"You're coming home with me," he said.

"No, I'm not."

"I didn't ask you. I'm telling you."

That's when a second man moved quickly to the table with both fists clenched; his eyes fixed on Jackson. The effort seemed to leave him breathless.

"Leave her alone," he said.

The three of us turned to greet him. He was two inches shorter than Jackson and at least fifteen years older.

"Did you hear me?" the man asked.

"David?" Megan said.

Jackson jerked a thumb at the man.

"No," he said. "You're here for him? You're cheating with him? Some fucking egghead?"

Egghead? my inner voice asked.

Fortunately, at that moment my outer voice proved to be just a tad more cognizant.

"Dr. Seeley," I said. I spoke like I had been expecting him. The way his head flinched told me that I had guessed his name correctly. I waved at Jackson and his wife. "I take it you all know each other?"

"Yes," Seeley said.

"Wait a minute," Jackson said.

"Thank you for coming on such short notice," I said. "I appreciate it. If you'll excuse me for just a moment . . ."

"Wait, wait, wait," Jackson chanted.

"Go away, Jackson," I told him. I turned toward Megan and held up the white envelope. "Ms. Jackson, thank your grandfather for doing this. Thank you for taking the time to bring it to me. I promise I will do my best to find his Andy."

"Wait," Jackson said again. "You're looking for the dinosaur?"

"That's what I've been asked to do. That's what this meeting was about. Why? Do you know where it is?"

"What? Me? No. How would I know?"

"Uh-huh." I spoke to Megan again. "I will very much keep in mind what you told me."

"What did she tell you?"

I lied some more.

"She said the skull is worth so much money that even people with money might be tempted to steal it," I said. "Do you have a lot of money, Jackson?"

"Why? Am I a suspect? Do you think I stole it?"

"Oh, for god's sake," Megan said. She grabbed her bag and brushed past her husband. "You can apologize when we get home."

She made her way toward the exit, looking neither to the left nor the right.

"You really should," I told Jackson. "Apologize I mean."

"It's just that she never looks that good when we go out."

"I wonder why."

"Listen—what's your name? McKenzie? Listen, McKenzie, you know nothing about our lives."

"I only know what I've seen."

Jackson's eyes settled on Seeley; they moved over him as if he still couldn't believe the man was standing there. I have no idea what he was thinking. As for me—*This is the guy Megan dressed up for?* my inner voice asked. *Huh.*

"McKenzie . . ." Jackson said.

I didn't let him finish.

"Go away," I said.

He bristled some, yet turned and moved quickly toward the door as if he was attempting to catch up to his wife.

"What just happened?" Seeley asked.

I turned toward the bar. Nina was standing behind it, her hands stretched, palms upward, as if she was wondering the exact same thing.

Seeley and I settled at the table. The customers sitting around us, sensing that the floor show had concluded, returned to their own worlds. Nina appeared. She set a drink in front of Seeley.

"You left this at the bar," she said.

"Nina," I said. "This, I presume, is Dr. David Seeley."

"Yes," Seeley said.

"This is Nina Truhler, my wife and owner of this fine establishment."

Seeley stood up and shook Nina's hand. He smiled at her, but then most men do.

"May I join you?" she asked.

"Please," I said.

Seeley's smile became brighter as Nina took a chair.

"I'm sorry for causing a scene in your place," I said.

"You didn't cause it," Nina said. "Besides, no one died. Dr. Seeley from the Science Museum of Minnesota?"

"Do you know me?" Seeley asked.

"Angela Bjork told us all about you."

"Nina," I said.

"Angela?" Seeley asked. "You know Angela."

Nina's eyes flicked from me to Seeley and back to me.

"I shouldn't be saying anything, should I?" she said.

"You know Angela?" Seeley repeated.

"An old friend," I said.

Seeley's scientist brain gave it a few beats and said, "You're some kind of investigator. Angela asked you to find the *An-*

kylosaurus skull. You met with Andy, Andrew Cooke. The envelope"—he pointed at it—"there's a letter in the envelope and it states that you're acting on his behalf. Megan came here to give it to you. And Jackson . . ."

"Jackson was convinced that his wife was stepping out on him—that's the expression he used. He came here tonight to confront her and her lover and found me instead."

"That's because Megan's real lover was sitting at the bar drinking an old-fashioned and waiting for her meeting to end," Nina said.

I glared at her.

"Sorry," she said and drew two fingers across her lips as if she was closing a zipper.

Seeley folded his hands around his glass and looked down at them.

"We never meant for it to happen," he said. "We met soon after we, meaning the museum, the U, and Macalester—you know about the dig?"

I nodded.

"Megan and I met while we were working out the details of a contract with her grandfather to prospect on his land. That was five years ago. Since then, she would often come to the museum as Andrew's representative to inspect whatever fossils we unearthed or just keep up to date on our activities. We would talk and we soon discovered—her husband is a complete jerk. You saw that for yourself. I keep asking her to leave him. I've begged her to leave him. She says she will; that she's going to, only . . ."

"It's not as easy as it sounds," Nina said. "I was in a relationship like that myself, once."

She glanced at me, only this time there wasn't a hint of apology in her eyes. She patted my hand and stood.

"I have work to do," Nina said and left the table. Seeley watched her go. Part of me was miffed. *That's my wife, pal.* Part of me wondered if Seeley's roving eye fell on anyone else besides Megan Jackson. The biggest part, though, wanted to get on with the job.

"Dr. Seeley," I said. He returned his attention to me. "I have questions about the *Ankylosaurus*."

"I don't want to talk about that, right now."

I pushed the envelope across the table until it rested in front of him. He sighed deeply, opened it, and removed the sheet of paper that was inside, read it slowly, returned the letter to the envelope, and pushed it back toward me.

"How can I help?" he asked.

"Where were you when the theft took place?"

"I was asleep inside the mobile home that we use as our HQ."

"Alone?"

Seeley smirked as if the question amused him.

"Yes, McKenzie," he said. "Alone."

"Tell me what happened."

"I heard the scream," Seeley said. "I was told later that Winter Billock—she's a student at the U."

"I know who she is."

"I was told later that Winter saw what happened and began to scream. That's what woke me. I put on a pair of pants and grabbed a shirt—that's when I heard the gunshots. I heard the gunshots and rushed to the door of the mobile home and stepped outside."

I flashed on what Professor Gary Phillips told Angela about running in the opposite direction when he hears gunshots but kept it to myself.

"At first I didn't see anyone," Seeley continued. "When I looked down, though, I saw Weston, Dr. Hegarty, on the ground in front of the pole barn. I ran toward him; tried to help him as best I could."

Good for you, Doctor.

"He appeared to be badly hurt," Seeley said. "Then Nick, Dr. Larsen was there."

"Where did he come from?"

"I presume from the mobile home; the three of us had bedrooms in the mobile home. I wasn't aware of him, though, until he started barking out orders."

"Orders?"

"Nick was anxious to get Weston to the hospital and at the same time keep everyone else calm."

"Tell me about that."

"You don't keep people calm by shouting at them."

"I meant the hospital."

"The hospital? There's not much to tell. Nick drove—it was his SUV. He kept asking me how Wes was doing. What was I going to say? He's still alive? McKenzie, it took so long to get to the hospital in Ekalaka. Eventually, we did, and the staff there took charge of Weston, and we were shoved into a waiting room and there we sat until the sheriff arrived."

"The Carter County sheriff?" I asked.

"He asked questions about what happened, and we answered as best as we could, but really McKenzie, there was very little we could tell him."

"Okay," I said. "Dr. Seeley, the *Ankylosaurus* was discovered in mid-May . . ."

"Who told you that? Angela?"

I didn't say if she had or hadn't.

"The *Ankylosaurus* was discovered in mid-May," I repeated. "In early August it was decided to transport the fossil, sandstone and all, to the science museum by the end of the month."

"Yes?"

"Who did you tell?"

"What do you mean?"

"Who did you tell about transporting the fossil?

"Everyone. About the *Ankylosaurus*? Everyone. Starting in May. It wasn't a secret, McKenzie. It was a terrific find. Of course we told anyone and everyone who would listen. I personally held meetings with the senior leadership at the museum, the staff. We had to prepare to accept the fossil, after all. The board of trustees were informed. Who else? The *St. Paul Pioneer Press*. It ran a story. We supplied the pics because the paper couldn't afford to send a staff reporter or photographer to the dig; newspapers aren't what they used to be."

"When did the piece run?"

"Early August."

That caused me to raise an eyebrow.

"Did it include a date for when the fossil would be delivered to the museum?" I asked.

"No, we didn't have an exact date then. We didn't decide until maybe a week before Dr. Hegarty hired the trucks."

"Dr. Hegarty hired the trucks," I repeated.

Seeley apparently took my response as an accusation.

"You can't possibly believe—" he said.

I raised my hand to interrupt him.

"I'm just gathering the facts," I said.

I don't think he believed me. I hit him with another question.

"Once you knew the exact date when the skull would be transported, who did you call?" I asked.

"I contacted the staff at the museum, of course. We had to prepare . . ."

Seeley paused for a long moment. His expression suggested that he felt I was now accusing him. I raised my hand again.

"I'm not accusing anyone of anything, least of all you," I said. "But the thieves knew when the skull was ready to be stolen. Someone must have told them, either on purpose or by accident. It's possible that someone called a friend and said, 'Hey, guess what?' and that friend told another friend who told someone else."

"Do you believe that's what happened?"

"I don't know what to believe yet," I confessed.

"I understand."

"Do you?"

Seeley nodded his head.

"Doctor, who else did you call?" I asked.

He paused before he answered—"Megan."

There were more questions and answers after that, only they didn't amount to much. Seeley said that everyone connected to the dig was excited and probably shared their excitement with who knows how many other people.

"Are you going to ask each one of them who they called?" he wanted to know.

"Yes," I told him.

Seeley seemed surprised by that.

Eventually, he made ready to depart. I gave him a card. I asked if I could visit him at the science museum. He said, "Sure. Just call in advance."

I told him I would.

As Seeley made his way from the club, I moseyed up to the bar. Nina greeted me there.

"Anything?" she asked.

"About what you'd expect. Are you okay?"

"Yes. Why wouldn't I be?"

"The way you left the table . . ."

Nina gave me a wave that was meant to dismiss my concerns.

"I'm fine," she said. "It was just when Seeley started talking about Megan—I hadn't thought about my ex, about Jason, in years; not even when he invited himself to Erica's graduation party last spring. He was just another guest as far as I was concerned. I only knew about half of them as it was, half the guests; the rest were all Erica's friends from college, from wherever. But hearing about Megan and Jackson, suddenly I felt so very, very angry. Not at Jason, but at myself for putting up with his crap for as long as I did. It's silly, I know. So many years ago. And now look at me."

"It's always been my great pleasure to do just that—look at you."

"I wonder what I would have done if I had known you back then. Would I have cheated like Megan is doing? Would you?"

Nina chuckled at the thought.

"No, not you," she said. "You have a code of ethics. Come to think of it, so do I. Dammit. Why am I feeling this way? There's probably a term for it. The residue of regret. Something like that. McKenzie, do you know what you do really well? You listen without interrupting; without pretending you have all the answers."

"Thank you," I said.

"You know what else you do really well?"

I didn't dare attempt an answer.

"Take me home and we'll talk about it," Nina said.

I must admit, I was feeling excited when I drove my Mustang out of Rickie's parking lot. That changed, though, after only a couple of turns.

"Hmm," I said.

"What does 'hmm' mean?" Nina asked.

"I think we're being followed."

Nina turned in her seat to look out the back window. It was about ten o'clock and all she could see were the headlights of a vehicle several car lengths behind us.

"Are you sure?" she asked.

"No."

She turned in her seat again, only this time she was watching me and waiting for an explanation.

"Whoever is driving started his vehicle when we started ours, left the parking lot when we left, and has been turning as we've been turning ever since," I said.

"What are we going to do?"

By then we were crossing a bridge that spanned I-94. I hung a left and followed the service road to the freeway entrance. A half minute later, we were driving toward Minneapolis at sixty miles per hour. The vehicle remained with us. The freeway lights told me that it was a white SUV but that was about it.

"Hmm," I said again.

"Who are they?" Nina asked. "Is it Kevin Jackson? You hit him. Twice. In public. Do you think he wants revenge?"

"I don't know."

"You're absolutely sure they're following us?"

I turned, this time without signaling, onto the exit ramp that led to Lexington Avenue. The SUV did the same. The traffic lights at the top of the ramp had just turned yellow as I hung a right onto Lexington, heading north. They were red when the SUV turned to follow us.

"Satisfied?" I asked.

"What are we going to do?"

"Keep moving for one thing."

I was starting to feel anxious. The turn onto Lexington proved that the SUV was following us. It should also have informed the driver of the SUV that we were onto him. Yet he remained on our tail. I started watching the vehicle behind me more than the vehicles in front; waiting for it to speed up, wondering if he would attempt to intercept us and what I would do if he did. At the same time, Nina hit me with a barrage of questions—why are they following us, are they trying to find out where we live, do they mean to hurt us when we stop the car? Answering them only underscored the potential danger we were in.

"I don't know why they're following us. Clearly, they know who we are; I mean they didn't pick us at random. If they know who we are, then they could easily find out where we live. Computers, you know. And yeah, hurting us is a possibility. The question is why."

"The *Ankylosaurus*."

"That's like admitting, 'You're on the right track, buddy; keep looking.' If they were smart, the thieves would lay low. They wouldn't do anything."

"You and Bobby are always saying that most criminals are stupid."

"That's what we say."

I steered the Mustang right onto brightly lit University Avenue and headed east, immediately adjusting my speed so we could hit all the traffic lights without stopping. The SUV stayed with us, always keeping a respectful two to three car lengths behind us. I couldn't make out the model. It could have been a Subaru, a Honda, a Volvo—all white SUVs seem to look alike these days. I asked Nina if she could make out the license plate. She couldn't; it looked to her like the plate had been covered up.

"Hmm," I said.

"I wish you would stop doing that and tell me where we're going."

"A safe haven. I hope."

We drove past the Minnesota State Capitol Building and Regions Hospital before crossing the bridge over I-35E. After that it was a matter of some quick turns: right on Pine, left on 13th, right on Olive, left on Grove. The SUV stayed with us. Finally, I turned left into the particularly well-lit parking lot of the Ramsey County-St. Paul Criminal Justice Campus. On our left was the James S. Griffin Building, headquarters of the St. Paul Police Department. On the right was the Ramsey County Sheriff's Department. Directly in front of the space where I braked were the Adult Detention Center and the Second Judicial District courtrooms.

The SUV didn't follow us into the lot, though, and it didn't stop. Instead, it picked up speed and fled down Grove Street, its taillights receding into the darkness.

"Hmm," I said again, just to be a smart aleck.

"I have to admit, this was one of your better ideas," Nina said.

"Yes, well, like I always say, we learn as we go."

"What did we learn?"

"Not a helluva lot. However, they, whoever they are, learned that we're not as dumb as they thought we were which, in retrospect, might not be a good thing."

"Do you think they might be waiting for us to leave the parking lot so they can follow us again?"

"No, but we'll be careful."

"Hmm," Nina said.

That's when we heard the hard rap of a knuckle on her passenger side window.

Nina recoiled at the sound even as she turned toward it; her hand went to her mouth stifling a shriek. I was much cooler, of course, although my hand did instinctively move to the spot behind my right hip where my semi-automatic SIG Sauer would have been holstered if I had thought to bring it.

There was another rap and a voice asked, "What are you guys doing here?"

I powered down the passenger window to reveal Bobby Dunston who, along with being my best friend dating back to kindergarten, was the best cop I knew.

"Good evening, Commander Dunston," I said. "Working late?"

"Oh my God, Bobby," Nina said. "You scared the crap outta me."

"Which brings me back to my question—what you are doing here? I was walking to my car when I saw McKenzie's Mustang."

"Just showing Nina where I used to work," I said.

"Oh, Bobby, some men were chasing us," Nina said, "and McKenzie drove us here . . ."

Bobby held up both of his hands.

"Wait, wait," he chanted. "What men?"

"We don't know," Nina said.

"Are you in danger?"

"We don't know."

Bobby leaned down so he could get a good look at me through the window.

"What is it this time?" he asked.

Yes, Bobby was aware of the favors I do for friends and, like Nina, he rarely approved of them.

"Remember Angela Bjork?" I asked.

"No."

"She's the girl who saved McKenzie's life when he went up to Libbie, South Dakota, that one time," Nina said.

"You mean the girl on the white horse?"

"Only she's not a girl anymore. She's a very attractive young woman."

"Of course she is. That's how things work in McKenzie's life."

"Right?"

"She lost a dinosaur," I said.

Bobby stared at me for a few beats before he repeated—"She lost a dinosaur."

"An *Ankylosaurus*," Nina said.

"All right, I have to admit, this is different, even for you."

"It was stolen in Montana," I added.

Bobby held up his hand like he was stopping traffic.

"Please tell me that this won't involve the Homicide and Robbery Unit of the Major Crimes Division of the St. Paul Police Department."

"God, I hope not," I said.

"Uh-huh. Listen, guys, I have to go. Shelby's going to be upset that I'm keeping such late hours as it is. She worries."

"Tough day at the office?"

"I'd say that you'd know how it is only you don't anymore, do you?"

"I have a vague recollection."

"See you at dinner Friday night?"

"We wouldn't miss it," Nina said.

"Shelby has something special planned."

"What?"

"Damned if I know."

SEVEN

Early the next morning, coffee cup in hand, I sat in front of my computer screen at my desk and opened the email that Maryanne Altavilla had sent. She included three attachments—an Incident Report filed by Martin Flor, Sheriff, Powder River County Sheriff's Office, a Supplemental Investigation Report issued by the Carter County Sheriff's Office, and a Case Report generated by the Montana DCI. She also wrote a note:

> I gave your name and number to Ben Dirnberger. He's an investigator with People's Financial Insurance Company. You'll like him; he'll like you. He'll explain why I took the liberty. G. K. sends her love.—MA

I was downloading the attachments when Nina walked up the three steps to the kitchen area and poured herself a cup of coffee from the French press I had set up.

"This is different," she said. "What is it?"

"Vanilla crème brûlée."

"I can taste the vanilla. I need to take a shower and go to the club."

"Umm."

What followed was a brief discussion during which I told

Nina that I was anxious about the idea of her going alone to Rickie's. She thought I was being sweet. My next remarks weren't sweet at all. Nina countered by assuring me that she was not going to spend the rest of her life in our condo no matter how nice the view and if she was followed by a white SUV, she'd do what I did, drive to St. Paul police headquarters and have Bobby protect her. I told her they, whoever they were, didn't need to follow her; they already knew where she worked. She said Rickie's parking lot was for customers only and if the SUV was there, she would have it towed. I told her that wasn't funny. Nina told me—well, it doesn't really matter what she told me. Let's just say that I lost the argument and let it go at that.

After she went into the bedroom, I left the condo and took the elevator to the ground floor and approached the security desk. The two guards sitting behind the desk smiled with anticipation.

I should point out that they were both friends of mine. Their names were Smith and Jones, and they were dressed in the identical dark blue suits, crisp white shirts and dark blue ties of their profession. For a long time, I couldn't tell them apart without reading their nametags. They had made it clear when Nina and I moved in a few years ago that they had checked me out—acting under building management's orders, of course; it was SOP for all new tenants—and they knew who I was and what I did. They had also made it clear that they were ready, willing, and able to assist me should ever the need arise.

"The job can get so boring," they had told me.

So, on occasion, I'd seek their help in exchange for items I'd find lying around the building like a case of Irish whiskey or Minnesota Twins tickets that I would turn into the Lost and Found because security personnel weren't allowed to accept gratuities from the tenants.

"McKenzie," they said in unison.

"Gentlemen, I need your help."

Their smiles grew even brighter.

I told them I was looking for a white SUV. I told them why. They motioned for me to step behind the desk and gave me a chair in front of one of their computer screens. They accessed the cameras that were trained on the perimeter of the building. We didn't see a thing that seemed out of place, certainly no white SUVs.

"It's just our block, though," Smith said.

"That's right," Jones added. "We can't see what's on the other side of Washington Avenue."

"I think I'll take a walk," I said.

"Want company?"

"No, I'm good."

"We'll be watching," Smith assured me.

I left the building and immediately discovered how chilly it had become. The temperature had dropped from eighty-two degrees to sixty-six in less than a day—welcome to Minnesota— and I told myself I should have worn a heavier jacket. I kept walking, anyway. I didn't even pretend to be nonchalant about it, gazing through the windows of every parked car I saw, knowing that if our stalker had been smart, he would have switched vehicles. I paid special attention to the area near the opening to our underground garage. I saw nothing that made me nervous, which of course, made me nervous. I returned to the building, gave Smith and Jones a wave, and took the elevator to our condo.

Nina seemed to be waiting for me just inside the door.

"Alert the boys, did we?" she asked.

"Why yes, yes we did."

"And?"

"The coast seems clear."

"I'll be careful," Nina promised. "Besides, if they had wanted to hurt us, they would have last night, wouldn't they? They followed us because they wanted to know what we were up to. Unless it was Kevin Jackson, in which case he's pissed at you, not me. Am I right?"

"Probably."

Nina kissed my cheek.

"Call me later," she said as she was walking through the door.

I told myself that calling every fifteen minutes would probably not be appreciated.

I returned to my computer after first pulling out a notebook as well as the notepad where I had transcribed all the information Angela Bjork had given me. It was my intention to compare her story with those of the various law enforcement agencies. I opened the first file; the one compiled by the Powder River County Sheriff's Department. It began:

> At 3:30 A.M. on August 29, 2023, a 911 call was forwarded to my cell phone informing me that an assault, an armed robbery, and an auto theft had all taken place at a remote site approximately twenty miles south of Powderville and that the victim of the assault was being transported to the Dahl Memorial Hospital in Ekalaka, in Carter County. I immediately contacted the Carter County sheriff and requested his assistance. He agreed to interview the assault victim at the hospital (see attached Supplemental Investigation Report). Deputy Derek Jones and I responded to the call at 5:00 A.M. We were met at the site by seven participants of an archeological dig . . .

Archeological? my inner voice asked.

> . . . that was being conducted on the property. They confirmed that they had made the 911 call and repeated that two or more suspects had invaded the site, assaulted one victim—Dr. Weston Hegarty from Minnesota—and stole a Ford F-150

pickup truck belonging to Peter Ralph of Minnesota, as well as the skull of an anklesaurus fossil . . .

He misspelled Ankylosaurus.

. . . valued at approximately six million dollars. (description below). We immediately issued a BOLO for a bronze-colored 2016 Ford F-150 pickup truck with a Minnesota license plate and the name Doyle Trucking printed on the doors. Afterward, Deputy Jones and I inspected the crime scene (see notes and photographs below) . . .

Angela didn't mention that.

. . . We interviewed all of the participants one at a time. NOTE: the dig was sponsored by the University of Minnesota, Macalester College, and the Science Museum of Minnesota, all located in the Twin Cities of that state. The dig was conducted on property owned by Andrew Cooke of St. Paul, Minnesota. (Contact info listed below.)

I had been very carefully taught that the purpose of an incident report was to document the exact details of an event while they were fresh in the minds of those who witnessed it. I was trained to be clear, concise, and comprehensive for the simple reason that these reports would become the foundation of the criminal cases adjudicated in court. I was also cautioned to never draw conclusions that were unsupported by the facts. You didn't write "the subject was drunk," for example. Instead, you wrote "the subject was unsteady on his feet and slurred his speech." What's more, you never, ever offered opinions—"I believe the subject was lying." Sheriff Flor's incident report was littered with those errors, though, which made me ask, "Who are you writing this for, pal?"

Winter Billock is a student at the University of Minnesota-Twin Cities studying geology. She was present at the dig as part of her studies. I interviewed her inside a recreational vehicle owned by Professor Ashley DeLuca, also of the University of Minnesota. I asked DeLuca to leave the vehicle while I spoke to Billock, but she refused. She said she would not leave Billock, who was clearly distraught. Billock was wrapped in a blanket. Beneath the blanket she was wearing only panties and a T-shirt. Billock claimed that she had left her tent where she was sleeping to go to an outhouse when she witnessed the assault. I allowed DeLuca to remain during the interview after cautioning her to remain silent. Billock seemed happy about that. The two women held hands during the interview.

According to Flor's report, Winter's story pretty much matched the one that Angela had told me. She said she saw the man who hit Dr. Hegarty in the head, although she could not identify him. She saw the man who shot at her, although she could not identify him, either.

Q: When did you go to sleep?
A: About ten thirty, eleven.
Q: In your tent?
A: Yes.
Q: Were you alone?
A: Of course.
Q: Why did you wake up?
A: I had to go to the bathroom.
Q: You might have heard a noise that woke you up.
A: I don't remember hearing a noise. At least not until I left the tent and started walking to the porta potty.

    I inspected her feet and concluded that they looked worn as if she had run barefoot over unbroken ground.

Wow, my inner voice said.

Next, Flor interviewed Professor Ashley DeLuca:

A member of the faculty at the University of Minnesota. De-
Luca claimed to be sleeping in her RV when the incident occurred. She became belligerent when I asked if she had been
sleeping alone. She insisted that she had. Her anger made me
believe that she was lying . . .

Really?

DeLuca claimed she was awakened by Billock's screams and
looked out of the window of her RV and saw a man that she
could not identify firing a handgun into the air as he pursued
Billock. She said she heard the pickup truck being started and
watched it drive past her RV. Almost immediately afterward,
DeLuca said she saw the taillights of a second vehicle following
the truck.

Which is what Angela told you.

DeLuca became belligerent again when I asked her who in the
encampment she suspected of the theft and refused to answer.

Flor wasn't particularly subtle, my inner voice told me.
*Still, you might have asked the same question in the same way
just to observe her reaction if nothing else.*

Next, Flor interviewed the drivers, Peter Ralph and Patrick
Bittle. He asked them when they were hired, when they arrived,
and what they did when they arrived at the camp. He was told
that they drove their pickup and flatbed trucks to where the dinosaur was discovered and watched as its skull was lifted by a
crane and deposited in the bed of the pickup truck. Afterward,
the pickup was driven back to camp. The drivers had dinner

with the crew and at approximately 10:30 P.M. retired to the tent that had been assigned to them when they arrived. They did not leave the tent, not even when they heard the screams and gunshots. According to Sheriff Flor, Patrick Bittle said, "Whatever was going on, it was none of our business."

What? No stories about bears?

Flor asked both men if they had contacted anyone after they took possession of the *Ankylosaurus* and they said they had not.

Did he ask anyone else that question?

Flor then interviewed Professor Gary Phillips of Macalester College in St. Paul, Minnesota:

The Black man . . .

Black man?

. . . claimed that he had been sleeping alone in a tent on the far side of the encampment, although it should be noted that his tent was located next to the tent used by Angela Bjork (see below) . . .

What's that supposed to mean?

The Black man said he was awakened by the sound of screaming. He said he stepped out of his tent and met Bjork. Together, they ran toward the pole barn where they believed the screams had originated. The Black man stopped running and took cover when he heard gunshots, leaving the woman to continue alone. Later he claimed that he had knocked Bjork to the ground when the gunfire continued "for her own protection." That claim was later substantiated by Bjork (see below). The Black man claimed he did not actually see the gunman or his accomplice. When asked if someone in the camp might have been involved in the theft he replied, "I don't know."

After Professor Phillips, Flor interviewed Simon Stevens.

. . . a student at the University of Minnesota-Twin Cities who participated in the dig as part of his studies. He said he went to bed in his tent located near the tent used by Winter Billock. Stevens said he was awakened by her screams and the gunshots. He said he saw nothing; that he had remained in his tent for safety's sake. He got dressed and later emerged in time to see Dr. Weston Hegarty being carried to the SUV and transported to the hospital (see below).

Next came Angela Bjork.

Bjork, an employee of the University of Minnesota, seemed to be the most concerned about the theft of the anklesaurus . . .

He misspelled it again.

When she was asked why, she claimed, "The skull was important to me."

The notes that Sheriff Flor recorded in his incident report closely mirrored what Angela had told me and Nina, except for her response when Flor asked her who she suspected among her friends and colleagues had a hand in stealing the fossil.

"Go to hell."

After they left the scene, Sheriff Flor and his deputy interviewed George Hankin, the man who had operated the crane. They interviewed him three times. Hankin said he was called to the scene to lift the *Ankylosaurus* skull from a bowl of sandstone and gently deposited it in the bed of a bronze-colored 2016 Ford F-150 pickup truck. By then it had already been wrapped in a plaster jacket. He was annoyed because "those dork scientists" kept chanting "be careful, be careful" at him. Afterward, he returned to his home on Broadus with the promise to return early the next morning to finish the job. He said he did not visit anyone, he did not make any phone calls, and he did not speak to anyone save his wife and children for the rest of the day.

From what he wrote in his report, I learned that Sheriff Flor and his deputy went to great lengths to verify Hankin's story and were unable to find any discrepancies. Which seemed to suit them just fine because, once Sheriff Flor decided that the crime had not been committed by someone who lived within his jurisdiction, he seemed content to conclude his investigation.

Next, I turned my attention to the Supplemental Investigation Report filed by the Carter County sheriff in which he recounted his interviews with Doctors Seeley, Larsen, and eventually Hegarty.

Dr. David Seeley claimed that he heard a woman scream followed almost immediately by what he believed to be gunshots. This caused him to leave his bed in a mobile home anchored very near the crime scene, get dressed, and step outside. He found Dr. Weston Hegarty on the ground and rushed to his side and immediately began providing first aid. Moments later, he was joined by Dr. Nicholas Larsen. Together they transported Dr. Hegarty to the Dahl Memorial Hospital in Ekalaka. Dr. Seeley said he did not actually see the assault take place and he did not see any of the suspects.

According to the sheriff's supplemental, Dr. Larsen's account of what happened was nearly identical to Seeley's.

In a separate interview, Dr. Nicholas Larsen said that he also was awakened by a woman's scream followed by gunshots. He said he put on a pair of pants and stepped outside of the mobile home that he shared with Doctors Hegarty and Seeley. He found Seeley aiding Hegarty, and rushed to their sides.

Except . . .

If both men were sleeping in the same mobile home, and both men were awakened by the same screams and gunshots, and both men dressed and rushed out of the same door, why didn't they trip over each other? How did Seeley reach Hegarty so much earlier than Larsen? Shouldn't they have reached him at the same time?

I wrote a note on my pad and circled it—"Did Seeley have a head start?"

The Carter County sheriff wasn't allowed by the medical staff to interview Dr. Hegarty until early the next morning. I assumed the sheriff recorded the interview because Hegarty's statement came out as one long quote. Among other things, he said:

I couldn't sleep. I blamed it on the excitement I felt at finally transporting the Ankylosaurus skeleton home. Finally, I got up and stepped outside. I guess it was around three o'clock. That's when I saw two men standing near the pickup truck. The door to the pickup was open. At first I thought it was the truck drivers I had hired—Peter Ralph and Patrick Bittle. I stepped up to them and I asked, 'What are you guys doing?' Suddenly, I felt something hit my head. I don't know what it was; I never saw it coming. Everything turned white after that, like I was in a cloud. I remember David asking if I was all right, and I told him I felt fine but when I spoke to him about it later he told me that I never said a word. The next thing I knew I was in the hospital.

According to the supplemental, Hegarty was unable to identify or even describe his assailants.

That brought me to . . .

MONTANA DIVISION OF CRIMINAL
INVESTIGATION

Case Master Report 2023–787

Agency: MONTANA DIVISION OF CRIMINAL INVES-
TIGATION

Division: Investigations Bureau

Section: Major Case

Unit: Billings Regional office

Lead LEO: Bruce Harmon (1386/Major Case/Montana DCI)

Type of Case: Theft/Assault

Case Description: Theft of dinosaur fossil/private land, theft
of the Ford F-150 pickup truck carrying it, and physical assault on one of the owners

Case Status: Open—no arrests

. . . which was considerably better written than what the
two sheriffs had put down on paper, yet contained virtually
identical information, although, the agent seemed to be more
impressed with the *Ankylosaurus* skull and its perceived value.
He made a reference to what he considered . . .

an escalation of stolen fossils taken from public and private
lands not only in southeastern Montana but other states as well
possibly by organized criminal groups (see internal memo).

Unfortunately, Maryanne didn't send me the memo. Probably she hadn't seen it herself, the word "internal" suggesting it
was for members of the Montana DCI only. Still, the line—an
escalation of stolen fossils taken from public and private
lands—made me wonder.

Is it possible that my list of suspects had nothing to do with the theft; that the crime was committed by criminals who have discovered that there's money to be made in them bones and were simply monitoring the dig?

I wrote another note, although I didn't circle this one—Think Special Agent Linda Ambrose would like another raspberry white chocolate scone?

EIGHT

The Minneapolis campus of "the U," as it was called in Minnesota, was divided into two parts—East Bank and West Bank. John T. Tate Hall was located on the East Bank of the Mississippi River. That's where the Department of Earth and Environmental Sciences resided. It was also home to the School of Physics and Astronomy as well as the university's observatory where, every Friday night while school was in session, you and your girl could spend a romantic evening viewing the moon, planets, star clusters, nebulas, and galaxies for free. Not that I did that while I was in school more than a dozen times.

The condominium in downtown Minneapolis that I shared with Nina was located on the West Bank of the Mississippi. Yet, because of the Washington Avenue Bridge, it was quicker for me to walk to Tate Hall than drive there and attempt to find a parking space, only twenty-six minutes according to my map app. I put on a black golf jacket that zipped up the front and left the condo. I also considered wearing a black fedora but decided that was too much.

It took me considerably longer to reach Tate Hall than the app predicted, though, because I allowed myself to be distracted by the Weisman Art Museum. And, of course, I had to stop at Coffman Union for a cup of coffee and a brisk jog down memory lane. Eventually, I found myself standing in the Northrup Mall as hundreds of students wandered past, whining to myself over how much the campus had changed since I graduated, yet marveling at how much of it had remained the same when I heard a voice behind me.

"Are you lost, old man?" it asked. "Do you need help?"

I turned to find a young woman. A young woman—when did that happen? She had the dark, almost brooding appearance of her father yet her smile expressed the outgoing personality that matched her mother's. She was standing next to another young woman who was staring at her, a look of shock on her face.

"Is there someone I can call?" the first woman asked. "An assisted living facility?"

"What are you doing?" the second woman whispered.

I was desperate for a clever retort, yet all I could manage was "Why, you young whippersnapper."

I opened my arms and Victoria Dunston stepped into my embrace. I hugged the daughter of my two best friends as if she were my own daughter.

"What exactly is a whippersnapper, anyway?" she asked.

"I have no idea. It's something old people call young people."

"If there are young whippersnappers, there must be old whippersnappers."

"I probably qualify, then. How are you, Vic?"

"Good, really good. Oh, this is my roommate, Melissa Mirth."

I half released Victoria and offered my hand.

"This is McKenzie," Victoria said.

Melissa squeezed my hand harder than I thought she meant to.

"Wait," she said. "*The* McKenzie."

"I guess," I said.

"Oh my God, Vic. It was a true story, wasn't it?"

"Didn't you believe me?" Victoria asked. "Geez, Missy."

"Story?" I asked.

"We had a gathering, all the girls in the dorm after we first moved in," Melissa said. "Our residence hall director decided that to break the ice we should all tell a fun fact about ourselves, and Vic said that she had been kidnapped when she was a child and held for a million dollars ransom but she was rescued by a swashbuckler . . ."

"Swashbuckler?"

"Named McKenzie who was her father's best friend who then helped the FBI catch the bad guys. Is that true?"

"I suppose, but swashbuckler?"

Victoria spread her hands and shrugged as if daring me to come up with a better name.

"The Jade Lily," Melissa added. "Was that true, too?"

I turned to Victoria.

"Don't you have anything better to talk about?" I asked.

"What are you doing here, anyway?" she replied. "McKenzie, is this because of the missing dinosaur?"

"How do you know about the dinosaur?"

"You told Dad . . ."

"That was late last night."

"He told Mom, and she told me."

"Already?"

"We text and talk all the time."

"Since when?"

"Since I moved out. Funny. We used to argue constantly and now we get along just great."

I nearly said something along the lines of two strong-willed women sharing the same house yet stopped at the word "women." I had literally been sitting in her living room when Victoria first learned to walk.

"Dinosaur?" Melissa asked.

"Mom says he's looking for a dinosaur," Victoria said.

"No. That can't—a dinosaur? Really?"

"It's complicated," I said.

"Oh my God."

"I'd be happy to blow off precalculus to help you," Victoria said.

"Me, too," Melissa added.

"Ladies," I said, "I'm just walking over to Tate Hall."

Melissa pointed at a huge brick building fifty yards away that was adorned with six Greek columns, the word PHYSICS carved in stone above them.

"There," she said.

"I know where it is."

"Do you have a student ID card so you can get inside?"

"Do I need . . . ?"

Victoria grabbed an arm and spun me around. Melissa took hold of the other arm and together they walked me to the hall.

"They don't let just anyone wander the school buildings," Victoria said. "You're lucky we came along, old man."

"I don't know what I object to more, that or swashbuckler."

"I have no idea what a swash is or why it needs buckling," Melissa said. "I'll look it up later. That and whippersnapper."

"Missy is an English major," Victoria told me.

We climbed the steps and Victoria used her U Card to open the front door. I thanked her. She appeared as if she was about to say something, but instead waved me off and said, "See you later."

Melissa followed her down the short flight of steps.

"He's kind of a zaddy, isn't he," she said.

What the hell is a zaddy? my inner voice wanted to know.

While the U might have been keen about who entered its buildings, once inside I was able to wander freely. Tate Hall's architecture was quite exquisite. While the pillars and dark brick façade gave the outside a 1920s vibe, inside it was all 2020s modern with a four-story atrium and a skylight in the center, the result of a

ninety-three-million-dollar renovation. A couple of diagrams attached to the walls and a question to a student who was passing
by led me to Room 150, which wasn't an actual room, but more
like a sprawling suite filled with offices and classrooms. Eventually, I found an office with the name Dr. Weston Hegarty attached to it. The door was open. I leaned against the frame and
watched a man with a raspberry-colored dress shirt and black
sports jacket sitting behind a desk and staring at a computer
screen. He was wearing glasses.

"Excuse me," I said.

If Hegarty was startled, he didn't show it. Instead, he lifted
his eyes from the screen and set them on me.

"Can I help you?" he asked.

I pointed at my head and asked, "How's your head?"

Hegarty lifted his hand as if he was going to touch his own
head and paused.

"Who are you?" he asked.

"My name is McKenzie."

Hegarty took off his glasses, tossed them on his desk, and
leaned back in his chair.

"Ah, yes," he said. "Angie Bjork's friend."

"She told you about me?"

"Yes. Come in, come in. She told me she spoke to you on
Monday. If you see a strange man . . ."

Strange man?

". . . hanging around and asking questions, that would be you,
she said. Apparently, you're some sort of investigator. Angie was
a little vague."

"'Vague' is the word for it."

There was a chair in front of Hegarty's desk and I sat there.

"How is your head?" I asked again.

"Fine."

"Fine?"

"I've been experiencing the lingering effects of a concussion if you must know. Headaches. Ringing in my ears. Occasional dizziness. Not that it's any of your business."

"Irritability?" I asked.

"That, too."

I reached into the inside pocket of my own sports coat, withdrew the envelope containing Andrew Cooke's letter and handed it to Hegarty.

"What's this?" he asked as he took it from my hand.

I let the letter speak for itself. After he finished reading it, Hegarty slipped it back in the envelope and handed it to me.

"How is Mr. Cooke?" he asked.

"Anxious to see his dinosaur returned."

"I don't blame him."

"Has anyone contacted the U with an offer to sell it back?"

"Not as far as I know. Do you expect that to happen?"

"It's a possibility."

"The university would never agree to something like that," Hegarty said.

"At least not out loud."

Hegarty's response was to nod his head.

"The community knows what happened, McKenzie," he said. "Certainly, in the United States. Probably Europe, too. Paleontologists talk, don't they? To my knowledge, though, no *Ank* has ever been sold at auction or appeared in a private collection. If one were to show up now . . ."

"Could you prove it was yours?"

"Of course. Practically every inch of the skull has been documented and photographed. Professor DeLuca accidentally chipped a one-inch size piece of bone from its snout and repaired it with Krazy Glue. That alone would prove provenance."

"The skull wasn't completely cleaned before it was stolen," I said.

"No, not at all."

"Who could do that?"

"Clean it? Someone with lots of patience."

"My experience, thieves aren't known for their patience; one of the reasons they become thieves."

"That's something beyond my area of expertise."

"Dr. Larsen believes the theft was well-planned."

"Nick might be right," Hegarty said.

"It's been suggested to me that Dr. Larsen might be upset that he was passed over as the director of the Earth and Environmental Sciences Department."

"Who told you that? Nick?"

I shrugged my reply.

What are you going to say—your wife?

"Paleontology is my great love, but earth sciences covers a great deal more than that," Hegarty said. "We're involved in geophysics, geobiology, geochemistry, hydrogeology, mineral physics, mineralogy, petrology, rock and mineral magnetism, seismology, and structural geology not to mention the study of natural hazards, climate and environmental change, groundwater, lakes, oceans, earthquakes, volcanoes, tectonics, minerals, fossils, soils, sediments, and rocks.

"McKenzie, there are twenty-seven professors of various ranks in my department not counting adjuncts and another fifty researchers and research support staff. Just about all of them think they can do a better job than me. As for Nick—he teaches his courses, does his research; writes his papers. That's all I care about. He'll be getting plenty of attention around Christmas, too, when the Minnesota Science Museum finally unveils the *Acheroraptor*. It was discovered in Montana under his watch, his and Dr. David Seeley's. Do you know Seeley?"

"Yes."

"It was Nick and David who arranged to establish a dig on Andrew's property in Montana long before I arrived here. In any case, I don't see how one thing has anything to do with the other."

"Angry people do amazing things," I said.

"Another area beyond my expertise."

"It was you who arranged to transport the fossils to the Cities."

"Yes."

"Doyle Trucking."

"Yes."

"Why Doyle Trucking?"

"Why not?"

I didn't answer his question. Instead, I waited until Hegarty answered mine. That seemed to surprise Hegarty.

"I had used them before," he said.

"When?"

"When I first moved here from State College in Pennsylvania. They brought most of my belongings."

"Were they recommended to you?"

"No. I found them on the internet. They promised door-to-door delivery, so . . ."

"They didn't mention that."

"You spoke to them?"

"They said you were very keen on keeping the *Ankylosaurus* move a secret."

"Not secret but I thought that the fewer people who knew about it, the better."

"Who did you tell?"

"Me? Only the people who needed to know. The staff at the dig." Hegarty pointed at my left lung, although I'm sure he meant the letter that I had returned to the inside pocket of my sports jacket. "Andrew Cooke. Who they told, I couldn't say."

"The night of the theft . . ."

"I couldn't sleep," Hegarty said. "I got up and walked outside. I saw two men standing by the pickup truck; the door of the pickup was open."

"If the door was open, the dome light would have been on."

"If you're asking if I could see their faces, no, I couldn't. I thought it was the drivers from Doyle Trucking, Patrick Bittle and Ralph Peters."

Peter Ralph, my inner voice corrected him.

"I walked up to them and said, 'Hey guys, what are you doing?' Then someone hit me with something and—and that's all I remember until I woke up in the hospital."

"Dr. Larsen said that you saw the two men hot-wiring the truck."

"I don't—no. I don't remember saying that. I don't even know what that would look like."

Nor was it referenced in the Carter County sheriff's supplemental.

"You keep mentioning Nick Larsen," Hegarty said. "Do you suspect he had something to do with all this?"

"Yes."

"Really?"

"I suspect you, too."

"Oh."

I assured Dr. Hegarty that I was conducting my investigation as a favor to Andrew Cooke and that probably nothing would come of it. I told him what I originally told Angela Bjork—that the skull was probably already locked in some rich prick's vault. He seemed to take comfort in that, yet when I offered Hegarty a card, he took it from my fingers and promptly dropped it on his desk as if it were too dangerous to hold.

Afterward, I went searching for Dr. Larsen's office. I didn't tell Hegarty that, though. Eventually, I found it. It was located about as far away from Hegarty's office as possible and still be on the same floor. I wondered if that was intentional.

Like Hegarty, Larsen was sitting behind his desk. Unlike

him, he was wearing a long-sleeved flannel shirt over a black T-shirt and jeans. He was also sporting a silver-and-gray goatee.

Angela didn't mention that.

When I knocked, Larsen said, "What?"

"My name is McKenzie."

"Yes? What can I do for you, Mr. McKenzie?"

Angela didn't tell him about you.

"I'm investigating the theft of the *Ankylosaurus* skull," I said.

"On whose behalf? Are you with the authorities?"

I reached inside my jacket for the envelope. The gesture made Larsen flinch and I wondered if he thought I was going for a gun. He seemed relieved when I offered him the envelope. He read what was inside and handed it back to me.

"I haven't spoken to Andrew for a week or more," Larsen said. "I gather he's still upset."

"Still," I repeated.

"How can I help you? I'm a little busy so please be brief."

"You were the first to appreciate the theft was an inside job."

"Inside job," Larsen repeated as if he liked the sound of the words. "I knew almost immediately that it was well thought out; certainly not a crime of opportunity, some kid boosting a car that was left running in a parking lot while the owner ducked inside a drugstore."

"Let's say, for argument's sake, that you stole the skull."

"McKenzie, please."

"Let me rephrase the question. Let's say, for argument's sake, that you were attempting to re-create the crime."

"Like you?"

"Like me. How would you go about it?"

"I suppose it comes down to resources. Who has the resources to not only plan and execute the crime, but profit from it."

"Do you?"

Larsen paused before answering and I wondered if he felt insulted. He answered, though, as if it were a question he hadn't contemplated before.

"I can't think of who I would call," he said. "I guess I've lived a sheltered life. McKenzie, I suppose there are people I might contact, people in the field of paleontology who might put me in touch with other people but—I don't know. Wouldn't the authorities find such incriminating behavior easy to identify and trace through phone calls and emails and such?"

Not necessarily, I nearly said. Instead, I asked, "Of all the people present at the dig, whom would you suspect?"

"The investigator from the State of Montana—I don't recall who he worked for."

"The Division of Criminal Investigations."

"Yes, yes, similar to our own Bureau of Criminal Apprehension, I suppose."

"Very similar."

"The investigator asked me the same question—whom do I suspect? Honestly, McKenzie, I have given this much thought, and I am unable to offer a response that's based on evidence and not personal animosity."

"Animosity toward Dr. Hegarty?"

Larsen smiled at the suggestion.

"No." He then wagged his hand as if he was wavering. "Everyone wants to be in charge. Me, too. Yet that doesn't mean I desire the responsibility of overseeing the entire department. Supervising the dig and my other duties is more than enough to gratify my ego."

"Professor Bjork?"

"*Ms.* Bjork"—he emphasized the Ms.—"is a promising academic. She must remember, though, that she is an academic. What might be acceptable in the real world cannot and will not be tolerated on a college campus."

"Such as?"

From his body language it was clear to me that Larsen didn't want to answer the question, yet he did anyway.

"Personal relationships," he said.

I flashed on both Jordan Wall and Professor Gary Phillips.

"Are you referring to what happens between teachers and students or teachers and teachers?" I asked.

Larsen didn't want to answer that question, either, and he didn't. Instead, he said, "In any case, the loss of the skull hurts Ms. Bjork far more than anyone else, I believe."

"Ashley DeLuca?"

"Professor DeLuca has also shown genuine promise . . ."

Professor, not Ms.

"I do not suspect her, however," Larsen added. "Like Ms. Bjork, she had much to gain from the discovery and study of the *Ankylosaurus*. No, I believe the truck drivers were involved. Or perhaps the man who operated the crane."

"People to look at," I agreed.

I offered Larsen a card and asked him to call if he thought of anything important.

"Thank you," he said. "I will."

That's when I gave him my best Columbo impersonation.

"One more thing," I said. "Dr. Larsen, according to the reports I read, you and Dr. Seeley both told the county sheriff that you were sleeping in the same mobile home. You were both awakened by the same screams, the same gunshots. You both dressed quickly and went outside. Yet, Dr. Seeley reached Dr. Hegarty long before you did."

"What are you suggesting?"

"That wouldn't have happened if you both started in the same place at the same time. Dr. Larsen, where did you start from?"

"I greatly resent your insinuation."

"That doesn't answer the question."

"Perhaps I dressed more slowly than David."

"Perhaps."

"I think we're done here."

Neither Angela nor Ashley DeLuca were in their offices and I could find no one who would tell me when they were expected to return. I decided to retrace my steps and head back to the West Bank and my condominium. I crossed the bridge, hung a right on Cedar Avenue and followed it through an area of Minneapolis known as Seven Corners. Instead of going directly to the condo, though, I decided to stop at Open Book, which housed the Minnesota Center for Book Arts, Milkweed Books, the Loft Literary Center, and the Weavers Guild of Minnesota among other businesses. What interested me most, though, was FRGMNT Coffee, which not only served a decent mocha, but also a very tasty assortment of Cardigan donuts. I bought a half dozen.

Because the donuts took me out of my way, I crossed the street at an intersection farther down from the condo than I would normally have used. It was while waiting for the traffic to clear that I saw it—a white SUV strategically parked so that the driver had an unhampered view of the entrance to our underground garage.

I beat a casual retreat so not to draw the driver's notice, maneuvered around a couple of city blocks, crossed the street, and came up from behind the SUV—it was a Toyota by the way. I was purposefully blasé in my movements, sipping my coffee and balancing my box of donuts like any other passerby might. When I reached the rear bumper, I glanced down and then slowly bent as if I was tying my shoelace. Instead, I was studying the SUV's rear license plate. It was one of those fakes that criminals buy from Amazon for $14.95 and hang on their bumpers despite the company's disclaimer that they should never be used in place of real license plates. I edged close enough to lift it up and memorize the number of the actual license plate that was beneath it. I slowly stood. The driver didn't seem to notice.

I moved to the passenger window and glanced inside. The driver was young, at least he was younger than me, and leaning against the door, his cheek resting in his hand, while he stared through half-closed eyes out the front windshield. I had the impression that a volcano could erupt across the street and he wouldn't notice.

Amateur, my inner voice proclaimed.

I rapped on the window.

He jumped high enough that I was sure he hit his head against the SUV's roof; certainly, he jumped much higher than Nina had when Bobby Dunston did the same thing to us the night before. The young man looked at me, an expression of alarm on his face. I motioned for him to lower the passenger window. He did.

"What?" he asked.

"Are you looking for me?" I asked.

"You? No."

"Are you sure? My name is McKenzie."

His eyes widened.

"Why would I be looking for you?" he asked.

"That's what I'd like to know."

The kid glared at me and reached under his jacket.

You can't be serious. A gun?

I tensed; nearly dumped my cup of coffee on him. Instead, I said, "Really? Really? In downtown Minneapolis with traffic cameras everywhere?" I gestured at the lights of the intersections directly in front and behind us. "Not to mention the cameras from the storefronts and apartment buildings."

He brought his hand out. He was holding a pack of cigarettes.

"What are you talking about?" he asked.

I waved my coffee cup at him.

"Those things will kill you," I said.

"Get lost."

"Tell your boss you don't have to follow me anymore. Tell him that I'll be happy to drop by to see him the first chance I get."

"Wait. You know Mr. DeLuca?"

DeLuca! my inner voice screamed. *As in Ashley DeLuca?*

"I do now," I said.

The kid's eyes betrayed his fear.

"Don't worry about it," I said. "I won't blow your cover. Just move along. I promise I'll catch up to you later."

I don't know if he believed me or not, but as I was following the sidewalk back to the condominium, I noticed that he started the SUV and drove off.

Amateur, my inner voice repeated.

NINE

Detective Jean Shipman and I did not get along. Shelby Dunston claimed that it was because we were both jealous of each other's relationship with Bobby and I suppose there was some truth to that. After I left the SPPD, she became Bobby's partner of choice on those occasions when he stepped away from his role as a practicing bureaucrat and actually did some investigating. Which was fine, except Bobby once told me that Shipman was "young, beautiful, smart as hell." He never said that about me. Mostly, though, Shipman and I didn't get along because I liked to tease her and she just hated to be teased which, of course, is why I did it. Yes, I can be a jerk sometimes. On the other hand, not too long ago a person or persons unknown attempted to murder me. Shipman helped find out whom. We've been at least on speaking terms ever since.

"What the hell do you want, McKenzie?" she asked when I called.

See?

"I have a question for you," I said in between bites of my cinnamon sugar cake donut.

"Go on."

"Who do you think will take over the Homicide and Robbery Unit in the Major Crimes Division when Bobby is finally promoted to deputy chief?"

"The best investigator."

"Who's the best investigator?"

Shipman didn't hesitate for a moment.

"I am," she said. "I'm the best investigator."

"Prove it."

"Excuse me?"

"Sure, you have an excellent clearance rate, but have you broken any really big cases lately?"

"You mean besides yours?"

"I don't know if you're aware, Detective Shipman, but about a month ago an *Ankylosaurus* dinosaur skull valued at approximately six million dollars was stolen from a dig in Montana that was jointly sponsored by the University of Minnesota, Macalester College, and the Science Museum of Minnesota."

"What about it?"

"I have been asked to try to find it."

"Let me guess—it's a favor for a friend."

"I have to think that helping to solve such a high-profile case involving such prominent victims could only boost your résumé."

I took another bite of donut while Shipman thought it over.

"I'm listening, but just barely," she said.

"Since I took the case, Nina and I have been followed . . ."

"Is Nina okay?"

Everyone loves Nina, even Shipman.

"She's fine," I said. "So am I by the way."

"Uh-huh."

"Anyway, we've been followed . . ."

"By whom?"

"I have a name and a license plate number."

Shipman paused some more.

"Why didn't you call Bobby?" she asked.

"You know Commander Dunston would never compromise his lofty position by doing favors for friends. Why, he might even call me names and hang up the phone."

In my mind's eye I could see Shipman leaning back in her chair and staring at the ceiling.

"I'm going to regret this, aren't I?" she asked.

"No guts, no glory."

"You sound like my old softball coach. I hated that guy. All right, let's start with the name."

"DeLuca."

"DeLuca? As in Martin DeLuca?"

"I don't have a first name."

"Martin DeLuca from South St. Paul?"

"I'm guessing he's known to the authorities."

"DeLuca owns a restaurant that he named after himself. He was charged a couple years ago in Dakota County with aiding and abetting racketeering and aiding and abetting in the business of concealing criminal proceeds. Apparently, he was selling things that fell off the back of trucks and laundering the proceeds through his restaurant, only charges were dropped before he went to trial."

"Why?"

"I don't know. It wasn't my case. But I've had dealings with the man. Let's just say I'm not surprised."

"That he was arrested or that he got off?"

"Both. What about the license plate?"

I gave her the number.

"It was hung on the back of a white Toyota SUV," I added. "Under a fake plate."

"Fake license plates—that's only a misdemeanor in Minnesota, but it would give us an excuse for a stop and search."

"You but not me," I said.

"I need a minute."

Shipman took about five.

"You still there?" she asked when she returned to the phone.

"Still," I said.

"The vehicle is registered to Martin DeLuca."

"It wasn't DeLuca driving unless he's about twenty-five."

"If his driver's license is to be believed, he's seventy-two. Why, McKenzie? Why are you being followed by an ancient, small-time wiseguy wannabe? How is this connected to the theft of a dinosaur fossil?"

"I don't know, although . . ."

"Although what?"

"One of the scientists at the dig in Montana is an assistant professor at the U. Her name is Ashley DeLuca."

"No kidding? What's their relationship?"

"I don't know yet."

"Okay, I'm officially intrigued."

"I'll keep in touch."

"You'd better."

My next call went to Angela Bjork. She didn't answer.

I was tempted to call Ashley DeLuca but decided against it. There are some conversations, I told myself, that must be conducted in person. I was debating whether or not to make another trip to Tate Hall; see if I could corner Ashley in her office. That's when I heard Judy Garland singing, "Clang, clang, clang went the trolley, ding, ding, ding went the bell." I answered my phone.

"McKenzie," Megan Jackson said. "Do you have a few minutes?"

"Sure."

"I mean do you have time to meet with me?"

Another private conversation in a public place?

"Sure," I said again. "Where?"

"At my house?"

"When?"

"Anytime you can get here."

"I'm on my way."

It took me over twenty minutes to reach Megan's two-story Victorian, partly because I wanted to make sure I wasn't being followed again and partly because I got lost—they don't call it Tangletown for nothing. She must have been waiting for me because she opened the front door before I could knock.

"Sorry I took so long," I said as Megan bade me enter. She was dressed like a casual housewife again in jeans and a sweatshirt that proclaimed her allegiance to the Minnesota Lynx basketball team. Megan patted my wrist as if we'd been friends since the beginning of time.

"Not at all," she said.

"I had the impression that it was important."

"Hardly. Please . . ."

Megan led me into the living room. Andrew Cooke was sitting in the same throne-like chair with the thick red cushions and carved arms as when we met the day before. He was sound asleep, and, in his sleep, he seemed so much paler and fragile than he had when we last spoke. Megan patted his wrist the same way she had patted mine.

"Grandfather," she said.

Andrew's eyes popped open, and he looked around as if he wasn't sure where he was.

"I'm awake, I'm awake," he chanted. "I wasn't sleeping."

"Grandfather," Megan said. "You remember McKenzie."

"McKenzie?" He found me standing behind his granddaughter. "McKenzie, yes, yes. McKenzie. Thank you for coming. Please."

He gestured at the sofa across from him. This time Megan sat next to me.

"So, why did I call you?" Cooke asked. "Megan?"

"Andy," she said.

"Yes, yes, Andy. Have you found him?"

"Not since yesterday."

"Yesterday?"

Cooke's eyes sought out his granddaughter.

"McKenzie was here yesterday," she told him.

"Seems longer. When you get old, McKenzie, you'll think that everything speeds up. That's because you become aware of how little time you have left. No, no. It slows down." Cooke paused. "What was I going to tell you? Oh yes, Andy. I don't have the time to sit around and wait for someone to find him. Meg doesn't like to hear that. Look at her."

I did. If I didn't know any better, I would have said she appeared like a mother who was concerned about her child.

"Darlin'," Cooke said. "We all die. Your grandmother died. She died way too soon. Although, McKenzie, it's better to die too soon than too late."

"Yes, sir," I said. I didn't necessarily agree with him. I was just trying to be polite. I think Megan knew it, too, because she patted me on the wrist again.

"The last time you were here you said that the thieves might be willing to sell Andy back to us."

"Yes, sir," I repeated.

"I've thought about it—do you think you could make that happen?"

"I could pass the word. If the right people hear it . . . Is this really something you want to do?"

"I've got plenty of money. You know what I ain't got? I ain't got a dinosaur with my name on it."

"Grandfather, the Minnesota Science Museum hopes to unveil the *Acheroraptor* by Christmas," Megan said.

Cooke stared as if he had never seen her before.

"*Acheroraptor*?" he repeated.

"Yes, Grandfather. The Science Museum . . ."

"*Acheroraptor* is a damn lizard." Cooke held his hand just below the arm of his chair. "It's only this tall. And they only have half of its bones. They had to use fake bones to complete the skeleton. Andy is a real dinosaur. Am I right, McKenzie?"

"It's certainly much bigger," I said.

"I want it back. No questions asked."

"How much are you willing to pay?"

"Oh, McKenzie, we'll let the crooks set the market. Then we'll find out how desperate they are to sell before we begin negotiating. But McKenzie—no more than five hundred thousand. I'm old and getting older; that doesn't make me senile. 'Course, I'd rather not pay anything. I'd be very happy to not pay anything. Do you understand me?"

"Yes, sir."

"Can I count on you?"

"Like I said, I'll pass the word. Hopefully, someone will respond."

"Can I count on you?"

"If the thieves take your bait, yes, sir, you can count on me."

Cooke pointed at me yet spoke to his granddaughter, repeating almost exactly what he told her the day before.

"Now this is the kind of guy you should have married," he said. "Someone you can depend on."

"Yes, Grandfather," Megan said.

I wonder how many times she's heard that.

"Yes, yes, now McKenzie, I'm counting on you." Cooke waved his finger in the air. "Do what needs to be done."

I took that to mean the meeting had concluded and stood

up. Instead of standing with me, Cooke waved his finger some more.

"I'm going to rest here for a while," he said. "Megan will show you to the door."

"Of course," I said.

Megan and I moved away from him.

"He sits there a lot just staring at the fireplace," Megan told me. "I don't know what he sees. Maybe my grandmother. Once I tried to build a fire and he—he didn't like that."

"I'm impressed that you're giving up so much to take care of him."

"What am I giving up?"

"I mean . . ."

"I know what you mean. Believe me, it's no trouble."

"Megan, did you know what your grandfather was going to ask me?"

"Yes. We spoke about it before I called."

"What do you think?"

We had reached the front door; Megan's hand rested on the knob.

"He's dying, McKenzie. He might not be here for Christmas. This, this"—she brought her hand off the knob and waved, taking in the entire house—"this is hospice care."

"I'm sorry."

"So am I. He's not, though. He keeps saying it's about time. McKenzie, if you could find his dinosaur before he goes . . ."

"I'll try."

"It'll make him so happy."

"I'll try," I repeated.

"Thank you."

"Megan, does your husband know that your grandfather is willing to buy back the *Ankylosaurus*?"

"Not yet. Grandfather made the decision just now."

"Tell him."

"I will. I'll tell everyone in the family but, McKenzie, I don't really believe Kevin stole it. That's just something I said because . . . I don't know why I said it."

"How dare I offer marital advice to anyone, much less you, but would it really be that hard to push him out the door?"

"Maybe I'm the one who should be pushed."

Since I was in the neighborhood, I decided it would be a good time to visit Professor Gary Phillips at Macalester College. Once again, though, my cell phone started playing "The Trolley Song." I had it synced to my Mustang's computer, so I was able to answer it while I drove. I must say, Judy Garland sounded so much better in stereo.

"Hey," I said.

"I'm sorry I didn't answer when you called earlier," Angela Bjork said. "I was teaching a class and afterward I became involved in some school-related matters."

"That's okay. I appreciate that you called me back."

"What can I do for you, McKenzie?"

"A couple of things but I'd like to talk to you in person."

"That can be arranged. When and where?"

"How 'bout dinner at Rickie's? I'm sure Nina would love to see you again."

"Seven?"

"Be there or be square. Oh, hey, Angela. What's a zaddy?"

"A zaddy?"

"I heard the word and I've been wondering."

"It's a Gen Z term, a twist on daddy. It refers to a sexually attractive older man with swag and style. Jon Hamm is a zaddy. So is Idris Elba."

"Oh, okay. See you tonight."

Angela rang off and I started laughing. I don't know why. Well, yes, I do.

You're a zaddy!

In contrast to the century-old exterior of John T. Tate Hall, the Olin-Rice Science Center looked like it had been built last month. It was located more or less in the center of the Macalester College campus. I was forced to park on a residential side street a couple of blocks away and walk to the building, parking being as big an issue there as it was on the U's campus.

While heading to Professor Gary Phillips's office on the first floor, I passed an exhibit of dinosaur fossils including a pair of ten-foot-high *Herrerasaurus* that were posed as if they were racing each other. According to the tablet, the name meant "Herrera's lizard," after the rancher who discovered the first specimen in South America. Unfortunately, the tablet also said the dinosaur skeletons weren't real, merely replicas. Oh, well.

Unlike at the U, I was escorted to Phillips's office by a receptionist who seemed very keen to know my name. It was she who introduced me to Phillips. He appeared glad to see me, which made the receptionist smile as she walked away.

"McKenzie," Phillips said. "I'm very pleased to meet you. Angie told me wonderful things."

"I'm sure she exaggerated," I said as we shook hands. "Thank you for seeing me, Professor."

"Unless you're taking one of my courses, call me Gary. Are you taking one of my courses?"

"Probably not."

"Pity. I teach an introductory course, Geology 101: Dinosaurs, but everyone calls it 'Gary's Dinosaurs.' I could teach you a lot."

"Speaking of which . . ."

"You want to know about that night."

"You tackled Angela to the ground when the bullets started flying."

"It seemed like the thing to do at the time."

"I was impressed that you left cover to do it. I like to think I would have done the same, still . . . As for Angela, after tackling her to the ground I would have spanked her."

"I wish I had thought of that at the time."

"Speaking of which . . ."

"You want to know if we have a sexual relationship."

"It's been suggested . . ."

"By whom? That cracker sheriff in Montana?"

Now that's an epithet you haven't heard for a long time.

"He was impressed that our tents were located side by side. I don't know if I should feel insulted by that or complimented—you've met the woman. I'll be honest here; liaisons are not unusual at a dig. There's not much to distract you in the middle of nowhere. Only not between Angela and me. It's possible, McKenzie, to be friends with a woman, even a woman as attractive as Angie, without sleeping with her. Or are you one of those guys who believe that a man and a woman can't just be friends."

I flashed on Shelby Dunston. She and I shared a bond that went all the way back to college. The joke, if you want to use that word, was that if I had been the one to spill his beer on Shelby's dress instead of Bobby, all of our lives would be different.

"I object to the term 'just friends,'" I said. "It makes it sound as if friendship has little importance."

"Like I said, Angie told me nice things about you."

"You were upset when Angela included Ashley DeLuca in her find and not you."

"She did what she did because of professional concerns. I didn't take it personally. McKenzie, this isn't my first dig. You'll notice that my name hasn't been mentioned in the discovery of the *Acheroraptor* that the science museum will soon put on display, either. You'd be amazed how much politics there is in academia. That's all right. You want to be known for who you are and not what you do."

"Isn't that the same thing?"

"You have a point."

"Tell me about that night."

Phillips did. His story closely resembled what Angela had told me, although I hadn't heard the term "po-po" used to describe the police before.

"According to the reports I read, the sheriff asked who you suspected was involved in the theft and you said you didn't know," I told him.

"That's not what I said. I said—actually, McKenzie, I believe I've used up my allotment of obscenities for the day."

"Do you suspect someone?"

"Yes and no. The paleontologists in Minnesota, there aren't that many of us. It's still a modest community, although it's growing, and we like to get together every few weeks and talk shop over a couple of beers. Not all of us. Dr. Larsen from the U is strictly a red wine man. We've talked about this, of course we have, and we just can't get our heads wrapped around the possibility that someone at the dig, that one of us, was involved in the theft.

"McKenzie, I didn't become interested in dinosaurs because I saw them in the movies for the simple reason that I didn't see anyone who looked like me in those movies, except maybe for Samuel L. Jackson in *Jurassic Park*. But he was an engineer not a paleontologist and he was killed, so . . . It wasn't until I was in college that I decided that this was something I could do. In many ways, I was ahead of my time. Now there's a prize, the Futures Award, that's presented by the Society of Vertebrate Paleontology. It was created to encourage people of color to enter the field.

"Only, if you erase the color of my skin, I'm just like everyone else. I study dinosaurs because I love it. My area of research deals with nourishment. Dinosaurs had varying diets. Not every dinosaur was a meat eater. If that were true, their environment would not have been able to sustain them. No, some dinosaurs ate plants, some ate meat, and some ate both. Most ate plants, though; I'd say at least sixty percent."

Phillips waved his hand as if he was reminding himself to stay on topic.

"I can't believe that any one of us would have betrayed"—he hesitated as if looking for the perfect word—"betrayed our dreams."

"It's like I tried to explain to Dr. Seeley . . ."

"You spoke with David?"

"I told him that it's possible that someone called a friend, and that friend is the person to blame."

"Yes, but wouldn't we know that by now; know what our friend did? How could we keep quiet about it?"

"When our actions do not, our fears do make us traitors."

"You're quoting Shakespeare at me? *Macbeth*? Seriously?"

Phillips started laughing at me, which I found annoying, although . . .

It's not like you don't have it coming, my inner voice said.

"Who did you tell about the skull?" I asked.

"When it was discovered; when we started to excavate it? Everyone."

"And the night it was taken?"

"No one."

"You should know—and I encourage you to repeat it to anyone who cares to listen—that Andrew Cooke is offering to pay for the safe return of the *Ankylosaurus* skull no questions asked."

"No shit?"

Professor Gary Phillips accompanied me to the exit of the Olin-Rice Science Center. Along the way I gave him a card. He asked if I had planned to meet with Angela anytime soon.

"I'm having dinner with her tonight," I said.

"Oh?"

"At my wife's club."

"Oh. Well, tell her I said 'Hi.'"

"I will."

I walked to my Mustang. Three hours later I was parked in the lot adjacent to Rickie's on Cathedral Hill in St. Paul not far from the St. Paul Curling Club where I occasionally sub in on Bobby Dunston's team. The white Toyota SUV was nowhere to be seen.

I entered the club and found an empty spot at the bar. Nina discovered me there a few minutes later.

"Were you followed?" she asked as dramatically as possible.

"About that."

I told her what I had learned. Her eyes grew wide.

"Ashley DeLuca did it," she proclaimed.

"I wish you would stop jumping to conclusions. Nora Charles would never do that."

"Yes, but . . ."

"I'll talk to her and this Martin DeLuca tomorrow if I can manage it and we'll see. In the meantime . . ."

"What?"

I told her about Andrew Cooke's offer to buy back the dinosaur skull.

"No kidding," Nina said. "What else?"

"I ran into Victoria Dunston when I was at the U."

"How is she?"

"Great. I also met her roommate, a girl named Missy. Very pretty. She thinks I'm a zaddy."

"What's a zaddy?"

I told her. Nina thought that was awfully funny and not for the same reasons I did.

"What?" I asked. "You don't think I'm attractive to young women?"

"You're forty-seven years old."

"I see younger guys ogling you all the time."

"There's a difference."

"What's the difference?"

"I'm a babe," Nina said as if she was daring me to contradict her.

"Yes, you are. I've said so many times. I'm meeting Angela here for dinner, but I didn't make reservations. Can you help us out?"

"Only if I'm invited. You know, in case she also thinks you're a zaddy."

Angela arrived a short time later. Nina managed to secure a booth for the three of us on the ground floor. After we settled in, I said, "Gary Phillips says 'Hi.'"

"How is he?" Angela asked.

"I saw him a few hours ago. He seemed fine. He said you told him that I was trying to find the *Ankylosaurus* skull."

"Yes."

"You also told Dr. Hegarty."

"Yes."

"But not Dr. Larsen."

"No. I only told Gary and Dr. Hegarty. And Dr. Seeley, but he already knew. I guessed you spoke to him. Oh, and Ashley DeLuca. I didn't want her to think I was freezing her out since we've been home; that I was only her Montana friend."

"Tell me about Ashley," I said.

"After we discovered the dinosaur . . ."

"After you discovered the dinosaur and brought her in on it."

"We started sharing personal stuff after that; our loves, fears, ambitions; our history. We became close. She told me that she was raised by a single mother that she just adored, who died of cancer while she was still in school. Ashley said that her great regret is that her mom didn't see her graduate; didn't see her become a professor at the U. What else? She said that her father, whom she despised, was killed in a car accident just a short time later."

"Why did she despise her father?" I asked.

"I don't know. I didn't ask. I know he didn't marry Ashley's mom, so that might have had something to do with it."

"What else?"

"McKenzie, I don't know why you're asking me these things. Ash had as much to lose by the theft of the *Ankylosaurus* as I did."

"That's what people keep telling me."

"She wants to be a full professor just like me. She wants to earn a PhD, just like me. Researching and documenting the *Ank* would help us both achieve those goals."

"Your name would come first."

"So what?"

I came *this*close to telling Angela about the white SUV and its owner, only I decided against it; decided not to burden her with the revelation until I learned more about both Ashley and Martin DeLuca. Instead, I pivoted.

"Tell me about Jordan Wall," I said.

"Ah, geez . . ."

"Angela . . ."

"What about him?"

"Based on what you already told me concerning your relationship with him and Dr. Larsen's undisguised animosity toward you . . ."

"Did you talk to Dr. Larsen?"

"This morning."

"What did he say?"

"Besides you being a promising academic? He talked about

what's not allowed on a university campus that's perfectly acceptable off of it."

Angela glanced at Nina and quickly looked away. When she spoke, though, she spoke to Nina.

"I don't know what I was thinking," Angela said.

"Having been there myself when I was young, I'd say you weren't thinking," Nina replied.

"It happened when we stopped in Bismarck, North Dakota, on our way to the dig. It was late and I couldn't sleep, probably because I kept dozing off during the six-hour drive it took to get to Bismarck. I stepped out onto the second-story landing overlooking the parking lot. It was very quiet. Jordan left the room he was sharing with Larsen, the one next to mine; he said Larsen was asleep. We chatted and then we—we went inside my room because it was getting cold. One thing led to another. I know what you're thinking, apparently Larsen is thinking it, too. Jordan wasn't my student, though, not then or now and he isn't going to be. Afterward, I was hard on him. I purposely made it hard because I realized what a mistake I had made. But Nina, McKenzie, we parted friends."

"Have you spoken to him since he left the dig last May?" I asked.

"No. Well, maybe twice, but only to nod and say hello. And both times were at the science museum. Winter has been a regular there; working to help free the remaining *Ankylosaurus* bones from its sandstone sarcophagus. Jordan was there because of her."

"You didn't call that night to tell him that the skull was sitting on the pickup and ready to be taken?"

"Of course not. Why would you say such a thing?"

"Jordan isn't an aspiring paleontologist, Angela. He was only tangentially involved in the find. By helping to arrange for the theft of the *Ankylosaurus* skull, he makes a few bucks and punishes you for refusing to be the love of his life."

"He wouldn't do that."

"I've known men who have killed their girlfriends for breaking up with them. I've seen husbands who murdered their wives because they wanted a divorce."

"What are you telling me?"

"I'm telling you that just because you like someone doesn't make them innocent."

"That's enough," Nina said.

"I'm just trying to make a point," I said.

"I think you've made it."

Nina rested her hand on Angela's and gave it a squeeze.

"I made a mistake, I know that," Angela said, the words spoken with an exhale.

"I'd like to speak to Wall," I said. "And Winter Billock and Simon Stevens, too."

"I can't speak for Jordan, only like I said, Winter, and Simon, too, have been working at the science museum to help extract the specimen."

"How's that going?"

"Slowly. We've recovered some nice fossils, though. I'll be there tomorrow afternoon after classes. Around four? Winter and Simon should be there, too."

"I'm sorry if I sound like a jerk, Angela. I really am trying to help you."

"I know. Thank you."

"Something you might want to tell the people at the museum or anywhere else for that matter—Andrew Cooke has agreed to buy back the skull, no questions asked."

"Will that make it easier or harder to get it back?"

"It depends on who stole it."

After my interrogation, the three of us had a pleasant dinner. Angela said she appreciated everything I was doing and hugged me as if she meant it. After she left, Nina held a quiet conference with her night manager and a couple of employees. A few minutes later, we started to leave together.

I saw the reflection of a white SUV in the glass of the front door as I held it open for Nina. I grabbed her elbow, pulled her back, and quickly closed the door.

"What?" she asked as I nudged her back into the club.

"It seems Mr. DeLuca wants to speak sooner instead of later."

"He's out there?'

"His Toyota is."

"What are we going to do?"

"Stay here," I said. "And when I say stay here, I mean stay right here. Don't go to the door and look outside; don't go to the windows. All right?"

Nina nodded.

I worked my way through the club to the back door that opened out onto the trash and recycling dumpsters in the alley and then hugged the building as I moved to the parking lot. The SUV was parked in the third row with the front bumper facing the street. I stayed low, moving from the first to the second row, using the parked cars for cover, and came up behind the vehicle. There was plenty of light. If the driver had been paying attention, he probably would have spotted me right away. Because of the light, I could see that the same kid I had met that morning was sitting in the driver's seat; the passenger seat was empty. The kid was gripping the steering wheel and staring at the front entrance. This time I came up to the driver's side window and gave it a rap with my knuckles. He jumped just as high as he had the first time. Again, I asked him to power down the window.

"What are you doing here?" I asked.

"Mr. DeLuca said to watch you."

"Didn't you tell Martin"—I used the first name to send the

kid a message—"that I would talk to him in his restaurant when I was ready?"

He hesitated before answering—"No."

He didn't want the boss to know he screwed up. Probably didn't tell him about following Nina and you to the Criminal Justice Campus, either.

"I don't think you're cut out for this kind of work, kid," I said.

He gritted his teeth—"I want to be a chef."

"Instead, you're being forced into a life of crime?"

"I'm not doing anything illegal," he said. "Am I?"

Actually, I felt a little sorry for him.

"Tell you what," I said. "Let's do this, get you on your boss's good side. Tell him that you found a stool at the bar inside Rickie's where you could eavesdrop on a conversation I was having with someone—you don't know who. Tell him that you heard me say that the owner of the *Ankylosaurus* skull has agreed to pay a ransom for the safe return of his property, no questions asked."

"Are you serious? Cooke said that?"

All right, confirmation that this is all about the dinosaur. There was never really a doubt.

"Yes, I'm serious," I said aloud. "Now beat it, will ya?"

"Okay, okay," the kid chanted.

"Wait. What's your name?"

The kid hesitated before he answered—"Tony DeLuca."

"Martin is your father?"

"No. God. My uncle—granduncle. He's my grandfather's brother."

"If you don't want to be his errand boy . . ."

"He hired me to be a chef in his restaurant but when he wants something done—keep it in the family, he says."

"He wants you to follow in the family business. I get it. My old man, he wanted me to be a cop."

Tony didn't know what to do with that. I stepped back. He started the SUV, and I watched him leave the parking lot. Afterward, I went inside the club and found Nina. I assured her that "It's all good."

She remained skeptical.

I escorted her to her Lexus; stood by while she started it and began the fifteen-minute drive home. No one followed her except me.

TEN

It was about ten thirty the next morning and Nina had just left to go to the club when Judy Garland started singing, "Clang, clang, clang went the trolley, ding, ding, ding went the bell" again. I glanced at my smartwatch, not to read the time, but the date.

Three more weeks before you're allowed to change the ring-tone to something less boisterous, my inner voice reminded me. *I can't believe you bet against the Minnesota Timberwolves. What were you thinking?*

My cell was unable to ID the caller, yet I answered anyway.

"Yo, is this Rushmore McKenzie, the world-famous semi-professional consulting detective?" a male voice asked.

"And you would be?" I said in reply.

"Name's Benjamin D. Dirnberger. I'm an investigator with People's Financial Insurance. Our mutual friend Maryanne Altavilla says you're the modern-day Sherlock Holmes."

"No, she doesn't."

"Not in those exact words. On the other hand, she mentioned a few of your exploits, so . . ."

"Maryanne said you would call. She said I would like you."

"I am likeable."

"I'll be the judge of that."

Dirnberger thought I was being funny.

"I would have called yesterday, but what can I say—life," he told me. "Maryanne said you're going to help us."

"Us?"

"Our respective employers might be at odds over who is going to compensate whom for what, but we, meaning the investigators, tend to be more cooperative. It's not unlike how members of the St. Paul PD might help out their colleagues in Minneapolis."

He has you there.

"I'm going after the *Ankylosaurus* skull as a favor for a friend," I said. "If that helps you out, fine with me."

"Fair enough."

"This is the part of the program where I'd offer to trade you what I have for what you have only I don't have anything tangible yet."

"How 'bout I tell you what I have and then you can owe me?"

"I always pay my debts," I assured him.

"That's what Maryanne said. McKenzie, the Montana Highway Patrol recovered the stolen Ford F-150 early yesterday morning. And no, they did not find the skull. The pickup was hidden under a pile of brush just off the Theodore Roosevelt Expressway near a small unincorporated hamlet called Raymond. Raymond is approximately ten miles from the Canadian border. There's a border crossing, Raymond Port of Entry it's called, not that we have any evidence our friends used it."

"So, the *Ankylosaurus* is probably now somewhere in the land of maple syrup."

"If I was going to bet the over-under, I'd take the over, yes, sir."

"Well, that'll complicate matters."

"You think?"

"Tell me, did the highway patrol dust the truck?"

Dirnberger seemed amused by the question.

"No, they did not dust the truck," he said. "For one thing, it would be tough to lift prints from the interior because of the vehicle's design and texture. DNA is just as bad. Plus, they would also need to lift the prints and DNA of everyone who had ever been inside the truck for elimination purposes. Then there's the why. Why would they go to all that trouble? McKenzie, for five hundred dollars, guess what is the single, most often stolen vehicle in Montana, and please, state your answer in the form of a question. Wait for it. Ding, ding, ding, ding. What is the Ford F-150 pickup truck?"

"Please."

"Would I lie?"

I let it all sink in for a moment.

"Ben," I said, "was the vehicle hot-wired?"

"Hot-wired? Who the hell hot-wires cars in this day and age? I mean besides the guys who go to antique auto shows. Just a sec."

A full minute later, he was back on the phone.

"The MHP suspects an OBD port attack. The thieves plugged a diagnostic systems reader into the vehicle's on-board computer port, the kind that mechanics use to tell you why your check engine light is on, and used it to access the truck's key code, start the engine and—you've heard this story many times before, I'm sure."

If he didn't know what he was looking at, Dr. Larsen might have confused that gag with an old-fashioned hot-wire.

"Yeah," I said aloud.

"What I tell people—lock your damn car doors."

"Ben, what's the status of the lawsuit?"

"McKenzie, c'mon, you know how these things work. The event took place in late August. It's now the first week of October. Ask me again around Valentine's Day. Of course, if we find the dinosaur skull before then . . ."

"Ben, if the thieves decided they wanted to sell the skull

back to its owners, which insurance company should they negotiate with?"

"Speaking from my oh-so-limited knowledge and experience in these matters, I doubt if either would make a deal. That would be like admitting that they were responsible for the skull in the first place and that's not going to happen until the lawsuit is settled."

Good. That would make Andrew Cooke the only game in town.

I told Dirnberger that Cooke had agreed to pay a ransom for the *Ankylosaurus*.

"Ah, McKenzie, so you do know a thing or two. Listen, I'm sure that would make both Midwest Farmer's and People's Financial very, very happy. Assuming the skull isn't already in a box and heading for the People's Republic of China."

Okay, maybe not the only game . . .

I thanked Dirnberger for his time and promised I would contact him as soon as I had something worth contacting him about. He said he'd do the same. After ending that call, I searched my contact list and started another.

"Special Agent Brian Wilson," he said in case I had forgotten who I had called.

"Harry," I said.

"So, we're back to that."

"Brian . . ."

"You know Brian makes me nervous. Brian makes me think you want something, again."

"How 'bout if I just say 'Hey, you'?"

"What do you need, McKenzie?"

"I'd like to chat with Linda."

"You mean Special Agent Linda Ambrose?"

"Since we're such close, personal friends now . . . I have something that might or might not interest her."

"Such as?"

"The violation of Section 2314 of the National Stolen Property Act, specifically the transportation of illegally obtained goods valued at $5,000 or more across foreign borders by persons knowing the goods to be stolen."

"She's in the field somewhere doing who knows what. I'll have her call you the first chance I get."

"Or you could give me her number and I'll . . ."

"No."

"Why not?"

"Guess."

"The FBI does not support much less condone my actions."

"Don't worry, McKenzie. She'll call you back."

"Thank you, Brian."

Since I was sitting at my desk anyway, I decided to fire up my computer and access Minnesota Court Records Online, a website where any citizen can search for the district court criminal and civil records of any other citizen in the state. I started with Kevin Jackson and discovered that the man hadn't been cited or arrested or sued for anything. Ever.

Even you have a worse record than he does, my inner voice told me.

Next, I tried Peter Ralph. He had only two hits, both for illegal parking. Afterward, I looked up Patrick Bittle. He was a career criminal compared with the others—three speeding tickets, one citation for failure to stop for a traffic control signal and, gulp, he was busted for driving under the influence when he was twenty-two.

There were other websites known to me that revealed

unsavory behavior, however, and I searched them, too. It took about an hour to discover that Doyle Trucking had been involved in three separate heists.

The first—five thousand pounds of furniture meant to be exhibited at the Steele County Fair in Owatonna, Minnesota, was stolen from a semitrailer truck driven by an unidentified Doyle driver between the hours of one and four A.M. while it was parked in the fairgrounds lot. There were no arrests, and the furniture was never recovered. The theft occurred three years ago.

Second—nine months later, between $10,000 and $15,000 worth of construction equipment was reported stolen from the back of a Doyle box truck while it was parked at a construction site in White Bear Lake, Minnesota. Apparently, the thieves cut a padlock and stole numerous cordless power tools including batteries, charging stations, nail and air guns, compressors, and drills.

Third—my favorite heist—took place just last year. According to the report I read, Doyle Trucking delivered $50,000 worth of cleaning supplies owned by Jackson Janitorial to a storage facility in Rochester, Minnesota. Twenty minutes after it was unloaded and the truck drove off, thieves broke into the facility and, well, cleaned it out. Again, no arrests were made.

I retrieved my cell phone, surfed my contact list, and tapped the call icon.

"This is Maryanne," a female voice answered.

"Maryanne Altavilla, the Jessica Fletcher of insurance investigators?" I asked.

"Yes, as a matter of fact, I am. What can I do for you, McKenzie? I take it you met Ben Dirnberger."

"Only over the phone. According to Ben, you two are supposed to be working together."

"Let's just say we're sharing information."

"Since it's probably more to your benefit than his, I thought I'd tell you what I found out."

I told Maryanne about the three robberies connected to Doyle Trucking that I had discovered.

"I know all about them," she told me. "Jessica Fletcher, remember?"

"Did you know that Jackson Janitorial is owned by Andrew Cooke's grandson-in-law?"

Maryanne paused before answering—"No, I did not."

"When I first met Jackson's wife, Megan, who's Cooke's granddaughter, she told me that she suspected her husband was involved in the theft. Later, she recanted, saying that she didn't actually believe it. Still . . ."

Maryanne paused again.

"That's interesting," she said.

"Also, I learned last night that Mr. Cooke is now offering a reward for the safe return of his dinosaur."

"You don't really think it's that easy, do you?"

"What do you mean, easy?"

"Jackson conspires with Doyle Trucking to steal the *Ankylosaurus* skull and sell it back to his wife's grandfather?"

"You know what, why don't I go over there and ask him?"

"Who? Jackson? The guys at Doyle Trucking? Can I watch?"

Maryanne couldn't see me shaking my head, but she could hear my voice.

"No," I said. "You might intimidate them with your stern countenance."

"Are you saying I look mean?"

"Love to G. K."

I drove to Doyle Trucking—the Flatbed and Heavy Hauling Experts—arriving just before one. The man I had met two days earlier was still standing behind the counter and staring at a computer screen; you couldn't prove by me that he had moved a single inch since then. This time he did look up, though.

"Peter Ralph," I said.

"Not here," he told me.

"Patrick Bittle?"

"Paddy!" he shouted.

A few moments later, a man stepped into the reception area. He was half the size of his partner and about a decade older with thinning gray hair.

"How can I help ya?" he asked.

"My name is McKenzie."

"McKenzie, McKenzie? Oh yeah, the dinosaur hunter, am I right?"

"Pretty much."

"Ralphie told me you guys talked the other day."

"Where is Ralph?" I asked.

"Out. The man got his insurance check yesterday. He's shopping for a replacement pickup as we speak."

"Is that right?"

"That's our main thing, right now, 'kay?" Bittle said. "Get the truck, get back on the road."

"I'd like to ask a few questions about the night the *Ankylosaurus* skull was stolen."

"Got nothin' more to tell you than what Ralph did; what he said he told you. We stayed in the tent and didn't come out until everything settled down. I mean, I'd like to help you, but we didn't see anything."

"Ralph said that you took the job in secret."

"Not secret, but you know, keep it to ourselves 'til it was done, that's what we promised."

"What you promised Dr. Weston Hegarty."

"Guy from the U who hired us, yeah, yeah."

"Did you tell anybody? Give someone a call when you saw the dinosaur, perhaps."

"No, no, no, nothin' like that. We said we would—wait? What are you asking?"

"Just what the county sheriff asked," I said.

Bittle thought about it and said, "Well, we didn't tell anyone, 'kay?"

"I was told that you worked with Dr. Hegarty before."

"We moved some of his furniture from Pennsylvania to here, when was that? A year and a half; two years ago? Something like that. And you know what? We didn't tell anyone we were doing that job, either, 'kay? Just so you know, this whole thing is becoming a court case, so from now on I'm not going to answer any questions about what we did or didn't do or should've done or anything like that. You wanna know something, talk to the lawyers at People's Financial."

"That's fair," I said. "You should probably know, though, the Montana Highway Patrol recovered Ralph's F-150 yesterday morning."

"Guess the insurance company owns a truck then, cuz we ain't giving back the check."

"The truck was found not far from the Canadian border. It was empty."

"So, you're saying the assholes took the goods into Canada?"

"That's the bet."

"What do I care? Look, if I sound pissed off it's cuz I am, 'kay? This whole thing has been bad for business. Hauling a dinosaur here would have been great. Think of the internet ads. 'We haul everything from dining rooms to dinosaurs.' A pic of the damn thing was going to be the first thing you saw when you pulled up our website. But losing a dinosaur? Being known as the guys that *lost* a dinosaur! Right now, it's not too bad. People who know what happened; they aren't connecting us directly to the crime. If it goes to court, though, and it becomes a big deal; if they say we're liable, you know WCCO, KSTP, all them others are gonna send their news crews down here to take pictures of the guys who lost a freaking dinosaur. Man, this job, it started so sweet. Then it went from terrific to catastrophic just like that. We're trying to—what is it the politicians say? We're trying to distance ourselves from what happened, 'kay?"

"I checked your website the first time I came here. You have a list of nice clients—3M, Cargill, Dairy Queen . . ."

"Yeah?"

"Jackson Janitorial."

Bittle shrugged his shoulders at me.

"We've done okay," he said. "What about it?"

"This isn't the first time you lost a load, is it? You've lost three in the past three years alone. The last one you lost belonged to Jackson Janitorial."

"That had nothin' t' do with us," Bittle insisted. "The load was stolen after we delivered it. It was stolen from the storage facility, not us. Even Jackson didn't blame us. Hell, we're still doing business with them."

"Did you know that Jackson Janitorial is owned by Andrew Cooke's grandson-in-law?"

Bittle thought about it before he responded.

"I don't know who that is," he said.

"Andrew Cooke is the man who owns the property where the *Ankylosaurus* was discovered," I told him. "He's offering a reward for the safe return of the dinosaur."

"You're telling me this for a reason, aren't you?"

"Cooke asked me to act as a go-between, just in case you're wondering."

"I'm not wondering."

I gave him my best shrug and reached inside my pocket for a card with my cell number on it. Instead of handing it to him, I set it on the counter.

"Just spreading the word," I said.

"That's not all you're spreading, is it?" Bittle took a deep breath and exhaled slowly as he pointed toward the entrance. "You know what? There's the door. What's your hurry?"

The junction of I-35W and I-494 just south of Minneapolis in Bloomington might be the busiest, most congested, and unsafe intersection in Minnesota. It carries over 250,000 vehicles every day and has as many car crashes as you might expect from the heavy traffic and high speeds; the traffic rooted in the fact that about twenty-one percent of all metro area jobs are located along the 494 corridor. As a result, it was ranked as the seventeenth worst commute in the United States, which angered a lot of residents who wanted to know, "Only seventeenth?"

It took me fifteen minutes to find Jackson Janitorial and that was after I reached the intersection. It was located in a business park in the southeast quadrant of the crossroads; a sprawling one-story building that seemed more like a warehouse than an office. I parked and walked into the lobby. A woman sat behind a counter. Behind her were a lot of people sitting at a lot of desks.

"Hi," I said. "I'd like to speak to Mr. Jackson."

"Do you have an appointment?"

"No. Tell Kevin that it's McKenzie."

I purposely used the man's first name to give the impression that we were friends. It seemed to work because the woman smiled at me, left the counter, and maneuvered around her busy co-workers to an office on the far side of the room. The door was opened, and she poked her head inside. I didn't hear what was said, but it only took a moment before Jackson appeared in the doorway and looked at me over the receptionist's shoulder. He surprised me by giving me a tiny wave that suggested I should join him. I passed the receptionist who was returning to her perch behind the counter and stepped inside the office. Jackson was standing behind his desk, hands on his hips. He was wearing jeans and a dress shirt; a blue suit jacket was draped over the back of his chair. Apparently, no one wears a tie at work these days.

"Did you come to apologize?" Jackson wanted to know.

"Yes," I said. "I'm sorry I hit you in the face with my elbow after you tried to hit me in the face with your fist."

I was surprised to see Jackson grin.

"Apology accepted," he said.

Jackson pointed at a chair in front of his desk. I sat there while he seated himself behind the desk.

"I'm sorry," he told me. "I'm sorry for the way I acted when we first met; for accusing you. Meg and I—we've been having our issues lately and when I saw you and her together, I jumped to conclusions. And then Dave Seeley showed up. I should have known better than to accuse him. If Meg was cheating with someone, it wouldn't be with the egghead. It would probably be with one of those college kids from the dig; the ones working on the skeleton."

Wow. Does he think his wife is a zommy?

"It's none of my business," I said aloud.

"No, it's not and I'm sorry I dragged you into it."

"Like I said, it's none of my business, but if things aren't working out why don't you two go your separate ways?"

"Lots of reasons. Money reasons. Business reasons. The fact that I love the woman; that I adore the woman. We used to work together. Here. She would schedule deliveries, work with the truckers, that sort of thing. Her desk was just outside my door. Sometimes, she would step into the office and close the door because we had important business matters to discuss. Amused the hell out of my employees. One of them hung a dirty athletic sock on the doorknob like we were in a college dorm; I never found out who. But it was great. That is until her grandfather moved in with us and she quit her job to take care of him.

Suddenly, I wasn't measuring up, somehow. We started arguing, drifting apart; looking at other people like they might have the solution to all our problems. You don't need or want to hear any of this, though. You want to talk about the dinosaur, isn't that right? Meg told me last night that her grandfather is now willing to buy it back from the thieves."

"That's what I was told, too. Apparently, Andrew wants me to act as his representative."

"Is that why you're here? You think I have it?"

"Something I learned from the insurance companies"— *Really, you don't want him to know you've been checking up on him?*—"is that you have a relationship with Doyle Trucking. You've worked with them in the past. Not only that, Doyle was involved in a robbery where fifty thousand dollars' worth of your products were stolen."

"They weren't involved in that. The theft took place after they delivered the goods and were long gone from the storage facility."

"Not long gone."

"I know what you're thinking, McKenzie, only the Rochester cops cleared them and so did the insurance company. Turns out that the storage facility had been hit several times over a period of months and it hadn't done anything to improve security. At least that's what I was told when they handed me a check covering my losses."

"People's Financial?"

"No, I'm with Midwest Farmers Insurance Group."

MARYANNE! DAMMIT!

"McKenzie," Jackson said. "I can't speak for the guys over at Doyle Trucking. I don't know any of them personally. Maybe they were involved, maybe not—what do I know? Only if I had that dinosaur and it meant saving my marriage, I'd give it to Megan wrapped in a bow."

"It's probably moot, anyway. The Montana Highway Patrol

found the pickup truck that was carrying the *Ankylosaurus* skull only a few miles from the Canadian border."

"So, whoever stole it has already smuggled it out of the country. Does Megan know?"

"I doubt it. I just found out myself."

"Well, I'm not going to tell her. She's already mad enough at me. You tell her."

"Only if I have to."

I returned to my Mustang and a few minutes later I was trying to drive it out of the business park. It only took a couple of turns before I realized that I was being followed by the white SUV again.

"Are you kidding me?" I yelled at no one in particular.

I nearly stopped, my plan being to leave the car and confront the kid in the middle of the street. I decided against it, though, when my inner voice asked a simple question—*How the hell did he find you?* I couldn't possibly have been so careless as to let him follow me from the condo first to Doyle Trucking and then to Jackson Janitorial without noticing, could I? Hell no, I decided. Which meant . . .

It wasn't hard to lose Tony DeLuca in the heavy traffic around the interchange. Afterward, I headed east on I-494 at a speed that invited police intervention. Finally, I took the 34th Street exit that led toward Terminal 2—Humphrey, the second terminal of the Minneapolis St. Paul International Airport; the one named after Hubert H. Humphrey. I pulled up to the pumps at the Holiday Stationstore and started gassing up. I knew it was just a matter of time before Tony found me again, only I didn't need much, just a few minutes to search the bumpers, wheel wells, and undercarriage of the Mustang. I found it without too much effort, a small, black, magnetized metal box attached to the rear axle. I didn't bother to open the box; I knew what was inside.

My first thought was to drop the GPS transmitter into the trash, yet where was the fun in that? Instead, I put it in the pocket of my black golf jacket. After I filled my gas tank, I jumped onto Highway 5 and drove east past Terminal 1—Lindbergh, this one named after Charles Lindbergh; past Fort Snelling, and over the Mississippi River into St. Paul where Highway 5 became West Seventh Street. That's when Tony finally caught up to me. He immediately fell back, allowing a couple of cars to slide between us, and continued following in the same lane.

He's getting a little better at this.

It was when we reached the Science Museum of Minnesota in downtown St. Paul that things became a little dicey for him. That's because the museum was built into a high bluff overlooking the Mississippi River. There was a parking ramp off Kellogg Avenue on top of the bluff that was easy enough to access. Yet instead, I drove to the ramp that was attached to the museum. The problem for Tony was that its entrance was located at the very bottom of the bluff, which required several sharp, descending turns to reach. Tony couldn't possibly keep up without revealing himself—which he did. That was okay. I didn't mind that Tony knew that I knew that he knew where I was. I wanted him to know where I was.

ELEVEN

After finding a stall, I took the parking ramp elevator up to the top
level of the museum and followed a short corridor to its entrance.
Beyond the front doors there was a sprawling lobby featuring the
large Explore Store gift shop, the Mississippi River Exhibit, a
Ginkgo Coffeehouse and multiple ticket stalls. In the center of the
lobby was the skeleton of a ferocious-looking *Tyrannosaurus Rex*,
although the kids surrounding it didn't seem particularly frightened. It occurred to me, though, that positioning the skeleton of
the *Ankylosaurus* so that the two beasts could be imagined growl-
ing at each other would have been a great way to greet visitors.

Each level of the museum was two stories high and there
was an open atrium in the center. Exhibits on each of the levels flowed into each other, so it was easy to wander from one
to another. I bought a ticket and made my way down the long
staircase to the third level, which was dominated by dinosaurs,
lots of dinosaurs, mostly replicas like the *T. Rex* upstairs. There
were also quite a few skeletons that were composites of the dinosaur's actual bones plus casts of missing bones; the casts, I
read, were made by using precise molds of the bones from other
fossils and then adding them to complete the skeleton.

I had arranged to meet Angela Bjork at the bottom of the
stairs on the third level, except I had arrived early, so I started

wandering among the exhibits. I quickly learned that what Angela and the others were doing at the dig was not unusual at all by the standards of the hundred-and-seventeen-year-old museum. For example, the *Triceratops* that was on display—only one of four nearly complete skeletons in the world and by far the largest—was discovered by Linda Erickson and dug up by a science museum crew led by her husband, the famed paleontologist Bruce Erickson, in, you guessed it, the Hell Creek Formation in Montana.

A bunch of high school kids from Anoka, Minnesota, helped develop the Poison Creek Formation in Johnson County, Wyoming, which resulted in the excavation of no fewer than eleven dinosaur skeletons including a ninety-two-foot long *Diplodocus* and a "flexible lizard" called *Camptosaurus,* both on prominent display at the museum.

Jean Adams, a rancher in North Dakota, once brought a box of sixty-million-year-old fossils that she and her family collected to the University of Minnesota, which sent them to the Science Museum of Minnesota, which led to a thirty-year study of the crocodiles, turtles, snakes, lizards, frogs, birds, and vegetation at what is now known as the Wannagan Creek Quarry.

There sure are a lot of creeks with dinosaur bones in them, my inner voice suggested.

I returned to the bottom of the staircase to find Angela staring at her watch.

"I'm sorry to keep you waiting," I told her. My gesture took in a large part of the museum. "I was distracted."

"I know exactly what you mean and please, don't worry about it. This way."

I followed Angela into the Light Gallery that dealt with, well, light and shadows and colors. It was an interactive exhibit so visitors could bounce light off reflective coils, peer through glass to find distorted images, and play with layered rainbow lights. We didn't stop for any of that, though. Instead, Angela

led me to a door in the back with a sign that read PALEONTOL-
OGY LAB. She opened the door and we stepped inside.

You hear the word "lab" and you expect to see a pristine,
well-lit room painted white and inhabited by people dressed in
white coats bending over microscopes. The Paleontology Lab
of the Science Museum of Minnesota reminded me of an overstuffed garage with tools hanging from the walls, ladders, shelves
stacked with boxes and rolls of paper, and a half dozen worksta-
tions manned mostly by people of retirement age dressed as if
they were cleaning out their own garages.

"Angela," a woman said in greeting.

She was wearing an apron over a blue sweater and brushing the top of a fossil I couldn't have identified if you gave me
a month to work on it. There was another woman with gray
hair and three men, all of them with brushes and picks in their
hands and fossils in front of them. Their concentration was such
that they didn't give Angela and me much more than a head
nod in greeting.

"Seen the kids?" Angela asked.

The woman in the apron pointed at the floor with her brush.

"Thank you," Angela said.

A few moments later, she was leading me to the levels directly beneath the exhibit halls. Along the way, I asked, "Who
were those people?"

"Volunteers," Angela said. "They're helping to prepare fossils
for research and exhibit; mostly stabilization work to keep the
fossils intact, picking, brushing, that sort of thing."

I nodded as if I knew exactly what she was talking about.

The lower levels were where the museum kept its collection
vaults; rows and rows of white cabinets containing literally
hundreds of thousands of fossils all kept under strict climate
control. And yes, the walls, the floor, and the cabinets were immaculate and white. Across from the vault was another lab, this
one very long and filled with gray-green cabinets and counters

and matching rolling chairs. It was as cluttered and messy as a frat house.

We walked the length of it, passing a four-wheel cart. On top of the cart was a *Prosaurolophus* fossil, a duck-billed dinosaur that roamed Alberta, Canada, during the Cretaceous period. I knew because of the handwritten note attached to it. On another counter we passed were the pieces of an ancient bison skull that were being held together with string. There were other fossils mixed with a few stuffed dinosaur toys including a *Stegosaurus*, a *Pterodactyl*, and a *Brontosaurus* the size of a small child. They could have been items on a supermarket shelf for all Angela was concerned. As for me . . .

This has to be one of the coolest things you've ever seen, my inner voice told me. I would have said the words out loud, only I was afraid of appearing uncool.

At the far end of the lab was a large thigh-high table. On top of the table was what looked to me like a long slab of rocks and soil. Two young people were jabbing at it; around them were plastic buckets filled with rocks and dirt. I heard them talking.

"I wish you would leave it alone, Simon," the woman said.

"He's a jerk," Simon said. "You gotta know that."

"I don't know that."

They stopped speaking when Angela and I approached.

"How's it going?" Angela asked.

"Fine," Simon said, although his tone of voice suggested otherwise.

The young woman looked up toward the very high ceiling and rolled her eyes.

The only person that Angela had described when she told me her story was Winter Billock, saying she was petite with short red hair, and betting that she would be carded in every bar and club she walked into until she was at least forty-five. The description was accurate. If Winter topped five feet tall it was because of the shoes she wore; if she weighed more than one hundred pounds it was because she had lead in those shoes. Plus, she had an open, almost childlike face. She reminded me of a doll. Not Barbie, but Skipper, Barbie's baby sister.

"This is McKenzie," Angela said by way of introduction. "McKenzie, this is Winter Billock."

Winter smiled brightly and held out her hand.

"Hi," she said. "Professor Bjork told us all about you."

I took her hand and for a brief and wholly shameful moment, I hoped that she thought I was a zaddy.

"She said you were going to help us find the *Ankylosaurus* skull," Winter added.

"Going to try, anyway," I said. I turned to the young man. "You must be Simon Stevens."

He seemed surprised that I knew his name. "Hey," he said without offering his hand.

"I'm hoping you two can answer a few questions for me," I said.

"I didn't see anything," Simon said.

"If I can," Winter said.

"Then you first," I said. "Excuse us."

Winter gave a cautious glance over her shoulder as I led her back down the length of the lab to where we could speak privately, halting near the *Prosaurolophus* fossil. We commandeered a couple of rolling chairs and sat facing each other. Winter was the first to speak.

"Mr. McKenzie . . ."

"McKenzie is fine," I told her.

"Then you must call me Winter; not that you wouldn't have, anyway."

"I don't understand."

"Most people automatically call me by my first name like we call children by their first names. Even in class. When professors call on students it's usually by their last names. Johnson. Freeman. Sometimes, Mr. Johnson; Ms. Freeman. With me, though, it's nearly always Winter."

"I'm sorry to hear that."

"McKenzie, I'd pay serious money if I could be six inches taller."

"My father used to say that dynamite comes in small packages."

"I don't want to blow anything up. I just want to be treated like an adult."

"I'll do my best, Ms. Billock."

"Thank you. McKenzie, what do you want to know?"

I told her.

Except for some minor variations, her story was nearly identical to what Angela had told me and what the Powder River County sheriff put into his report.

"At the risk of insulting you—"

Apparently, Winter knew what I was going to ask because she interrupted, saying, "I was sleeping alone. If I was going to hook up with someone, it sure as hell wouldn't be in a tent surrounded by my college professors." Winter slapped her hand over her mouth as if she was trying to catch the words she had just spoken. When she lowered it, she added, "Not that I would, anyway."

"Tell me about Jordan Wall," I said.

"Oh God." Winter looked up and away and around. When her eyes settled on me again, she said, "We've been seeing each other. We started seeing each other at the dig and then he went home and I stayed, but when I came back here we started seeing each other again. I don't know why that's a big deal."

"Who says it's a big deal?"

"Simon for one. He thinks—he says that Jordan is just using me."

Geez, I hope not.

"After Jordan left the dig, did you two keep in touch?" I asked. "Did you call each other?"

"Text mostly."

"Did you tell Jordan when the team would be transporting the *Ankylosaurus* skull home?"

"No. I mean yes. I mean—I told him when I was coming home; when we were all coming home and that we would be bringing the *Ankylosaurus* back with us in a couple of trucks, but that wasn't a secret, was it?"

"Did you tell him that you would be loading the skull onto the pickup truck that Tuesday?"

"I didn't know we were loading it on Tuesday. I thought it would be later in the week; we were scheduled to abandon the dig on Saturday. I spoke to him that Tuesday. I spoke to him just before I went to bed. I told him that we had loaded the skull and that it wouldn't be long before I was coming home."

"That was . . ."

"Ten, ten thirty. Something like that. McKenzie, you don't think that Jordan could have had anything to do with this, do you? I mean how could he have?"

"Right now I'm just trying to find out where everyone was that night and what they were doing. I don't know anything about Jordan."

"If you ask Simon about him, he'll probably say nasty things."

"Why is that?"

"He's jealous. Simon is my friend. I love Simon, I really do. He's so sweet. But—but I'm just so tired of being treated like a child. Jordan treats me like a woman."

So we're back to that. Move on.

"For what it's worth, I spoke to Andrew Cooke last evening," I said.

"Oh, I love that old man. He is so cool."

"He said he's willing to pay for the safe return of the *Ankylosaurus* skull."

"Pay who?"

"The people that stole it."

Winter gave it a few beats before she replied.

"If I knew who that was I'd tell you."

I gave her my card.

"You never know," I told her.

Simon was using a small pick on the sandstone slab when we returned; Angela was rummaging through the plastic buckets. I saw her lick a rock—at least it looked like a rock to me—and set it on the counter.

"Mr. Stevens," I said. "May I trouble you for a moment of your time?"

"I didn't see anything," he repeated.

"Just a moment."

He set his pick on the counter and wiped his hands with a rag. He moved past Winter.

"Simon, please," she said. "Smile for me."

Simon smiled, but I don't think his heart was in it.

We ended up sitting on the same chairs near the *Prosaurolophus.*

"How's it going?" I asked.

"Fine. McKenzie, I know what you're going to ask me, but honestly, I don't know anything. I didn't see anything."

"Bear with me," I told him and then asked pretty much the same questions as the Powder River County sheriff had. Simon's answers were nearly identical to the ones I read in the incident report except, unlike with the written word, I could hear regret in his voice.

"Did you tell anyone about the dig?" I asked. "About the *Ankylosaurus*?"

"A lot of people. My parents; my friends."

"How about after it was decided they were going to transport the *Ankylosaurus* home?"

"Herschel. He was there when Professors Bjork and DeLuca first discovered it. He was curious about what was going on and we kept in touch a little bit."

"The day you loaded the skull onto the truck . . ."

"Nobody. Not Tuesday or Wednesday, either."

"Okay." I handed him as card, as well. "If you think of anything . . ."

He took the card and stared at it.

"Simon?" I asked.

"I messed up."

"Excuse me?"

"I did something unforgivable."

Simon shook his head even as he lowered it so he could stare at his shoes.

My God, he's going to confess!

"McKenzie, when Winter screamed, I stayed in my tent. I didn't—I didn't rush out to help her."

Never mind.

"Did she ever say anything about that?" I asked.

"It's never come up in conversation."

"Then she probably doesn't hold it against you. Listen, kid, I'm going to give you some advice whether you want to hear it or not. Play the long game. Be the woman's friend—woman, not girl. Be her friend through thick and thin. Don't criticize. Don't lecture. Don't give advice unless she asks for it. Don't threaten or cajole or seduce. Just be there for her. Always and forever. If things eventually turn your way, fabulous. If not, you get to see your friend being happy."

"Yeah? Did that work for you?"

I flashed on Shelby Dunston's face.

"As a matter of fact, it did," I said.

Dr. David Seeley was chatting with both Angela and Winter when we returned to the sandstone slab. How he entered the lab without my seeing him I couldn't say. He turned to face me.

"McKenzie," he said. "Still on the job, I see. Any good news?"

"I don't know if it's good news or not but Andrew Cooke has agreed to pay a ransom for the safe return of the skull."

"Yes, Megan told me."

"Did she?"

Seeley didn't like the question. He looked at me as if he thought I was judging him, which of course, I was.

"I'm concerned," he said. "We would all like to see the *Ank* returned, only I worry for the reputation of the museum."

"In my experience, these things are rarely reported."

"In your experience? You've done this sort of thing before?"

"You're referring to the ransoming of stolen art?"

Seeley nodded.

"Let's just say I've seen it done," I said.

"Without anyone knowing about it?"

What exactly is he asking you?

"Without anyone knowing," I said.

"That's a good thing," Seeley said. "I mean for the reputation of everyone involved."

"Partly it's about reputation. Partly it's because the parties paying the ransom don't want to encourage future thefts."

"Yes, yes. I can see that Angela chooses her friends well."

"I don't know about that."

I meant the remark as a joke on me, yet his expression suggested that Seeley thought I was judging him, again.

"For what it's worth . . ." I waved at the lab and quickly mentioned all of the exhibits I had seen that afternoon. "This is wonderful."

"Yes, we think so, too. You know, we're always looking for support. There are eight different membership levels you can join."

"I'm going to do that. Thank you for your time, Dr. Seeley. Professor Bjork. Mr. Stevens." I looked at Winter and smiled. "Thank you, Ms. Billock."

She smiled back as if I had just given her a compliment.

As I was walking away, I heard Winter say, "I need to go, too."

"I can walk you to the Green Line," Simon said.

"I have a ride coming."

"Okay."

"Why don't you join us?" Winter asked. "Jordan and I can give you a lift back to campus. It's certainly better than taking the light rail."

"No, I'm good."

"Are you sure?"

"You know what? I'd appreciate the ride. Sure your BF won't mind?"

"Not at all."

The long game, kid, my inner voice said. *Play the long game.*

A few minutes later, I was in my Mustang and pulling out of the parking ramp. Tony DeLuca was waiting for me. He didn't even pretend to be worried that I knew he was there, moving right up to my rear bumper when I stopped at the intersection of West Seventh Street and Kellogg Boulevard. Straight ahead was the ramp that led to I-94 and Minneapolis. Hang a right, though . . .

Oh hell, my inner voice told me. *You've been putting this off for long enough.*

TWELVE

DeLuca's was an old-school Italian restaurant. Old-school in that it was dimly lit and all the tables and booths were draped with white tablecloths; wax candles were burning in the center of each of them. A small bar was in the corner with wooden stools where customers could linger until their tables were ready. The waitstaff was dressed in immaculate black slacks and skirts and starched white shirts. The music playing on invisible speakers was strictly Italian-American: Frank and Dean and Tony and Louis Prima, Buddy DeFranco, Mario Lanza, Perry Como, Vic Damone, Al Martino, even some Dion, Frankie Valli, and Lou Christie. There wasn't a TV in sight.

It was late afternoon when I arrived; the dinner rush was just starting to ramp up. A woman clutching several menus to her chest greeted me at the door.

"Good evening," she said. "Do you have a reservation?"

"No. I'm here to see Mr. DeLuca."

The hostess tilted her head. "May I have your name?" she asked.

"Just tell him that McKenzie is here."

"No." The voice came from behind me. "I'll do it."

I turned to see Tony DeLuca. I had given him the slip in a tangled intersection of freeways and highways that even the traffic guys on the radio called "Spaghetti Junction." I had not seen him in my rearview when I took the Concord exit off Highway 52 and drove into the heart of South St. Paul, but he must have known where I was heading. He was not happy about it.

"McKenzie . . ." He spoke my name like it was an obscenity. The hostess stepped away, clearly not wanting to hear what next came out of Tony's mouth. I, on the other hand, was all ears.

"This is not a good idea," he said.

"Tell me, Chef—do you want to keep following me around or get back to the kitchen?"

"This is, this is . . . Dammit. Come with me."

Tony led me deep into the restaurant. Before we hit the kitchen, though, he hung a right and I followed him to an unmarked door. He rested his hand on the knob yet turned to look at me before opening it.

"Wait here," he said.

A moment later, he stepped inside, closing the door behind him. I moved close and tried to eavesdrop while pretending not to. Tony Bennett was singing in the background. In between the lyrics to "Once Upon a Time" I heard a voice shout, "He followed you here?" Another voice answered, "No, I followed him." A few seconds later, the door opened, and Tony bade me enter.

Behind the office was a long desk made of dark wood with a large leather chair positioned behind it; photographs of famous and semi-famous personages in non-matching frames both large and small covered most of the walls. In front of the desk, I found a man sitting at a table that seemed identical to the ones inside the main restaurant right down to the tablecloth, candle, napkins, and silverware including an imposing steak knife. He was dressed in a perfect dark gray suit, white shirt, and a black tie; a pink carnation was attached to his lapel. Detective Jean Shipman had told me that he was seventy-two years old and he looked it, with a wrinkled face, neck, and hands. He was wearing a gray toupee.

"McKenzie," he said. "How good of you to come."

"How good of you to invite me."

Neither of us smiled at the lie.

"I'm Martin DeLuca," he said.

He gestured at the chair across the table from him. I sat. Tony stood behind and to DeLuca's left, his hands folded over his belt buckle. The whole scene was playing like something you'd see in a gangster movie directed by Martin Scorsese or Francis Ford Coppola or even Brian De Palma. My inner voice started cracking wise about tropes and clichés, only I beat it down. DeLuca sure as hell didn't think he was a cliché and I wasn't about to call him one.

"What can I do for you, McKenzie?" DeLuca asked.

"First, you can tell me why you're having me followed."

"Am I having you followed?"

I gestured at the kid with my chin. I promised that I wouldn't blow his cover and I didn't.

"He's not bad," I said. "But you should know that a one-car surveillance is impossible." I reached into the pocket of my sports coat for the black metal box and tossed it in the center of the table. "Even if he has help."

DeLuca made a production of looking at the box, at Tony, and finally back at me.

"I know you, McKenzie," he said. "You used to be a cop; a pretty good one, too, I'm told. Then you sold your badge to collect a reward on an embezzler. Now you do favors for friends, some of them of dubious character."

"The favors or the friends?"

"McKenzie . . ."

"I know you, too, Mr. DeLuca."

"What do you know?"

"I know what the Major Crimes Unit of the St. Paul Police Department knows."

"If the MCU knew anything, I'd be preparing to have my dinner in Oak Park Heights instead of my own place."

"There's knowing and then there's proving what you know."

"The authorities can't verify any wrongdoing on my part, yet they continue to make scurrilous remarks behind my back. Perhaps I should sue them for defamation."

"Yeah, you do that, but first, tell me why you're having me followed."

"Rumor has it you're looking for a dinosaur skull."

"Why is that a concern of yours?"

"I would very much like to know where it is."

"Do you expect me to lead you to it?"

DeLuca didn't say if he did or didn't.

"I understand your interest," I said. "The skull is, after all, worth a great deal of money. I've heard a figure as high as six million dollars being bandied about."

DeLuca locked his eyes on mine as if he were daring me to look away.

"Is that why you're looking for it?" he asked. "The money?"

I didn't trust DeLuca as far as I could throw his restaurant which, let's face it, wasn't very far. Yet I couldn't think of a good reason to lie to him.

"No," I said.

"You're doing it as a favor for a friend."

"That's right."

"I don't believe you."

About six replies flashed through my head. I picked the one where I raised my hand a few inches and let it fall indifferently onto the arm of the chair.

DeLuca stared some more. Finally, he said, "I want the dinosaur returned to the University of Minnesota."

I could guess the answer, yet I asked anyway—"Why?"

"Professor Ashley DeLuca. Know her?"

"Know of her. We haven't met."

"Let me tell you a story. My brother's daughter, Sophia, was raped when she was twenty years old by the son of her mother's best friend. We did not learn this until Sophia was five months pregnant. My brother and I had every intention of killing the rapist. Sophia and Sophia's mother, my sister-in-law, begged us not to. They were both very insistent. Against my better judgment, we acquiesced to their wishes. However, we made it abundantly clear to Sophia's rapist that he was to stay as far away from her as humanly possible for the rest of his life. Four months later, Sophia gave birth to a baby girl. Ashley grew up to be the most beautiful, most intelligent, most considerate, most caring woman I know. Seven years ago, while Ashley was away to college, Sophia died of cancer. It was then that Sophia's rapist"—I noticed DeLuca refused to give the man a name—"reached out to Ashley. He said they should be family. Ashley declined. He was persistent. She was persistent in her rejections. He refused to listen. Shortly after, he was hit by a car while jaywalking. McKenzie, if you want to kill someone, I suggest you use a car. Pedestrian fatalities that are not directly linked to drunk driving are rarely prosecuted."

Wow!

"The point being," DeLuca added, "my family is everything to me. There's not much left of it. My brother's gone. So is my sister-in-law. All that remains is me, Ashley"—he threw a thumb over his shoulder—"and Ashley's brother, Tony. Tell me, McKenzie, what does your family mean to you? Hmm? Do any of them jaywalk?"

I've never been one to intimidate people or threaten them with bodily harm. Instead, friendly persuasion was my preferred weapon of choice. Only I didn't think DeLuca would respond well to that. More likely he would view it as a sign of weakness; an indication that he could threaten my family; that he could do whatever he desired to my family without fear of consequences. I decided those assumptions needed to be addressed in no uncertain terms.

With that in mind—I lunged toward DeLuca, grabbed his

steak knife, and plunged it as hard as I could into the table directly in front of him. Either the wood was soft or the knife was far stronger than one might expect because the blade did not snap. Instead, it sank a full inch into the table. Meanwhile, DeLuca recoiled in fear. His arms came up to protect himself as he fell backward. He would have hit the floor along with his chair if not for the quickness of Tony, who was in time to grab his granduncle and keep him from falling.

I left the knife standing upright in the table and returned to my seat. Teddy Roosevelt was in my head. "Speak softly and carry a big stick," he once said. I took his advice and spoke quietly as if nothing had happened.

"As I promised my friend, I intend to recover the *Ankylosaurus* and return it to its rightful owners. That can only be good for your grandniece. Unless you're the one who stole it. Did you steal it?"

I might have said more, only I was interrupted by a shrill voice shouting, "What the hell is going on?"

A woman was standing just inside the doorway. She quickly closed the door—I could only imagine what the restaurant patrons outside must have been thinking—and moved to the old man's side. Together with Tony, she helped hold the old man until he was steady on his feet. She glared first at the knife sticking out of the top of the table and then at me.

"Who are you?" she shouted.

"My name is McKenzie."

"Angie's friend? What is happening?"

"Are you Professor Ashley DeLuca?" I asked.

Her eyes grew wide at the sound of her own name.

"What is happening?" she repeated.

"Nothing, nothing, my dear," DeLuca said. He brushed Tony and Ashley's hands away and bent to pick up his chair. They tried to help him, only he wouldn't have it. "It's okay, it's okay. McKenzie and I were just coming to an understanding."

He adjusted his pink carnation and settled into the now up-right chair.

"What understanding?" Ashley wanted to know. "What have you done, Martin? I told you to stay out of this."

If he was listening to her, DeLuca didn't show it. He reached out and pulled the knife from the table—it took some effort—and set it next to his napkin.

"As you were saying, Mr. McKenzie," he said.

Mister, he called you. You should take that as a conciliatory gesture.

"Mr. DeLuca," I said, "have you ever had any dealings with Doyle Trucking?"

"No, I don't believe so."

"How about Jackson Janitorial?"

"I buy my cleaning supplies from Jackson, why do you ask?"

"Jackson Janitorial is owned by the grandson-in-law of Andrew Cooke."

"Andrew?" Ashley asked.

"Mr. Cooke owns the land where the *Ankylosaurus* skull was discovered."

"I told you about him," Ashley said.

DeLuca raised his hand as a sign for her to keep quiet.

"Mr. Cooke has announced that he is willing to pay for the safe return of his dinosaur, no questions asked," I said.

"So I've been informed," DeLuca said.

I glanced at Tony; decided to throw him another bone.

"Good for you," I said.

He smiled in return.

"Are you willing to make that deal?" DeLuca asked.

"It's not my deal to make. I'm merely acting as a go-between."

"To return the dinosaur to the University of Minnesota."

"As well as Macalester College and the Science Museum of Minnesota, yes."

"It would seem that we have the same goal then."

"Will you stop having me followed now?"

"You were following him?" Ashley wanted to know.

DeLuca waved his hand at her again.

"I hope you will keep me abreast of future developments," he said. "It is possible that I might be of use to you. I have many contacts."

"I shall keep that in mind, sir."

I stood up.

DeLuca stood up.

We shook hands across the table.

I headed for the door, had a thought, paused, and turned back.

"Professor DeLuca," I said. "May I have a moment of your time?"

"Dinner, drinks, whatever you like," DeLuca said, "on the house."

I stepped outside the office. Ashley reluctantly followed me.

I decided I could use a drink but not at DeLuca's. I asked Ashley to accompany me, and together we stepped out of the restaurant. Once we were outside and moving along the sidewalk, Ashley said, "Mr. McKenzie, I have no idea where to begin. What was going on in there? What did Martin do?"

"Like he said, we reached an understanding. I must tell you, though, the man has a flair for the dramatic."

"You have no idea. The stories I could tell . . ." She shook her head as if deciding that wasn't a good idea. "But the knife . . ."

"Just playing my part in the drama. I'm terribly sorry about your mother. I lost my mother when I was young, too. It must be very hard, even now."

"Martin told you that?"

I nodded.

"What else did he tell you?"

"He told me about your father."

"Why would he do that, I wonder?"

"He wanted to impress me with how he died."

"By getting hit by a bus?"

"Your father was hit by a bus?"

"He was staring at the screen of his smartphone and stepped into the street without looking."

I started laughing and then stopped myself.

"I'm sorry; I don't mean to be disrespectful. Only it's like I said, that old man has a flair for the dramatic."

"McKenzie, I spoke with Angie this morning at the U. She told me that you were interviewing everyone who was at the dig when the *Ank* was stolen. She also told me about Mr. Cooke's offer to buy back the skull. Do you think that will happen?"

"It depends on who stole it."

I explained that there was a real possibility that it had already been ensconced in someone's vault. By then we had reached the Black Sheep Coffee Cafe. I would have preferred a bar, yet decided caffeine would have to do for now. I asked Ashley if I could buy her a coffee and she agreed. A few minutes later, we were sitting next to each other on two overstuffed orange chairs and sipping from actual white cups instead of cardboard.

I asked Ashley all the questions that I had asked everyone else. Her answers didn't tell me anything I didn't already know. She insisted that she hadn't told anyone about when they were transporting the *Ankylosaurus* home, especially her granduncle and brother.

"They didn't know anything," she said then repeated herself. "They didn't know anything"—in case I wasn't paying attention the first time.

I saved one question for the end and finally let her have it.

"Dr. Nicholas Larsen thinks highly of you," I said.

"Does he?"

"He told me that you have shown genuine promise."

"Asshole."

"Is he?"

"Ha."

Ashley took a long sip of her coffee and very deliberately set the cup on its saucer.

"McKenzie, you seem to already know so much about my personal life," she said. "What more can I tell you?"

"I'm concerned with the timing of the theft; when and where everyone was."

"You want to know where I was?"

"No, I want to know where Larsen was."

"He was with me when Winter started screaming and the shots were fired."

"Okay."

"Should I tell you what we were doing?"

"No, I'm good."

"McKenzie, I made friends at the dig, and I don't make friends easily. Angela is now my friend. Winter is still a child . . ."

She would hate to hear that.

"But I consider her a friend because of what happened that night. And Gary Phillips. Have you met Professor Phillips?"

"Yes."

"I consider him a friend, too. Dr. Larsen, though. He's only a means to an end. The end being professional advancement, and before you dismiss me as an opportunistic whore, know that it's at his—shall we call it a suggestion?—and not mine."

"Does your granduncle know?"

"Of course not. If he did, there's a very good chance that Martin might have him killed."

For a moment, I flashed on the death of Ashley's father while my inner voice pondered a thought—*I wonder who was driving that bus.*

I was driving toward Rickie's with the intention of mooching a free drink off my wife when my cell phone started singing to me. I used my onboard computer to answer it.

"McKenzie," Special Agent Linda Ambrose said. "I'm sorry it took so long to get back to you. I was in the field."

"A long day?"

"A productive day. You'll probably hear all about it. I know the assistant U.S. attorney is going to hold a press conference. Brian says you have something for me."

"I do. Can we meet? I know a nice bar near the FBI field office."

"So do I but honestly, McKenzie, I'm fried. Can it wait until tomorrow?"

"Sure."

"Meet me at Caribou Coffee first thing in the morning."

"Nine?"

"That's your idea of first thing?"

"Eight?"

"See you there."

Dammit!

Still, I told myself, there was another place where I could get a drink, although I knew it would be costly; a place I had been meaning to visit since I first spoke with Angela Bjork and learned about the theft. I put it off for the same reason I had delayed the meeting with DeLuca—I wasn't sure what I would find.

"Well, no time like the present," I told myself.

The Phillips neighborhood in the center of Minneapolis was a contradiction. It had some of the city's oldest and most historic buildings as well as some of the newest. It was home to many immigrant families as well as young professionals. It featured plenty of top restaurants, coffee shops, and parks alongside low-income housing, slum apartments, and crack houses—yes, they still exist. The schools were rated above average, the politics tended to be liberal, and most of the residents were less than thirty-five years old. It also had a violent crime rate that was 962 percent above the national average.

In the center of the neighborhood was a bar. I knew it was a bar because I had been there before, although I wondered who else knew. There was no name above the door, no neon lights flashing the logos of pasteurized beers from St. Louis or Milwaukee; no sign saying it was open for business or that customers were welcome. Only a black-and-white notification taped to the window that read NO FIREARMS ARE ALLOWED ON THESE PREMISES, which was the owner's way of saying if you carry a gun inside, they just might shoot you as you walk through the door. I am not exaggerating.

It was dark inside the bar. The lights were kept low, and a thick curtain had been pulled across the one and only window. There were a dozen people sitting in old-fashioned booths, the kind with high backs that you can't see over, and at small wooden tables. Most of them were male; all of them white. They looked at me with appraising eyes when I entered, as if wondering if I was trouble, how much, and whether they could handle it. A younger man sat alone at a table in the center of the bar with an unobstructed view of the front and back doors. He held a tablet with both hands, yet was looking over the top of it at me. There was a folded *Minnesota Star Tribune* on the table within easy reach. I knew the newspaper was hiding a gun just as it had been the last time I was there. I slowly unzipped my jacket and spread it open so he could see I wasn't carrying.

"You sonuvabitch," a voice called out.

I followed the voice to a booth directly across from the young man's table. A man was sitting there, his hands flat on the table; his eyes glaring at me. Between his hands there were two cell phones and a closed laptop. He was wearing a red dress shirt, jeans, and black cowboy boots. There was a half-filled glass of beer next to the laptop.

"El Cid, my lord," I said.

"Fuck that, McKenzie. You got balls coming into my place, again."

"Your place? I didn't know you were the owner, Cid. I thought it was just where you hung out. You know, like the people who work remotely from coffeehouses; where they write their books or poetry or whatever it is that they do that takes up most of the day."

"Still as funny as ever—not."

The young man continued to watch every move I made, so I tried not to make too many of them and none that were quick. In return, he kept both hands on the tablet.

"Don't tell me you're still holding a grudge after all this time," I said.

"Why would I hold a grudge? Just because you gave me up to the cops?"

"You told me that you weren't afraid of the cops."

"I'm not. You'll notice that I didn't spend five minutes in jail. Men in my line of work aren't afraid of the police. We can always make deals with the police. Do you know who we're afraid of?"

"Yeah, and I am sorry about that, Cid, I really am."

"Fucking IRS." He waved at the bar. "I work so hard to keep my visible assets to a minimum to avoid the IRS, but now I'm on their fucking radar. You don't think the IRS hasn't been studying my returns with a goddamned magnifying glass?"

"I had nothing to do with that."

"If you hadn't come here looking for the fucking Jade Lily, none of that would have happened."

"Cid." I gestured at the empty bench across from him. "May I?"

"Fuck," he said.

I took that as a yes and slid into the booth. A bartender appeared. He looked at the kid. The kid nodded and the bartender approached the booth.

"Maker's Mark on the rocks," I said.

The bartender glanced at Cid. Cid shook his head and the bartender left.

Cid—aka El Cid—aka David Wicker—I had asked him once, "How does one get the nickname of a Spanish lord?"

"I don't know," Cid had replied. "People just started calling me that. Perhaps they were impressed by my regal bearing."

I liked the answer, yet I knew it was a lie. "El Cid" was a nickname that Wicker gave himself, pilfering it from Rodrigo Díaz de Vivar, the Spanish knight and mercenary credited with driving the Moors out of Spain in the eleventh century. To survive, much less flourish in his line of work, a fence must be able to negotiate with the most dangerous sellers as well as the least scrupulous buyers. The fear of betrayal, of being ripped off, of being arrested, was always present so it was important to demonstrate a certain amount of fearlessness. El Cid—the Lord—was an affectation, just like his barroom office; just like the barely concealed muscle pretending to watch videos on his tablet while carefully watching us. It was designed to make associates believe that he was someone not to be trifled with.

The bartender returned and set the drink in front of me. I handed him a fifty and said, "Keep the change."

Cid smiled and shook his head.

"All right, McKenzie," he said. "You didn't come here to throw your money around. What can I do for you?"

"As the most accomplished fence between Chicago and the West Coast . . ."

"I prefer the term 'facilitator' and why bring Chicago into it?"

"Cid, what can you tell me about dinosaur fossils?"

Cid leaned against the wooden back of the booth.

"Dinosaurs?" he asked.

"Specifically, an *Ankylosaurus* skull pilfered from a dig in southeastern Montana a month ago."

Cid stared at me, yet the way his eyes lost focus, I knew that it wasn't me he was seeing but the world as he knew it.

"Dinosaur fossils," he repeated, his voice soft as if he was speaking to himself. "I know there's a market . . ."

Cid's eyes sharpened and he leaned forward.

"Nothing, McKenzie," he said. "I'm embarrassed to say I don't know what you're talking about."

"Yeah, well, it's new to me, too. I've been treating it like an art heist."

"As well you should."

"It's entirely possible the skull was stolen on commission. It's just as possible that the thieves were hired to acquire the item and hand it over to a facilitator, like yourself. Possibly the facilitator had a buyer lined up. Possibly he intended to place the skull in a vault for a few years and then secure a buyer. Possibly he meant to hide it until the statute of limitations expired, pretend to discover it while hiking through the Badlands, and sell it at auction. Possibly he meant to sell it back to the insurance companies and now is stuck with it because the insurance companies are fighting over who's liable for the loss."

"Possibly," Cid said.

"Or it could be amateur night in Montana and now that they have the skull, the thieves have no idea what to do with it."

"Amateurs?"

"All we can be sure of is that they knew how to steal a pickup truck."

"I could do that when I was twelve," Cid admitted.

"It's possible that they might reach out."

"To me?"

"Who else?"

"There are a few others." Cid shook his head slowly. "McKenzie, I'm aware that there's a thriving market for dinosaur fossils only . . ." He gestured at the table between us. "Nothing's crossed my desk."

"It's possible, maybe even probable, that the skull has already been smuggled into Canada."

"I know people in Canada."

"I'm sure you do. Do you think you could reach out to them for me?"

"Why would I? Why am I even giving you the time of day?"

"I have been tasked by the original owner of the skull to act as his representative. He is offering a reward for the safe return of his property, no questions asked."

"That doesn't answer my question."

"How much commission does a facilitator usually make to match a seller with a buyer?" I asked.

"How much is your client willing to pay?"

"The amount is subject to negotiation."

Cid leaned against the back of the booth again and crossed his arms. I took a long sip of the bourbon while he studied me.

"I know you, McKenzie," he said. "Is this going to be a straight-up business transaction or are you looking for retribution; looking to put someone in prison or worse?"

"My client is an old man. He's dying. I'm told he might not make it to Christmas. He wants to get his dinosaur back before he passes."

Cid studied me some more.

"I'll see what I can do. You at the same number?"

I nodded.

"Anything else?"

"What do you know about a guy named Martin DeLuca?" I asked.

"Martin DeLuca from South St. Paul?"

"Yeah."

"He's a poser."

Like you? my inner voice asked.

"Is that all he does—pose?" I asked aloud.

"He's been involved in a few jackings; money laundering; some extortion. Nothing big, although he likes to pretend it's big."

"Do you think he could pull off a gag like this?"

"I don't think he'd have the wit for this kind of job. On the other hand . . . I don't know. Let me ask around."

"Thank you, Cid."

"McKenzie, don't fuck with me. I mean it. Way I look at it, your money's just as good as the next guy's, but if this becomes a police matter . . ."

"I'll keep you out of it."

"That's what you said last time."

THIRTEEN

The next morning, Special Agent Linda Ambrose and I sat at the same table as we had when we first met. Apparently, she liked her raspberry white chocolate scones because she had another one with her mocha. She asked me what I had been up to in the past few days. Instead of answering, I asked her a question.

"Are there bands of rustlers roaming the Great Plains in search of dinosaur fossils?"

"That sounds somewhat fanciful. To answer your question, though—yes, McKenzie, there are. More often than not, they simply buy fossils from those individuals who scour public and private land looking for product to sell. That's basically what our friends in Salt Lake City did. Occasionally, they'll secure fossils from individuals who shoplift . . ."

"Shoplift? Now who's being fanciful?"

"Who acquire the fossils at authorized digs and keep them for themselves instead of handing them over to their sponsors. There have also been incidents, although uncommon, of gangs that ransacked digs the moment the owners' backs were turned. The theft of your *Ankylosaurus* skull, I admit, was slightly more sophisticated. Your turn."

I told Ambrose that Andrew Cooke had agreed to buy back the stolen skull. I also told her that I had carefully spread the word among all the people who were at the dig when it was stolen. Her expression suggested that she already guessed why I had done such a thing yet kept the knowledge to herself. Finally, I told her what Ben Dirnberger told me about the Montana Highway Patrol discovering the stolen Ford F-150 near the Canadian border.

"So, the fossil could have been smuggled into Canada anytime during the past thirty days," Ambrose said. "Probably sooner instead of later. Probably that very night."

"That's my guess, too."

"I can give the Mounties a shout. The border crossing is in Saskatchewan, so I'll contact the Regina field office. I know people up there. Only McKenzie, it looks like the *Ankylosaurus* has slipped beyond our reach."

"You think so? I guess we'll just have to lure it back, then."

Ambrose sipped her coffee, giving it a good ten beats before setting her cup down and looking at me across the table.

"I see it," she said.

"Do you?"

"Be very, very careful, McKenzie. What you're planning is illegal."

I raised my right hand.

"I promise Special Agent Ambrose, I personally will not be caught doing anything illegal."

She smiled. It was a soft, knowing kind of smile as if she could see snippets of the future.

"You have my number now," Ambrose said. "Feel free to call when you're ready."

"Thank you, Linda," I said.

The "something special" that Shelby Dunston had planned for dinner Friday night turned out to be meatloaf Wellington—a meatloaf wrapped in puff pastry and served with a rich red wine sauce, fingerling potatoes, and green beans with capers.

I had to admit it was very good and immediately had me wondering what I was going to cook next month to top it.

We were sitting at the dining-room table in the house where Bobby grew up, where I practically grew up, Bobby's mother all but adopting me after my own mother passed when I was twelve years old. She told me there were things my jarhead father simply couldn't teach me, "jarhead" being a reference to the fact that the old man was a former marine and therefore devoid of human feeling, which wasn't even close to being true, although he was a stern and taciturn fellow. Bobby bought the house from his parents when they retired to their lake home in Wisconsin, and Nina and I were frequent visitors, coming to dinner at least once every other month while Bobby and Shelby came to our place during the months in between. Originally, the meals were just an excuse to get together, yet they had evolved into an ongoing duel between Shelby and me. The meatloaf Wellington put her ahead.

Throughout the meal I kept checking my smartwatch while pretending not to. I didn't think anyone noticed.

"I had a brief but interesting conversation with Jean Shipman the other day," Bobby said.

"Really?" I answered. "What about?"

"What about," Bobby muttered. "McKenzie, my people never keep secrets from me."

"As far as you know," Shelby said with a smile.

"Let's just say they don't keep secrets from me the way my wife and daughters do. DeLuca? From South St. Paul? Really, McKenzie, he's involved in your dinosaur heist?"

"Yeah, what is that all about?" Shelby asked. "Vic told me that your investigation took you to Tate Hall at the U."

"Oh, it's crazy," Nina said. "It was Tony DeLuca who followed us to police headquarters that night. I guess he's actually a chef but somehow his uncle . . ."

"Granduncle," I said.

"Granduncle got him involved in all of this."

"Tell us," Shelby said.

Nina glanced my way, her silver-blue eyes glittering with expectation.

"By all means, Nora," I said. "Dish."

"Well, it all began with a pretty girl on a white horse . . ."

Nina told the story; I interrupted from time to time to provide specific details. Shelby was delighted—"Things like this never happen to me," she said—while Bobby seemed somewhat bored. I knew he had a few comments, though, and was merely waiting until Nina finished before he made them.

"So, that's your plan?" he asked. "You spread the word to all of the suspects that you're willing to buy back the dinosaur and just sit back and wait for the phone to ring?"

"Something like that," I said as I checked my smartwatch.

"Guy calls up and says, hey, I found your *Ankylosaurus* skull in a ditch, now where's my reward?"

"A distinct possibility."

"Then you pay 'em Andrew Cooke's money, they deliver the goods, and everyone lives happily ever after. It's bullshit."

"I know."

"You're rewarding thieves for being thieves. I don't like it."

"I know. But, Bobby, we've both seen it before whether it's a Lily carved from jade, a Stradivarius violin; newly discovered paintings from a long-dead artist . . ."

"Don't give me that," Bobby said.

"I don't believe it, anyway," Shelby said.

"What don't you believe?"

"That that's your plan. Even when you paid the ransom to get Victoria back you had a plan."

"The plan was to get her back safe and sound without a scratch on her. Same with the *Ankylosaurus*."

"Except once Vic was returned you squashed those bastards like a bug."

"She is my goddaughter after all and Bobby couldn't do it because, you know, sworn officer of the law and all that."

Bobby studied me for a few beats.

"You're going about this all wrong," he said. "You know that, right?"

"Who really knows what's right and wrong?"

"Stop it."

I thought I was being funny, although no one else laughed. After I stopped chuckling, I said, "I'm always open to good advice."

"McKenzie, when the city seemed to be under siege by thieves stealing catalytic converters, and later when they were tearing apart streetlamps for copper wire, it wasn't the thieves that we went after," Bobby said. "I mean, what were we going to do? Stake out lampposts? No. We went after the buyers. Put them away and the rest takes care of itself."

"Now there's a thought."

Bobby gave me a few more beats.

"What aren't you telling me?" he asked. "Why aren't you telling me? Is it because you like your surprises or because, you know, sworn officer of the law and all that?"

And the front doorbell rang.

And I glanced at my smartwatch.

And Bobby said, "Is this what you've been waiting for all night?"

And you thought he wasn't paying attention.

I stood up.

"I took the liberty of inviting a guest," I said. "I hope you don't mind."

The doorbell rang a second time.

Shelby rose from the table.

"My house," she said.

We watched as Shelby left the dining room. The fact that I didn't chant "No, no, no" seemed to be enough to assuage any fears that Bobby might have held.

The three of us couldn't see the front door from where we sat but we could hear it being opened and Shelby's shriek of delight followed by her proclamation, "Look at you!" That was quickly accompanied by an "Oh my God"—the words seemed to be wrapped in a hug. A moment later, Shelby guided a woman into the dining room. She was immediately met by Nina, who happily hugged her just as Shelby had done.

Heavenly Petryk was a chameleon; she could change her appearance to fit any occasion. Tonight, she was wonderfully wholesome-looking; a thirty-year-old woman-next-door who just dropped in to say "Hi"—her smile bright, her blue eyes glittering, her golden hair falling to her shoulders, her skin resembling fresh buttermilk. She was wearing jeans that hugged her long, sculptured legs, and a black sweater that clung to her athletic body. She was the most beautiful woman I had ever met in person, although I would never admit that to Nina. She was, at times, also shockingly treacherous. Only not to me, at least not anymore, and not to the two women standing at the dining-room table who had adopted Heavenly as if she were a long-lost sister from another mister; who had often wondered what it would be like to shed their conventional lives and live as she did.

I was also standing. Bobby had remained seated; his expression was unreadable.

"Heavenly Elizabeth Petryk," he said.

Heavenly smiled down at him.

"Commander Dunston," she said. "Or have you been promoted to chief of police since we last met?"

"The last time we met, you said you were on your way to Edinburgh."

"So I was."

"Something about a jewel-encrusted broach that once belonged to the Queen of Scots that had somehow gone missing from a display at the Palace of Holyroodhouse. A couple of days later, to everyone's great surprise, it was discovered in a mailbox near the entrance to Edinburgh Castle at the other end of the Royal Mile."

"Yes, I read about that in the *Scotsman* newspaper. Quite a coincidence, don't you think?"

"Very much so. Rumor had it that someone, not the royal family, but someone had paid nearly half a million pounds for its safe return."

"Rumored yet never confirmed. Oh, and it was euros, not pounds."

Bobby didn't know what to say to that, so he said nothing. Heavenly's smile didn't flicker for a moment.

"I've tried to explain it to you once before, Commander," she said, "I'm not a thief."

"What are you?"

"An acquaintance of McKenzie's once called me a mercenary bitch who profits off the misfortune of insurance companies," she said. "I can live with that. How 'bout you?"

"Stop it," Shelby said. "Both of you. Heavenly, please have a seat. Are you hungry?"

"What is this? Is this meatloaf Wellington? My mother used to make this."

No, she didn't, my inner voice insisted. And then it reconsidered. *Maybe she did.* With Heavenly it was always difficult to know what was real and what wasn't.

Shelby filled Heavenly's plate.

"What do you have for me?" I asked.

"A pleasure to see you, too, McKenzie," Heavenly said.

"Thank you for coming."

"I have almost nothing for you."

"Almost?"

"I've spread the word since we spoke last Monday . . ."

"Wait," Nina said. "You spoke on Monday?"

"Monday night," Heavenly said.

"McKenzie, why didn't you tell me?"

"I wanted it to be a surprise," I said.

Nina showed her gratitude by punching me in the arm and calling me a jerk.

"Almost?" I repeated as I rubbed the spot where Nina hit me.

"Apparently, no one has an *Ankylosaurus* skull to sell; no one had even heard that there was one on the market. I spoke to El Cid on Wednesday . . ."

"Funny, he didn't mention that when I spoke to him last night. In fact, he acted as if he didn't know what I was talking about."

"And that surprises you?"

At the end of the table I heard Bobby moan, "Noooooo . . ."

"Did you tell him that you were working for me?" I asked.

"Of course not. He thinks I have my own client. Only, Mc-Kenzie, he didn't have anything to say or he would have said it."

"I had the same impression."

"It looks like you were right," Heavenly said.

"Amateur night in Montana."

"More likely a crew that's looking to move up in the world rankings."

"You'd think they'd be making some noise by now. It's been over a month since the theft."

"Jesus," Bobby muttered.

"Enough," Shelby announced. "Heavenly, eat your dinner. It's getting cold."

Heavenly ate. The conversation turned to wholesome chatter.

"How are the girls?" Heavenly asked.

"They're wonderful," Shelby said. "Victoria is a freshman at the University of Minnesota, now; she's living on campus in one of the dorms. Katie is a junior in high school; she's been getting a lot of attention from colleges for her basketball skills."

"If only her grades were as noteworthy," Bobby added.

"Katie is out with her pals tonight," Shelby said. "They're both going to be upset that they missed you."

"Erica?" Heavenly asked Nina.

"She graduated from Tulane last spring," Nina said. "She's an economist now. She works for an investment company. I'm not entirely sure what she does but it seems to be very lucrative. She has an apartment in Uptown. She says she's going back to school part time in the spring to get her MBA."

"You don't know how happy that makes me."

"The girls will be so happy to see you." Shelby said. "What are you doing tomorrow?"

"Unfortunately, I'm flying to Toronto tomorrow morning."

"What's in Toronto?" Bobby asked; his voice filled with suspicion.

"The Hockey Hall of Fame. Did you know that they keep the original Stanley Cup in an open vault where visitors can just come and go as they please?"

Bobby stared at Heavenly as if he didn't know if she was kidding or not.

"Seriously," I said. "What's in Toronto?"

"A man positioned near the top of the hierarchy who almost never talks over the phone," Heavenly said. "We'll be flying out of MSP at 11:15 A.M."

"We?"

"Yes, we. Well, not we. Me and Nick Dyson."

"Oh, could it get any better?" Bobby asked.

Four and a half years ago, I did an off-the-books undercover job for my close personal friends at the FBI and the Bureau of Alcohol, Tobacco, Firearms and Explosives. To make it work, they gave me a false identity—with birth certificate, social security number, passport, credit cards, extensive criminal record—much of it available online for anyone to find including my photograph. When the job was over, though, they neglected to delete it. I've been hiding it in my safe ever since, taking it out and dusting it off on those rare occasions when pretending to be a hardened criminal might prove useful. Like now.

Nina drove Heavenly and me to the airport; Heavenly had spent the night in our guest room—Nina insisted. She didn't have much to say during the trip although she and Heavenly seemed to have plenty to talk about the night before and early that morning. I had no idea what they told each other and neither would give me a hint later although, on at least one occasion, I saw Heavenly brush away tears with the back of her hand and the two women embraced.

After my mother and father passed, my friends became my family; the Dunstons, Nina, a few others. I wondered if Heavenly had the same experience. Over the six and a half years that I'd known her, she occasionally invoked a mother, who apparently lived in three different cities, yet never mentioned a father or anyone else who might be related to her. I wondered, if like me, she was desperate for people and a place that would be home.

Nina found an empty spot at the curb next to the Air Canada sign at the Lindbergh Terminal, put the car in park, and turned toward Heavenly; they were both in the front seat of Nina's Lexus.

"Why do you do what you do?" Nina asked.

"I told you."

"Tell me again."

Heavenly gestured toward me in the backseat.

"Why does he do it?" she asked.

"McKenzie thinks he's actually making the world a better place."

"Just this once I'm going to help him."

Nina spoke her last word with resignation—"Fine."

The two women embraced and kissed each other's cheeks.

"What about me?" I asked.

"Get out of the car," Nina said.

I did. She popped the trunk, and I removed both Heavenly's and my bags. Nina circled the Lexus and hugged me. She didn't speak, just hugged. We hugged for a long time as cars weaved past us. A couple of people applauded. Someone beeped his horn. We released each other and Nina retreated to her car and drove off. I took my bag, Heavenly took hers, and together we entered the terminal.

"You two didn't have much to say to each other," Heavenly said.

"Yes, we did," I told her.

We moved toward the TSA checkpoint.

"Heavenly," I said.

"Ms. Petryk."

I glanced at her. Heavenly was already in character. She was now a haughty member of a Nordic royal family with perfect teeth in a perfect mouth formed into a perfect smile. Her eyes were as hard as azurite. Her hair, styled in a loose bun, resembled polished gold. She wore a high-waisted pencil skirt and a white silk top beneath a tailored blazer that fell to her knees. She looked like a woman who traveled first class or not at all. More to the point, she looked like a woman who expected to be *treated* like she flew first class or not at all.

"Ms. Petryk," I said.

"Yes, Nicholas?"

"There are people who love you."

She didn't speak until we reached a TSA agent who directed us to the precheck line.

"Thank you, Nick," Heavenly said. "I'll keep that in mind."

FOURTEEN

We boarded a small plane and made it to Toronto in just under two hours. I was not a fan of Toronto Pearson Airport mostly because it required us to make a long, meandering, up-and-down march from the gate to customs. We were waved through easily, though, and soon found ourselves in the ground transportation hub. I made for the escalator that I knew from past experience led to the platform where we would find an express train that would take us to Union Station. Heavenly did not follow, halting behind me and calling, "Hey."

I stopped.

"What?" I asked.

"We are what we appear to be."

"And what is that?"

Heavenly answered by leading me through the sliding doors to a stand where we could rent an airport limo. Not a Lyft, not an Uber or even a taxi—a limousine. Thirty minutes later we were let off outside a forty-one-story skyscraper on the corner of Peter Street and Adelaide in the heart of downtown Toronto.

"Not a hotel?" I said.

"Part Airbnb, part apartment building."

We passed through a sliding door that faced a security desk. Heavenly signed in, took two key cards, and headed to the elevator. I dutifully followed behind, carrying both of our bags. The elevator took us to the penthouse floor—that's how it was labeled. A few minutes later, we were in an elegantly furnished apartment with a small kitchen, bathroom featuring both a shower and a tub, large bedroom, and even larger living room. There was a balcony that ran the length of the living room behind a floor-to-ceiling glass wall with a splendid view of the CN Tower and the northwestern shore of Lake Ontario.

"Nice," I said.

"It used to be an office building, but Toronto has been having the same problems with people working remotely as New York, Chicago, and other cities, so it was converted. I prefer it because it has better security; only guests and tenants allowed in and out."

"You're going to let me pay for all of this, right?"

"Oh, Nick, you'll see a bill, trust me."

That's my girl, my inner voice said.

"So, what happens next?" I asked aloud.

Heavenly glanced at her smartwatch.

"Hungry?" she said. "I'm hungry. I know a place just down the street."

I was expecting Restaurant 20 Victoria or Jacobs & Co. Steakhouse or any of the other Michelin-star restaurants to be found in the city. Instead, Heavenly walked us to a comfortable joint called Ravi Soups where I had a very good chicken wrap with corn chowder and she had a wrap with curried lamb, yams, and baby spinach. While she ate, Heavenly consulted her smartwatch.

"Okay, we've been fed," I said. "Now what?"

"Nick, it's important that you remember your place."

"I'm pretending to be your bodyguard . . ."

"Pretending?"

"If I'm to be your bodyguard, it's important that I know what's going on."

"We're going to meet a man in about two hours."

"What man?"

"There's a Hilton that's a ten-minute walk from here. We'll get a taxi there."

"And take it where exactly?"

The Royal Ontario Museum was the largest museum in Canada and one of the largest museums in all of North America. Apparently, the people who worked there were very proud of that fact because the guidebooks they handed out made sure we knew it.

Heavenly decided we had plenty of time, so we began our visit on the top floor and worked our way down. I was careful to walk behind Heavenly, taking note of all exits, examining the other visitors more than the exhibits, as a bodyguard should, while also making sure I was the first one through the door when we went from one exhibit to another.

There was a special art exhibition by Islamic women from Egypt, Iran, Pakistan, and other parts of the Middle East on the fourth floor. The artists were very creative in expressing their concerns with how women were treated in their cultures. Heavenly didn't linger at most of the exhibits, yet I noticed she took her time examining this one.

Afterward, we walked casually among the artifacts and displays from Africa, the Americas and Asia-Pacific, plus an exhibit depicting the evolution of European style that we discovered on the third floor.

Heavenly kept glancing at her smartwatch throughout our visit. Finally, she said, "Okay," and we descended to the second floor where we found—dinosaur fossils—and plenty of them; hundreds of specimens in fact, the vast majority hailing from the fields of Alberta, Canada. I examined the exhibits carefully, a careless thing to do considering I was acting as Heavenly's bodyguard. *Lambeosaurus, Camptosaurus, Barosaurus, Stego-saurus, Allosaurus, Anzu wylei, Deinonychus, Albertosaurus, Protoceratops*—I didn't know that most of these dinosaurs even existed much less how to pronounce their names. Many of them were reproductions, although more than a few were actual skeletons—diagrams let visitors know which bones were real and which were cast from other fossils.

Among them I found the entire skeleton of an *Ankylosaurus*.

"I thought it would be much bigger," I said.

"This particular fossil comes from the late Jurassic period," Heavenly said. "It's over 150 million years old. Your *Ank* is from the late Cretaceous period making it about 60 million years old. You'll notice that this one doesn't have a boned tail. That feature evolved much later."

"And you know this because . . ."

Heavenly pointed at the plaque mounted in front of the exhibit.

"I read. Nicholas, we're on."

I immediately stepped away from Heavenly and turned my back to the *Ankylosaurus*. I positioned myself so I could watch the visitors around us. I saw two of them approaching. The first was an older man, I placed him to be at least fifty, who was dressed as if he was about to accept an award for wearing the most elegant men's business attire. The man behind him was half his age and a foot taller. He was wearing a much less expensive suit and an expression that suggested he wanted to punch someone.

Let's hope it's not you.

The first man moved up to Heavenly. She was leaning against the railing of the *Ankylosaurus* exhibit, her arms crossed in front of her. She was smiling. Her smile made the older man smile.

"Ms. Petryk," he said.

"Mr. Bergeron."

"My friends call me Louis."

"Then please, you must call me Heavenly."

"A lovely name."

"Thank you, sir."

They shook hands.

I listened carefully while pretending not to, instead concentrating my attention on the visitors that approached and left the exhibit. Bergeron's man, on the other hand, stared at me and nothing else. I found it very disconcerting yet worked mightily not to show it.

"It's a pleasure to meet you at last," Bergeron said.

"And I you."

"I know your reputation, of course. But Heavenly, I must say, I am disappointed. You insist on meeting me in a public place and then you bring a bodyguard? What is a man to suppose?"

"I asked you to meet me at the ROM because there is something I wish to show you. As for Nicholas—you know how it is, Louis. A young woman alone in a strange land, who doesn't know the language, doesn't know the customs."

That caused Bergeron to smile.

"I must say I admire how he is so obviously observant of all the movement around us while not so obviously listening to every word we speak," he said. "I wish my own man behaved so professionally."

Bergeron's man bristled at the remark and his gaze became even more intense.

Yeah, he wants to hit someone. Guess who?

"Louis, I contacted you because I have a request that is quite confidential in nature."

"How may I help you?"

"I have been approached by a gentleman of means; perhaps you've heard his name, perhaps not. The man owns four houses located on three continents, eleven cars, a helicopter, two private jets, a yacht the size of an aircraft carrier, and a cache of priceless art, some of which he is even free to display in public. What he doesn't have is a dinosaur."

"Excuse me?"

Heavenly gestured at the skeletons surrounding them.

"Apparently, my client has a friend who owns one and now he wants one, too."

"A dinosaur?"

"Specifically, he is seeking the skull of an *Ankylosaurus*."

Heavenly turned and gestured at the *Ank* on display directly behind her. Bergeron gave it a hard look.

"That is very specific," he said. "Why an *Ankylosaurus*, if I may ask?"

"He is aware that the skull of an *Ankylosaurus* was stolen from a dig in eastern Montana in the United States about a month ago and smuggled across the border into Canada. It is his intention to acquire it."

"The reason he knows about this theft?"

"He subscribes to *The Journal of Paleontology*. The magazine printed an account of the incident in its latest edition. As for the skull now residing in Canada, I recently discovered that the vehicle that contained the skull when it was stolen has been located by the Montana Highway Patrol very near the Raymond Port of Entry."

"Where is that?"

"Exactly a hundred and nine miles, according to Google maps, from Regina, Saskatchewan. Excuse me, a hundred and sixty-three kilometers. I only learned this a few days ago or I would have come to you sooner."

"This is a little out of my area of expertise."

"Are you saying I've come to the wrong place?"

Bergeron smiled at the suggestion.

"I know people in Regina," he said.

"I was sure you did."

"How long will you be in Toronto, Heavenly?"

"As long as I need to be."

"Let me make a few inquiries and I will contact you. Possibly as early as Monday."

"Thank you, Louis."

"Where can I reach you?"

"You have my number."

Bergeron smiled again, probably I decided, because he realized she wasn't about to give him her location.

"Of course," he said.

Bergeron hesitated long enough to stare at the skeleton of the *Ank* some more.

"I'm told that the skull in question is actually much larger than this specimen," Heavenly said.

"What is your client's price range?"

"Depends on his mood. He once bought a mansion for twice its market value and then bulldozed it to improve the view from his balcony. I've also known him to gripe over the price of a latte at Starbucks."

Heavenly spread her hands as if to say, "These are the people we work with." Bergeron nodded his head like he understood completely.

"Monday," he said.

Bergeron turned and left the dinosaur exhibit as if he was in a hurry. His taller henchman followed behind, yet not before giving me a menacing grin and a head shake, the shake suggesting that we would meet again.

I waited until they were out of sight before I asked, "Who is he?"

"Remember that time in Philadelphia when we were going after the Countess Borromeo, the fence who tried to have us killed? That's who Bergeron is if we're not careful except he's much more fashionable."

"Yeah, I liked his suit. Now what?"

"I thought we'd hang around for a time then head over to

a restaurant I know. It's about a twenty-minute walk from here."

"Clever girl," I said.

We returned to the third floor of the Royal Ontario Museum where we found an exhibit with a focus on ancient cultures: Byzantium, Ancient Greece, Ancient Cyprus, Bronze Age Aegean, Rome, Nubia, and Egypt. Heavenly seemed very interested in it. I was only interested in the visitors that we passed.

Eventually, Heavenly decided it was time to leave. We exited the ROM on Bloor Street and started walking west. It was when we were passing the offices of the Consulate General of the Republic of Angola that I made him, a man about thirty wearing a Toronto Maple Leafs sweatshirt beneath a black sports coat.

We kept walking until we reached Church Street and turned south. The man continued to follow us except he removed his jacket and slung it over his shoulder, hanging on to the collar with his left hand, a poor attempt at camouflage if you ask me. Or maybe he was hot. It was about sixty degrees, which was warm for Toronto in early October.

"See him?" I asked.

Heavenly continued walking, her eyes staring straight ahead.

"Yes," she said.

Four and a half blocks later we were standing outside Storm Crow Manor, the building looking like something out of the movie *The Addams Family* or maybe *Psycho*. The restaurant promoted itself as "Toronto's geekiest bar." I would suggest it was the geekiest bar in North America, but what did I know? The waiting area featured creepy clown dolls in a Ferris wheel, crows in cages, a mechanical fortune-teller and décor celebrating everything from *Star Wars* and *Star Trek* to *Blade Runner, The Shin-*

ing, and all things Marvel, not to mention *Game of Thrones* and every zombie movie ever made. Its drink menu featured concoctions with names like Pan Galactic Gargle Blaster, Romulan Ale, and the Mango-lorian. I ordered an Intellect Devourer, which was actually a pretty good old-fashioned except it was glowing red from a light-up ice cube, while Heavenly had a Princess Peach's Bourbon Iced Tea.

The drinks were served in a small, private room labeled HEAVEN. Next door was another room with the name HELL. Our room had stained glass windows that looked out onto the street. They gave us a clear view of our friend leaning against the bumper of a GMC pickup across the street and a half block up where he could easily see the entrance to the restaurant.

"Bergeron?" I asked.

"I wouldn't think so. Why would he have us followed when all he has to do is make a phone call and I'll come running?"

"He wants to know where we're staying."

"Perhaps."

"He wants to know if we're also dealing with his competitors."

"Maybe."

"What else?"

"You know, Nicholas, we could always ask."

Heavenly dipped a hand into her bag and retrieved a no-frills cell phone; its value made me think it was a burner. She found a number and called it. Someone answered.

"Louis," Heavenly said. "I thought we were friends."

Heavenly held the phone against her ear so I could not hear what Bergeron said.

"We're being followed . . . He's not . . . ? Honestly, Louis, I didn't think he was. I just wanted to be sure before . . . No, no, thank you for your concern. We have this. Like I said, I just wanted to be sure in case something nasty happens to him . . . Thank you, Louis. I look forward to your call. Good night."

Heavenly ended the conversation and put the cell back into her bag.

"Not Louis," she said.

"So he says. Do we trust him?"

"Of course not, still . . ."

"If not him, who else? Who knows we're in Toronto?"

Heavenly sipped her drink.

"El Cid," she said.

"I asked him if he had friends in Canada and he said yes."

"I'm willing to bet he knew I would be contacting Bergeron."

"At the Royal Ontario Museum?"

Heavenly leaned against the back of her seat and stared at the ceiling.

"The tail followed Bergeron," she said. "Bergeron led him to us."

"A distinct possibility. On the other hand, I made a lot of people aware that I was going after the *Ank* for Andrew Cooke including Cid."

"Yes, but how did they know you'd be in Toronto? You didn't even know you were coming until last night. We weren't followed to the airport. I checked. Didn't you?"

DeLuca put a GPS tracker on your Mustang. Did he also put one on Nina's Lexus that she drove to the Air Canada drop off?

I told Heavenly what my inner voice told me.

"It's not always about you, McKenzie," she said.

McKenzie, not Nicholas.

"You know, we could always ask," I said.

Heavenly and I ordered dinner. I had a Cloudy with a Chance of Meatball pasta dish and she ordered Chicken Pesto Boba-Fettuccini. While we ate, I studied the street-view of the area around us provided by the map app on my cell phone. Afterward, I showed her what I had in mind.

"I'd be much happier if at least one of us was armed," Heavenly said.

"No one carries a gun in Canada."

"If only that were true."

The front door of Storm Crow Manor was only about forty yards from Dundonald Street, a narrow, sleepy one-way lined with apartment buildings on one side and old duplexes with porches and balconies on the other. There were also plenty of trees and foliage and it provided a pleasant stroll toward the Wellesley subway station. Heavenly and I left the manor and started toward it. Our friend was half a block down and on the opposite side of Church Street. We turned down Dundonald and as soon as we were out of his sight, we sprinted to the locations that we had selected earlier. Our friend followed quickly, yet we were both well hidden by the time he reached the entrance to the street and started down it. He increased his speed, his head turning from right to left as he half walked, half jogged toward the Continental Tower apartment building where the subway entrance was located.

As he neared it, Heavenly stepped out from behind the largest oak tree I had ever seen. The man stopped and glared at her.

"You," he said.

By then I had moved from where I was hidden in the doorway of a redbrick apartment building and approached him from behind.

"You," Heavenly repeated.

It took a few beats before the man realized what was happening. He turned to leave and found me standing there.

"You," I said.

He tried to stiff-arm me in the face. I pushed his hand away and hit him just as hard as I could in the nose with a hammer fist just like I had practiced at Gracie's Power Academy. The blow sent the man to his knees and brought blood from his nostrils. He covered his face with both hands, only that didn't stop the bleeding. I took the opportunity to use a series of quick taps with my hands to search the areas where he might have been carrying a weapon and a few where no one goes armed. He was clean.

"We don't have a lot of time for this," Heavenly said.

She was right, of course. I had no idea what the Toronto Police Service response time was, only it couldn't have been more than a few minutes. That's assuming a neighbor saw what was happening and called it in.

I found the man's wallet and removed his driver's license. It was blue and white with Ontario's trillium logo and printed in both English and French. The name read Cloutier, Noah.

"Why are you following us, Noah?" I asked.

He didn't answer. Instead, he tried to stand up. Heavenly pounded his collarbone from behind and he yelped in pain; one of his hands continued to cover his nose while the other went to his shoulder.

I kept looking through his wallet and found—"Wow"—another blue plastic card. This one also featured Ontario's trillium logo. It read Private Security and Investigative Services in both English and French and claimed "Cloutier, Noah is licensed as Security Guard and Private Investigator." I gave it to Heavenly. She glanced at it and tossed it into the street.

"Who are you working for?" I asked.

Cloutier shook his head.

"Let's not make this any harder on you than it already is."

He shook his head some more.

"This isn't getting us anywhere," Heavenly said.

Cloutier turned his head and looked up at her.

"Bitch," he said.

"Now why would you say a thing like that?" I asked.

Unlike mine, Heavenly's response was nonverbal. She pounded his collarbone again; I thought I heard a crack, yet that might have been wishful thinking. In any case, Cloutier fell on his shoulder, the one she had hit, and moaned like he was dying. Heavenly spun around and moved toward the subway station. I dropped the PI's wallet in the street and followed her.

Ten minutes later we were on the subway. Fifteen minutes after that we emerged from the St. Andrew station not far from our penthouse. In another ten minutes we were seated at the bar of an English-style pub called Fox on John.

"Well, that could have gone better," I said.

"Not Bergeron," Heavenly declared.

"I'm still leaning in that direction. I get that he has his own people. Noah could have been one of them, though."

"I'm leaning more toward El Cid."

"Or DeLuca."

"Or someone else is involved. We don't know them, but they know us."

"They guess we're going to Toronto, make a call to a local PI requesting surveillance . . . How did Noah make us?"

"Noah saw us meet Bergeron; we must assume that. We also have to assume he knows who Bergeron is and what he does and reported those facts to his employer."

"*Dem bones Dem bones Dem dry bones, Hear the word of the Lord*. It would seem the market for dinosaur fossils is expanding."

"I thought this would be an easy gig, a favor for an old friend," Heavenly said. "What have you gotten me into?"

"What are we going to do now, is the question. Spend the next couple of days in the penthouse watching curling on TV and eating takeout while we wait on Bergeron?"

Heavenly smiled her bright smile, took a sip of her drink, and smiled some more.

"Do you want to have some fun?" she asked.

"Always."

"Drive these guys a little whacky?"

"By all means."

At seven forty-five the next morning we met a tour bus across from Ripley's Aquarium of Canada not far from Rogers Centre where the Blue Jays played ball. The tour director was from Malta and for a moment he had trouble finding our names on his tablet.

"Oh, here they are," he said. "Heavenly Petryk and Nick Dyson. You signed up late last night. Welcome, welcome. Have a seat."

We climbed aboard the tour bus, finding a pair of vacant seats near the front. Heavenly was well rested; me not so much. 'Course, she had slept comfortably in the penthouse's king-size bed while I camped out on the sofa in the living room. I barely had time to get dressed—"Think layers, it'll be in the high fifties," she said—much less have a cup of coffee before she had us walking from the Airbnb to the bus stop. It took only fifteen minutes, yet it seemed longer. At no time did we look to see if we were being followed. We just assumed that we were.

It didn't take long before the bus was filled with tourists. The bus driver stood in the front and greeted us.

"It'll take about two and a half hours for us to reach our destination, including a couple of stops," he said. "I think you'll find it to be a very pleasant drive mostly along Lake Ontario. I'll point out a few sights along the way. Enjoy."

I hope the guys following us enjoy it, too, my inner voice said.

Heavenly squeezed my arm.

"Have you ever been to Niagara Falls?" she asked.

"Nope."

"Never took Nina?"

I shook my head.

"Where have you taken her?" Heavenly asked.

"Paris. Jamaica. Martinique. London. Edinburgh."

"I loved Edinburgh. It was very profitable."

"One day you'll have to tell me your story."

Heavenly squeezed my arm again.

"One day I will," she said.

The bus was passing over the Burlington Skyway, a pair of high-level freeway bridges located between the cities of Burlington and Hamilton, when Judy Garland started singing, "Clang, clang, clang went the trolley, ding, ding, ding went the bell." Heavenly looked at me with a shocked expression on her face while I answered my cell phone. There was no name, only a phone number on the caller ID, so I said, "This is McKenzie, who's calling please."

"None of your goddamn business," a voice replied.

"Okay," I said and hung up.

I glanced at Heavenly.

"He'll call back," I said.

"That's your ringtone?"

"Yeah. What's yours?"

"The sound of a bell ringing."

Judy started singing again. The caller ID identified the same number.

Good.

"This is McKenzie, who's calling please?"

"You don't fucking hang up on me, asshole."

"Good manners are how we show respect for one another. Call back in an hour if you learn some."

I hung up again. I held my cell in my left hand while I switched from my phone app to the message app.

"Who was that?" Heavenly asked.

"The number had a 612 area code. That's Minneapolis, so I'm

guessing it's someone who wants to talk about the *Ank*. Right now, I'm the only game in town so I'm sure he'll call back."

"What are you doing?"

"Sending a text."

"To whom?"

"Special Agent Linda Ambrose."

"No. The FBI? Nicholas . . ."

"You seem concerned. Why? Are you doing something illegal?"

"Ah, geez . . ."

I sent the text. It listed the phone number with the message:

I wonder who might be calling me with information about the Ankylosaurus

The call might have come from a burner phone; probably it had. Yet despite what you see in the movies and on TV cop shows, burners can be traced. I can't do it. Neither can you. You know who can? The Federal Bureau of Investigation. Usually.

The bus made two "photo stops" before we reached the falls. The first was Maple Leaf Place, a tourist trap that claimed to have the largest carved wooden moose in the world, although it wasn't any bigger than a real moose. Heavenly and I each enjoyed a flight of maple syrups—light, amber, and dark. Only the dark tasted like maple syrup, though. I might have bought some, only I knew I couldn't bring a bottle larger than 3.5 ounces back home on the plane.

It was while we were sampling the syrup that I heard a ping that told me I had a message. The text was from Agent Ambrose. It read:

So do I

The second stop was to see the Floral Clock, a forty-foot clock, its face consisting entirely of colorful flower beds, that actually gave the correct time. It's where Marilyn Monroe conspired to kill Joseph Cotton in the thriller *Niagara*.

In both places I noticed a red Subaru Outback parked not too far away. I was tempted to give the driver a wave yet thought better of it.

Finally, we reached Niagara. The bus was halted in a small parking lot dedicated to tour buses about a mile from the falls. The Subaru kept moving down the street, turned a corner, and disappeared. As we disembarked, our guide made it clear to us that the bus would be leaving at exactly 3:25 P.M. He even made each of us repeat the time. He said anyone not on the bus at 3:25 P.M. would be left behind.

Why three twenty-five? Why not three thirty? my inner voice wanted to know only I didn't ask.

The tour guide recommended a couple of restaurants.

Heavenly and I decided food was a good idea and we started walking to one of those restaurants—Chuck's Roadhouse Bar and Grill. To get there we passed through an area that reminded me of the midway at the Minnesota State Fair. We encountered two Ferris wheels, kiddy rides, water slides, a Ripley's Believe It Or Not museum, miniature golf course, cart racing track, laser tag court, a rock and roll bowling alley, haunted house, house of mirrors, and a wax museum not to mention several casinos, breweries, distilleries, sports bars, pizza parlors, BBQ joints, Tim Hortons, Applebee's, Dairy Queen, Wendy's, and a Hard Rock Cafe. Because of the many visitors all of that attracted, it was difficult to know if we were being followed or not.

"So," I said. "Welcome to Niagara Falls."

"My, my, aren't we being cynical," Heavenly said.

Eventually, we reached the restaurant. I had a steak sandwich, Heavenly ordered bruschetta flatbread. No one put the arm on us; no one threatened our lives.

After lunch, we took a shorter, more direct route to the falls, working our way past a couple of hotels and a casino. My cell started singing while we were passing the Skylon Tower and its observation deck. I paused to answer it.

"This is McKenzie, who's calling please?"

"Okay, we'll do it your way this time."

The male voice wasn't shouting. I took that as a good sign.

"That doesn't answer my question," I said.

"You don't need to know my name. All you need to know is that we have the *Ankylosaurus* skull."

We?

"All right," I said.

"If you want it back, it'll cost you one million dollars."

"I'm going to put you on speakerphone so my friend will know why I'm laughing."

"What?"

I switched to speakerphone before I answered.

"One million dollars is ridiculous. There's no way that my client"—I didn't know how else to refer to Andrew Cooke—"will pay that amount."

"The skull is worth six million dollars."

"No, it's not. The entire *Ankylosaurus* skeleton might be worth that much, but the skull alone? No way."

"What?"

"Besides, how many people do you think are interested in buying a stolen *Ankylosaurus* skull?"

"We want one million and we want it in cash . . ."

We, again.

"Cash?" I asked.

"Oh my God," Heavenly said with a giggle.

"Who said that?" the voice asked.

"My friend. Listen, I don't think you've thought this through. One million dollars, half in twenties and half in fifties, would weigh seventy-seven pounds and fill a hockey equipment bag. And where do you think that money is going to come from? You think you can walk into a branch office of Wells Fargo with a withdrawal slip and walk out with a wheelbarrow full of cash? There isn't a bank in North America with that kind of cash on hand. No, you'll need to get it from the Federal Reserve Bank in Minneapolis. Now make no mistake. It's Mr. Cooke's money. If he wants it, they'll give it to him. Only the United States Treasury Department is going ask him if he's going to ship all that cash overseas. The FBI will ask if he's using it to pay off a kidnapper. The National Security Agency is going ask if he's using it to support terrorism. And none of them are going to take no for an answer. Not only that, how are you going to spend it? Are you going to wheel your barrow into the lobby of your bank and make a deposit? Are you going to take a bag of cash into a dealership and tell the guy you want to buy a Subaru?"

Even as I said the word, I glanced around. There were no red Subaru Outbacks to be seen; no one was leaning against a lamppost and watching us while pretending not to. That didn't convince me that someone wasn't watching from somewhere, though.

The caller paused for a long time. I heard some muffling sounds as if he was talking to someone with his hand covering the mic on his cell. Finally, he said, "What do you suggest?"

"You mean besides just giving back the skull?"

"Fuck."

"Accept the reward. Mr. Cooke is offering a reward for the safe return of his property. You take the skull to the Science Museum of Minnesota; he hands you a check; you deposit it in your bank account. Simple. Oh, and don't forget to pay your taxes."

"If he doesn't pay?"

"You take him to court. Once he announces the reward it becomes a contract; he's legally obligated to pay it, assuming you keep your end of the bargain. Look it up."

"The police . . ."

"What police?"

The question caused him to pause again.

"Look, pal," I said. "There are two kinds of crimes. Crimes against specific victims and crimes against the United States. Stealing an *Ankylosaurus* skull from private property is not a crime against the U.S. The Feds don't care. A crime against a specific victim—if the vic isn't interested in prosecuting, the cops are going to shrug and move on. There are plenty of more pressing matters for them to prioritize."

That caused the caller to pause some more.

"Think about it," I said. "In the meantime, I'll contact Mr. Cooke. I can tell you right now, though, a million bucks is not going to happen. Better start thinking smaller. A lot smaller."

"Fuck you."

"Do you kiss your mother with that mouth?"

"I never liked you."

"Oh? Have we met?"

Have we?

He replied by hanging up the phone. I slipped my cell into the pocket of my golf jacket and Heavenly and I continued moving toward the falls.

"You were right," she said. "Amateurs."

"Which might not be a good thing. With professionals you usually can guess what they're going to do and why they're going to do it. With these guys, who knows?"

"Commander Dunston would not approve. Giving them a crash course on how to profit from the theft of stolen property— who are you, Fagin?"

"If I am, does that make you the Artful Dodger?"

"If they follow your advice, that means we won't need Bergeron."

"We'll see."

"You know, if Bergeron does locate the *Ankylosaurus* and

makes a deal with these guys, there's a better than even chance that he'll cut me out."

"He needs your client."

"Unless he finds a client of his own like, I don't know, Andrew Cooke."

"That's one of the reasons why I have no intention of speaking to him. I don't want him to recognize my voice over the phone if he somehow gets McKenzie's number."

Heavenly didn't have anything to say to that until we were on the sidewalk walking past the statue at Nikola Tesla Plaza.

"Please tell me that this is all part of your plan," she said.

"What plan?"

"That's what I was afraid of."

The Horseshoe Falls were spectacular. I can't think of a description that would do it justice. There was a large complex called the Table Rock Centre that provided tourists with everything from handmade cashew buttercrunch dark chocolate to sweatshirts to a restaurant meal to the entrance to a tunnel that would take visitors behind the falls. Fortunately, it was located so that it didn't obstruct the view of the falls. The carnival that we passed through earlier was well behind us and out of sight, too.

Heavenly and I leaned against the stone wall and watched six million cubic feet of water fall one hundred and eighty feet every minute. We watched quietly for many minutes.

"I love this," Heavenly said, although I wasn't sure if she was talking to me or herself. "I love the sound of rushing water, the moisture in the air, the incredible green color of the water as it flows over the rocks. I love water in all its forms."

Meanwhile, instead of enjoying the dazzling scene in front of me, my mind turned to a story I heard about a teacher named Annie Edson Taylor who went over the falls on her sixty-third birthday in a barrel constructed of oak and iron and padded with a mattress. She did it in order to make enough money to retire on but died penniless because her manager stole her barrel and, without it, her ability to earn money.

Sometimes I worry about you, my inner voice told me.

FIFTEEN

Early the next morning, we were drinking coffee brewed from the cache supplied to us by the owners of the Airbnb while enjoying the view outside our penthouse windows. We didn't have anything to say to each other, so we didn't say anything, which sounds uncomfortable, yet wasn't. Heavenly's phone rang; the ringtone sounded like one of those tiny bells that rich aristocrats in the movies use to summon servants. Heavenly stepped away from the window, picked her phone up from the coffee table, and answered it.

"Yes," she said.

Once again, she held the cell close to her ear so I couldn't hear what was said on the other side.

"Louis," Heavenly said. "It sounds as if you intend to conduct an auction . . . That's not what I came here for . . . Do you have possession of the *Ankylosaurus* skull . . . ? Then what are we . . . Just so it's understood that no one will see a penny of my client's money until the skull is in my possession . . . No, no, no, no. If I were dealing directly with you, it would be a different matter . . . Mr. Bergeron . . . You want to have a friend, be a friend . . . Do you agree to my terms . . . ? Then yes, I will participate . . . Yes, I can come to your office. Thank you, Louis . . ." Bergeron said something that made Heavenly laugh. "I look forward to your call. Goodbye."

Heavenly deactivated her cell.

"Does Bergeron have the skull?" I asked.

"No, although it seems he's in contact with the people who do. They have agreed to let him act as their broker for a percentage of the selling price."

"Well, that complicates matters."

"You think?"

"How many parties will be involved in the auction?"

"At least two. Me and McKenzie. He'll probably get a call any minute now. If Bergeron has his way, though, there'll be a lot more participants. If he has his way, I'm sure he'll put the auction off for as long as possible, spread the word: build interest. Really, Nicholas, it'll depend on the sellers; how motivated they are to make a deal and get on with their lives."

"Let's go for a walk," I said.

"Why?"

"When Bergeron calls, if he calls, I want him to hear McKenzie's voice surrounded by a lot of ambient noise."

"To help disguise it, sure."

Heavenly grabbed her bag and a light coat and the two of us left the penthouse and headed for the elevator. A few minutes later we were on Peter Street and walking south until it became Blue Jays Way, apparently because it led directly to Rogers Centre. At Wellington Street we hung a left going nowhere in particular at a casual pace. If we were under surveillance, the people conducting it were quite good at their job because I didn't see them and I searched very hard.

Eventually, we arrived at David Pecaut Square, a park that was surrounded by office towers including the Metro Centre complex that housed the Municipality of Metropolitan Toronto. We claimed a couple of the multicolored wooden lounge chairs that lined part of the square's perimeter and watched the world spinning around us. Like most urban parks, this one was built of concrete and granite, and featured a fountain and reflecting pool. It also had nineteen small and generic-looking bronze animals displayed on the grass just off the sidewalk. Half of them appeared to be heading for a feeding dish while the other half seem to be wandering away. I have no idea what the sculptor was thinking.

Bergeron did not call.

After a while, we resumed our walk, again heading along Wellington. We passed the Hockey Hall of Fame, and I was tempted to wander inside to see if the original Stanley Cup was still in the vault—with Heavenly, you never know—only I had been there before and I knew it was as quiet as any museum you've ever been in.

A block later we discovered Berczy Park. In the center was a two-tiered fountain that incorporated cast-iron sculptures of twenty-seven dogs and one cat. All of the dogs were looking up toward a large bone perched on the fountain's peak, water sprouting from each of their mouths. Meanwhile, there was a ground-level trough where real live dogs were allowed to drink. The cat, meanwhile, was gazing at the statues of two small birds perched on a lamppost.

"This is different," Heavenly said.

I was about to agree with her when my cell phone started singing. I switched to speakerphone before answering and set it on the bench between Heavenly and I. If we were being followed, I didn't want it reported back to Bergeron that I was seen speaking on the phone at the same time he was calling McKenzie.

"This is McKenzie, who's calling please?"

"My name is unimportant. I am calling . . ."

"Oh, I don't know. You know my name; it seems only fair."

I glanced at Heavenly. She silently mouthed the name "Bergeron" in case I was unsure.

"Mr. McKenzie, I am reliably informed that you are acting as a representative of Mr. Andrew Cooke in the matter of his missing *Ankylosaurus* skull."

"So, I am." I deliberately gave my voice a singsong timbre. "Who reliably informed you, may I ask?"

"Does it matter?"

"Well . . ."

"What matters is that I have access to the skull."

"You have access? I got a call yesterday from some guy who claimed that he had access."

"I am in contact with the gentleman in question."

"Yeah, how much does he want now? He already knows what I thought of his original asking price."

"The amount will be determined at auction."

"Whoa, whoa, whoa—an auction?"

"That is correct. It will be incumbent on you to determine with Mr. Cooke exactly how much you are willing to pay for the skull's safe return before we begin."

"Where is this auction going to be held?"

"It will be conducted as a conference call."

What, no Zoom? You can't see the faces of the people you're dealing with?

"When?" I asked aloud.

"You will be contacted immediately before it begins, possibly as early as this afternoon. I advise you to make arrangements with your Mr. Cooke."

"So, I'm supposed to just sit around and wait for your call?"

Bergeron sounded exasperated when he answered, "That's exactly what you're going to do."

"Just so you know—Mr. Cooke is dying. He could go at any time. If he dies before the deal is made, there will be no deal. Instead of a reward for the safe return of his property, his estate

(252)

just might post a reward for the arrest of you and everyone else involved in the theft."

"Goodbye, Mr. McKenzie."

Bergeron ended the call. I casually slipped the cell into my pocket and looked up at Heavenly.

"Did I sound barely competent?" I asked her.

"No less than usual. Nicholas, how are you going to manage this?"

"What do you mean?"

"I was asked to be at Bergeron's office during the auction. If you, my bodyguard, don't accompany me, Bergeron will become apprehensive. So, again, how are you going to manage this? How will McKenzie be able to participate in the auction if Nick Dyson is standing next to me?"

You didn't think of that did you, smart guy?

"You could always tell Bergeron that Dyson has COVID or something," I said.

"I'm sure that won't arouse his suspicions."

"It isn't essential that McKenzie participate in the auction." *Are you trying to convince her or yourself?* "I would be perfectly satisfied if you win it. In fact, you should, considering that you have unlimited resources."

"That's not the point. If McKenzie doesn't participate, Bergeron will suspect . . ."

"When he calls to set up the time, I'll tell him that Andrew Cooke decided to withdraw on moral grounds."

Heavenly turned her attention back to the sculptures surrounding the fountain. She seemed much more interested in the cat that was staring hungrily at the birds than she was in the dogs.

"McKenzie, you and Mr. Cooke have no intention of paying for the skull, do you?"

"Not if we don't have to."

"If word gets out that I screwed over Louis Bergeron . . ."

"Don't worry, Heavenly. I have a plan."

"God help me."

Bergeron did not call back on Monday. We didn't hear from him again until early Tuesday morning. The number displayed on my caller ID did not match the one that he had used during his first call.

Clever, my inner voice decided.

I stepped out onto the balcony before I answered the call. I stood with my back against the building, as far from the railing as possible, because I have a thing with heights. The sound of traffic rose up to me.

"This is McKenzie, who's calling please?"

"The auction will take place at exactly three P.M. today," Bergeron said. "I will call back at exactly two fifty-five P.M. to connect you with the other participants."

"How many other participants?"

Instead of answering, Bergeron merely said, "Two fifty-five P.M."

"Listen," I said.

Bergeron didn't listen. Instead, he hung up.

Now what?

I stepped back into the penthouse and closed the sliding glass door. Heavenly stepped out of the bedroom, her cell phone pressed against her ear.

"Three P.M.," she said. "I'll be at your office fifteen minutes earlier . . . Business before pleasure, Louis, business before pleasure . . . See you then."

Three P.M.—the words brightened my heart.

Heavenly deactivated her phone and set it on the coffee table. I was smiling at her.

"What?" she asked.

"He screwed up."

"How?"

"Do you know what they have on virtually every street corner in Toronto, I mean besides a Tim Hortons and a cannabis shop? They have a Starbucks. Let me buy you a cup of coffee and I'll tell you what I have in mind."

"Be still my heart."

That afternoon we walked to Bergeron's office. We did a lot of walking in Toronto. It didn't bother me, yet I wondered how Heavenly managed the long distances in heels. We followed Adelaide Street West to Bay Street and headed north across Queen Street and past Toronto Old City Hall.

"Do you know where we are?" Heavenly asked.

"No idea."

"This is the center of Toronto's financial district. Think Wall Street."

"Okay."

"El Cid has his nickname and bar. This is the image Bergeron tries to project—he's not a fence, a receiver, a mover, a facilitator, a middleman, a go-between. He's a serious man of commerce; a transactional mediator."

"Okay," I repeated.

Heavenly led me past the revolving doors of a glass tower. We checked in with the guards in the lobby—"Yes, we were expected"—and took the elevators to the fifteenth floor. I followed Heavenly to an office, making sure that I entered first. A receptionist—*Bergeron has a receptionist?*—seemed happy to see us. She led us into a very plush office where we found Bergeron sitting behind his mahogany desk. His suit looked as if it cost more than the desk. His young man stood off to the side. Once again, he locked his eyes on me and never turned away. Because of his height, he was looking down on me. I found it just a tad intimidating which, of course, is exactly what he was going for.

Bergeron came around his desk and gave Heavenly a warm handshake, virtually ignoring me. He led her to a comfy chair in front of his desk.

"May I get you something?" he asked. "Anything."

Heavenly tilted her head as if she hadn't expected the question. Bergeron raised his finger and smiled.

"I forgot," he said. "Business before pleasure, business before pleasure."

Bergeron reseated himself behind his desk.

"I must tell you, Heavenly," he said. "As happy as I always am to see you, I admit again that I am disappointed."

"In what way?"

Bergeron gestured at me with his chin. I was leaning with my back against the wall next to the door, attempting to appear as nonchalant as possible.

"The company you keep," he said.

Dammit, he made you!

I felt my body seize up; my eyes fell on Bergeron's man who kept staring at me even as I silently warned myself to remain calm.

"Mr. Dyson's reputation is somewhat less than sterling," Bergeron added.

Or maybe he didn't.

Heavenly shifted in her seat to smile at me.

"In what way?" she repeated.

"His criminal record," Bergeron said. "Armed robbery seems to be his specialty although there's a newspaper story that alleged he was a suspect in the theft of an undisclosed amount of cash from a remote vault in northern Minnesota. He's a career criminal."

Heavenly shook her head sadly.

"Tsk-tsk, Nicholas," she said.

"Do you know how we learned your name?" Bergeron asked me.

Apparently, he expected me to act surprised. Instead, I answered in a near monotone, deliberately speaking low and avoiding all contractions. It seemed to work because Bergeron didn't leap to his feet, point at me, and shout, "It's you!"

"The security guards at the Airbnb or the tour guide that took us to Niagara Falls," I said.

The way he grinned made me think that I had guessed right.

"Did you enjoy the trip?" Bergeron asked.

I gestured at Bergeron's man.

"Did he?" I replied.

Bergeron glanced at him.

"You should not follow someone in a red SUV," I said. "They tend to stand out."

Bergeron's glance turned to a glare. His man seemed embarrassed. His gaze became harder as if he was trying to kill me with his eyes.

"You followed us, Louis?" Heavenly said. "Now I'm disappointed."

Bergeron pointed at me.

"I don't trust him," he said. "Should I tell you what my people discovered?"

His people? my inner voice asked. *Does he mean the private investigator you slapped around Saturday night?*

It would have been easy for Noah Cloutier to find plenty of files on the internet that suggested Nicholas Dyson was a career criminal who specialized in robbing banks, jacking armored cars, and burgling the occasional jewelry store. They had been uploaded by my friends at the ATF and the FBI and were meant to be found along with a photograph of me with a scraggly beard and long hair that didn't appear faked at all.

"I am aware of Mr. Dyson's history," Heavenly said.

Bergeron pointed at me some more.

"Tell me, Dyson—do you know a man named Rushmore McKenzie?" he asked. "McKenzie is also from Minnesota."

Heavenly turned in her seat and looked at me as if she also wanted to hear my answer.

"No," I said.

"I don't trust him," Bergeron repeated.

"I do," Heavenly said.

Bergeron shook his head.

"I will be responsible for Mr. Dyson," Heavenly added.

Bergeron still wasn't satisfied, only a glance at his watch told him he was running out of time.

"I will hold you to that," he said.

He started making conference calls. The first was answered by a man that Bergeron called "Number One."

"We will not use names during these proceedings," Bergeron warned everyone.

Number One had an accent that sounded like New York to me or possibly Boston.

Number Two had a French accent, although I suspected that he wasn't from France.

Montreal? my inner voice wondered.

Number Three was Heavenly.

Number Four didn't answer his phone, although I could feel it vibrating silently in the inside pocket of my sports jacket.

Bergeron became frustrated. He excused himself to Number One and Two; put them both on hold and attempted to call McKenzie again. Again, there was no answer. He glared at me like it was my fault.

"I told McKenzie I would call at exactly two fifty-five," he said.

I didn't say a word. That didn't please him.

"Well?" he said.

I made a production out of glancing at my smartwatch.

"Eastern time or central time?" I asked. "It is one fifty-five in Minnesota."

Bergeron's eyes grew wide as he realized the simple error

he had made. I folded my arms and looked up and away as if I were dismissing him. He didn't like that, either. Bergeron swore under his breath and took Numbers One and Two off hold.

"Gentlemen, I would like to postpone this event for at least an hour," he said.

"Hell no," Number One said. "What the fuck, Louie?"

"I do not wish to wait, either," said Number Two.

"One of the participants has been delayed . . ." Bergeron said.

"Tough shit," said Number One. "You snooze, you lose."

"Are we to be penalized for our punctuality?" asked Number Two. "Let us begin, as scheduled."

Bergeron looked to Heavenly for support. She spread her hands to indicate her agreement with Numbers One and Two.

"As you wish," Bergeron said. "Just a moment."

It took more than a moment for the Supplier, as Bergeron called him, to join the conference call. I recognized his voice. After nameless introductions were made, he asked "Where's McKenzie?"

"He is unavailable," Bergeron said.

"Well, fuck . . ."

"So are we going to do this, what?" Number One asked.

"Supplier?" Bergeron asked.

"Yeah, yeah, okay."

"What we have for sale is a complete *Ankylosaurus* skull dating from the late Cretaceous period, approximately sixty million years ago. The skull is not completely cleaned; I'm told it is only sixty, sixty-five percent free of debris. What's more, it is encased in plaster to protect it during transportation; the plaster supported by a wooden frame exactly thirty-six inches long, forty inches wide, and thirty inches high."

"It's about the size of a washing machine if you lay it on its side," Supplier said. "Two guys with moving straps can carry it."

"Supplier, please," Bergeron said.

"When, where, and how can we expect delivery?" Number Two said.

"That will be determined by you and the Supplier."

"And you, Louie," Number One said.

"Of course. The value of this skull on the open market was set at six million dollars in U.S. currency by Dr. David Seeley of the Science Museum of Minnesota . . ."

Who did he tell that, too? Oh, yeah—everyone who was at the dig.

"In the ancillary market," Bergeron continued, "the skull's value is estimated at—well, you tell me. Lady and gentlemen, I recommend an opening bid of six hundred thousand dollars."

"We're talking American money here, right?" Number One asked.

"Yes."

"Then one hundred thousand."

"That's crazy," Supplier said.

"Please, Supplier, control yourself," Bergeron said. "We are only just beginning."

"One hundred and fifty," Number Two said.

"What?" Supplier said.

"Sir, if you refuse to remain quiet, we can conduct these proceedings without your presence."

"Fine, fine, I'm just . . . Okay."

"I have a bid of one hundred and fifty thousand dollars," Bergeron said.

"One seventy-five," Number One said.

"One ninety," Number Two said.

"Two hundred."

"Two ten."

"Two twenty-five."

"Three hundred thousand," Heavenly said.

Her bid silenced both Numbers One and Two.

To fill the silence, Bergeron said, "We have a bid of three hundred thousand dollars."

He was about to say something more when Number One said, "Three hundred and ten."

Heavenly countered immediately—"Three fifty."

The silence became deafening.

"I have a bid of three hundred and fifty thousand dollars," Bergeron said. "Going once, going twice . . ."

"Wait a minute," Supplier said.

"Sold for three hundred and fifty thousand dollars."

"No," Supplier said.

"Gentlemen, thank you for your participation."

"You come across any more dinosaurs, you let me know, Louie," Number One said before he signed off.

"Congratulations, Number Three," Number Two told Heavenly. "Louis, a pleasure."

"This isn't what I wanted," said Supplier.

Bergeron ended the conference call with Numbers One and Two.

"Supplier," he said. "I told you when you agreed to this . . ."

"You told me six hundred grand minimum."

"I also told you that there was a possibility we might not reach that amount."

"This is bullshit. Where is McKenzie? I know I can get a better deal from McKenzie."

"Supplier . . ."

"I'm not going to do this."

"We had a deal," Bergeron said.

"Fuck your deal," Supplier said.

If this was thirty years ago, I'm sure we would have heard him slamming the telephone down on its receiver. Instead, we heard nothing.

Bergeron leaned back in his chair and looked at Heavenly.

"I don't know what to say," he said.

"How about 'I'm sorry, Ms. Petryk, for wasting four days of your precious time'?"

I think "Ms. Petryk" stung the most.

I continued to lean against the wall of Bergeron's office, my arms folded over my chest. I sighed dramatically.

"Do you have something to contribute, Mr. Dyson?" Bergeron asked.

"I have already expressed my opinion on this subject to Ms. Petryk," I answered in a monotone.

"Would you care to enlighten the rest of us?"

"You referred to him as Supplier. Do you know the thief's name?"

Bergeron stared at me as if he was unsure of exactly what I was asking. Finally, he answered, "Yes."

But he's not going to tell you.

"Do you know where we can find him?" I asked aloud.

"No," Bergeron said.

"How did you learn that he had the skull?"

"I am acquainted with a man who owns many storage facilities across the country including Regina. He studiously maintains detailed inventories of what his customers store in his units . . ."

Without their knowledge, I'll bet.

"I reached out to him, and he mentioned"—Bergeron quoted the air—"'an exceptional package' that had been placed in one of his units shortly after theft of the skull had been reported. He supplied the name and number of the owner. I contacted him . . ."

"The thief rented a storage unit using his real name and phone number?"

"He rented it with a credit card."

I thought that was funny and I laughed out loud.

Yeah, these amateurs need to be taught a few lessons.

"Anyway, I made my pitch," Bergeron said. "I thought we had an understanding until, well you heard . . ."

"If you had not screwed up with McKenzie . . ." I said. I saw Bergeron grimace at the remark and his henchman smile ever so slightly. For some reason he suddenly reminded me of Lurch in the old *Addams Family* TV show.

"Who is McKenzie?" I asked.

"He's an ex-cop friendly with Andrew Cooke, the original owner of the skull," Bergeron said. "Beyond that we've learned little about him. What are you thinking, Dyson?"

"Is the skull still inside the storage unit?" I asked.

Bergeron glanced at his young man who was standing across from me and looking menacing. I was beginning to wonder if that was his natural look; his face at rest.

"And if it is?" Bergeron asked.

I shrugged my reply.

"If it isn't?" Bergeron asked.

"The thief, whose name you have not yet given me, will not come back to you; he has burned that bridge. Instead, he will make a deal with McKenzie for whatever that amounts to. We might not know where the skull is, but we can guess where it is going."

Heavenly stood up abruptly. She gathered her light coat and bag and turned toward me.

"I thought I had made this clear to you—I am not a thief. I am not a smuggler. I stay away from the bad thing."

"However," Bergeron said. "You have many times acted as a middleman, middle-woman, between people who have acquired stolen goods and their customers."

"So I have," Heavenly said.

"An interesting distinction."

"Mr. Bergeron . . ."

"Ms. Petryk, if we should acquire the *Ankylosaurus* skull,

would you be interested in completing the transaction we began here?"

Heavenly paused for a few beats before answering.

"My bid was $350,000," she said. "Payable when the fossil is delivered to me in the United States."

"Where in the United States?"

Heavenly didn't pause for a moment.

"Lebanon, Kansas," she said.

Bergeron seemed confused by the answer. It caused me to chuckle, which only confused Bergeron more.

"Gentlemen," I said. "Lebanon, Kansas, is the geographic center of the continental United States."

Bergeron understood that to mean Heavenly had no intention of telling him where her client wanted the skull delivered.

"Thank you," he said.

Heavenly made for the office door without replying. I stood aside and opened it for her. I made to follow her out. Bergeron intercepted me.

"Mr. Dyson, what are your intentions?" he asked.

"To acquire the skull."

He gestured at the young man.

"With our assistance?"

I glanced at Heavenly who was standing in the doorway.

"If that will satisfy Ms. Petryk."

She nodded.

"I will pay you twenty percent," Bergeron said.

"You will pay me fifty percent."

Bergeron pointed at his man again.

"My assistant will accompany you," he said.

"How else will I know where I am going? Hey, pal, what is your name?"

"Max Love."

"Of course it is." I deliberately hid my smile because I knew he wouldn't like it. "Do you have a passport?"

He nodded.

"Give me your cell phone number."

He did. In return, I gave him and Bergeron the number of the burner phone I purchased the day before.

"I will call you in about an hour. Be ready to go."

"Go where?" Max asked.

"Haven't you been paying attention? The storage facility in Regina, Saskatchewan."

I followed Heavenly out of the building. Together we made our way back toward the penthouse.

"I'm surprised McKenzie hasn't heard from our friend by now," she said.

"The phone in my pocket has been vibrating every ten minutes since he hung up on Bergeron. Oh, there it is again. Want to listen?"

"Please."

I answered the call and put it on speakerphone.

"I've been trying to get a hold of you for an hour," the voice said. "Don't you answer your phone?"

"I didn't want to tie it up. I had an important call coming in from Canada, but it looks like he screwed me over."

"You and me both."

Heavenly smirked at that.

"What are you talking about?" I asked.

"Never mind. Do you want the skull or not?"

"We won't pay a million dollars for it."

"Six hundred thousand."

"No."

"Look . . ."

"No, you look. I talked it over with Mr. Cooke. The most he'll pay, the absolute bottom line, is $500,000. And don't forget the get-out-of-jail-free card."

There was a muffled sound; apparently, he had covered his cell phone while he discussed the matter with his co-conspirators.

"We'll take it," he said. "When you deliver the money—and we want it in a cashier's check so there won't be any funny business at your end . . ."

Perish the thought.

"When you deliver the money, we'll tell you where we hid the skull."

"No, no, no, no. What do you think? We're going to give you a check and then take your word that the skull will be where you say it is? You will deliver the skull—undamaged—in person to the Science Museum of Minnesota as we discussed earlier."

"Where the cops will be waiting for us? No way."

"I told you—if you deliver the skull . . ."

"I know what you told me but we're not taking any chances."

"Fine. I'm open to suggestions."

"There's a small town in Canada . . ."

"Canada? Are you kidding me? If you want your money you're going to have to bring the skull to the United States. You're going to bring it to Minnesota or there's no deal."

"Where in Minnesota?"

"I already told you our preference. If you have something else in mind . . ."

The caller paused for several beats.

"I'll call you back once we decide," he said and hung up.

I slipped the phone into my pocket.

"Okay," I said as if I were in complete control of the situation.

We walked all of a half block before Heavenly told me, "I'm leaving Toronto as soon as possible; getting far away from Bergeron in case he thinks I have an unhealthy relationship with Dyson. If he—you—do acquire the skull, he might try to use me as leverage against you."

"You're saying he might take you hostage; hold you for ransom?"

"I'm saying I wouldn't put it past him."

The moment we reached the penthouse, Heavenly began packing. I sat in the living room with my phone making calls. Heavenly must have done the same thing because just a few minutes after she finished packing, she stepped into the room, pulling her suitcase behind her.

"My limousine is here," she told me.

"Where are you going?"

"I thought I'd go back to the Cities; visit the girls. Besides, I want to see how this ends."

I held my arms open, and she stepped into them.

"Thank you," I said.

"Apparently, Nina didn't need to say it out loud when you and she said goodbye at the airport, but I do—please be careful."

SIXTEEN

Max Love and I left Toronto at 6:55 P.M. It took us three hours and twenty minutes to fly to Regina on WestJet, an airline I had never heard of until I booked the flight, yet since we were going from Eastern to Mountain Time, my smartwatch claimed it was only 8:15 P.M. when we landed.

I had attempted several times to strike up a conversation with him, only Max would have none of it. "We are not friends," he told me. Twice. Which made me feel better about our seats. I had booked the first flight out that had space for both of us, meaning we were flying economy, and he was clearly uncomfortable folding his large frame into the narrow seat. Hearing him moan as he stood when we finally reached Regina International Airport made me wish I had done it on purpose.

We moved directly from our gate to the car rental counter. Well, not directly. Along the way, Max insisted on visiting the restroom near the escalators that led from the second level to the ground floor. I waited outside for him. He was gone for less than sixty seconds.

Not even a full minute, my inner voice told me. *Take note.*

Fifteen minutes later, we were sitting inside a Toyota Prius, our suitcases nestled in the trunk. Max was disappointed that I had rented a small car, but I had my reasons besides watching him fidget uncomfortably on the small seat.

"Where to?" I asked.

"What do you mean?"

"Where's the storage unit?"

"We're going there now? It's almost nine."

"No time like the present. Besides, we don't want to give the thief time to move the goods, do we?"

Max used his cell phone to pull up the address on his map app and show me the route—take a right on Regina Avenue when we leave the airport parking lot, follow it to the CanAm Highway, and head south for thirty minutes toward a small town named Corinne.

Glancing at the map told me exactly what the thieves must have done once they had stolen the *Ankylosaurus* skull in eastern Montana. They drove to Ekalaka and headed more or less due north, picking up the Theodore Roosevelt Expressway and following it to the Raymond Port of Entry where they had abandoned the Ford pickup. How they crossed the border with the skull, I didn't know. Yet once they were in Canada, the expressway became Highway 6 and eventually merged with the CanAm Highway at Corinne.

Did they just drive north until they found a storage unit? my inner voice wondered. *Or was it planned?*

I returned Max's cell phone.

"Call the owner," I said. "Tell him to meet us at the storage unit. Drop your boss's name if you need to."

Unlike the rest of Canada, Saskatchewan did not observe daylight savings time, so the sun had set long before we left the airport. Once we put Regina's city lights behind us, we drove in heavy darkness punctuated only by the headlights of the occasional vehicle moving in the opposite direction. Max Love was his usual silent self until a sign informed us that Corinne was just a few miles ahead, at which point he said, "Corinne is just a few miles ahead."

Thanks, Max.

We passed a historical landmark called the "Red Barn With Two Trees," although I couldn't see any trees or the color of the barn. In fact, I couldn't see much of anything—no homes, no farms, no ranches, no businesses, nothing with a light burning in the window. We were at the northern edge of the Great Plains, after all. It reminded me of what Gertrude Stein once said about her home in East Oakland—"There is no there there."

Eventually, we passed a sign that said we were approaching the intersection with Highway 39. Before we reached it, though, the headlights of the Prius picked up another sign, this one advertising StorageGuard Public Storage. It was on the right, a large, silver building with a flat roof squatting in the middle of a gravel parking lot. If it weren't for the two light posts, one on each side of the building, I might have missed it. A gravel road led from the highway to the parking lot.

"Turn in," Max said.

Thanks again.

I parked between the two light posts and turned off the engine.

There's silence and then there's silence. This was silence. I couldn't even hear the sound of crickets. Or wind rustling the leaves of trees. There were no crickets; there were no trees. I could hear Max breathing, though. To escape it, I opened the door of the Prius and stepped outside. Max quickly did the same as if he were afraid I'd wander off somewhere.

"Where's your man?" I asked.

"He's coming."

I nodded, although I doubted Max would have noticed. Two passing vehicles raised my excitement level and then lowered it again. A third car, though, kept it high. It pulled off the highway and approached us, stopping about ten feet away, its headlights illuminating me, Max, and the Prius. The driver turned off the engine and got out while leaving his headlights burning. He was about a foot shorter than I was which made him two feet shorter than Max, with a balding head and an expanding waistline.

"This better be good," he said. "I don't care what Louis has to say."

"We need to look inside one of your units," I said.

"Why?"

Instead of answering, I gestured at Max.

"Tell him which one," I said.

Max hesitated.

"Oh for God's sake," I said. "Do you want me to put my hands over my ears and pretend not to listen?"

"Milo Richardson," Max said.

Never heard of him.

The owner gave Max a hard look. He must have remembered passing the name and contact information to Bergeron because without consulting the cell phone he held in his hand, he walked directly to the unit. We followed. When he reached it, the owner input a code on the garage door pad. The door opened automatically; about halfway up it triggered the fluorescent lights overhead.

In the middle of the concrete floor of the storage unit stood a block of plaster and sandstone wrapped in a cocoon of wood, and yes, it was about the size of a small washer that was resting on its side.

I took a step forward.

Max took a step backward.

I took a deep breath, spun around, and hit him just as hard as I could in the solar plexus.

His solar plexus was exposed because Max was reaching for something behind his back.

Max doubled over at the unexpected attack to his nerve center; I have no doubt even his gallbladder felt it.

He fell to his knees with a little help from me.

I reached behind him and grabbed the Colt 1903 Pocket handgun that he had slipped between his belt and the small of his back. It wasn't particularly big; a .32 caliber with a four-inch barrel, yet it was big enough.

The owner of the storage facility saw the gun in my hand and made a sound that was part surprise and part whimper.

"It's okay," I said. "No one is going to be hurt. Just please, stand over there."

I didn't specify exactly where "over there" was, yet the owner moved to the far corner of the storage unit with the *Ankylosaurus* skull between us.

I bent to Max. He was leaning on his arms and retching like he wanted to throw up yet didn't. I tapped his head with the barrel of the Colt just to make a point.

"It's the little things that matter," I told him. "You couldn't have brought a gun on the airplane with us so it must have been handed off when you stepped inside the restroom after we landed. But Max, here's the thing—no one who hurries into a restroom after a three-and-a-half-hour flight stays there for less than a minute."

Max turned his head. He saw the Colt in my hand; the barrel pointing at his face. He looked away.

"This and conducting surveillance in a red SUV; it makes me question your career choices," I added.

Max coughed a couple of times yet said nothing. For a moment I realized how young he was. 'Course, when I was that young, I was driving a patrol car out of the Phalen Village Storefront in the St. Paul Police Department's Eastern District.

"The gun, Max," I said. "Is that your idea or Bergeron's?"

He didn't respond.

I rapped him on the head again.

"Max, c'mon, talk to me."

"It was Bergeron who arranged for me to get it. He said you can't be trusted."

"How 'bout you? Can you be trusted?"

"What do you mean?"

"Do you like your boss?"

He didn't say that he did; he didn't say that he didn't.

"Are you okay?" I asked. "Can you stand? Here, let's get you up."

I helped Max to his feet. He seemed surprised by that.

"What are you going to do?" he wanted to know.

"*We*"—I emphasized the word—"What are *we* going to do?"

"I don't get it."

"We'll talk about that later." I gestured with the barrel of the Colt at the owner of the storage facility. "In the meantime—Mr. . . . I don't know your name. It doesn't matter. Do you have an empty storage unit?"

"What?"

"Do you have another storage unit that we can rent?"

"There's one right next to this, but . . ."

"Open it, please."

"Why?"

"Because we're going to move this"—I motioned at the block—"into there."

"We're not taking it with us?" Max asked.

"What are we going to do? Put it in the trunk of the Prius?"

Max gave it a moment's thought.

"You're taking the skull for yourself, aren't you?" he said.

"All will be explained," I told him. I held the Colt up for him to see. "I'm going to hang on to this for a while. I hope you don't mind."

Ninety minutes later, Max and I were sitting at a table in the Canadian Brewhouse, mostly because it was the only place we could find that was still serving food by the time we transferred the skull to the empty storage unit, half bribed, half threatened the owner into silence, returned to Regina, and checked into a motel off Highway 6. I ordered the Little Italy chicken parmesan with a side of fettuccine. Max loaded up on chicken wings and fried pickles. I drank Madrí Excepcional, a light beer that originated in Madrid. Max glared at me like I was a traitor. He ordered a Molson Ultra, brewed in Canada.

"You said you would explain," he told me after we were served.

"So, I did. During your last restroom visit, did you happen to call Bergeron and tell him that we acquired the skull?"

Max seemed surprised by the question.

"No," he said.

"Why not?"

"I thought"—he paused as if he was trying to remember what he thought—"I thought that I would wait until I heard what you had to say."

Hmm, do you believe that?

"Here's the thing," I said. "We did what we said we were going to do. We acquired the *Ankylosaurus* skull."

"Uh-huh."

"Now what?"

"What do you mean?"

"What are we going to do with it?"

Max paused before he answered—"Give it to Louie."

Louie, not Louis; not Mr. Bergeron.

"What is he going to do with it?" I asked.

Max seemed confused by the question.

"He's going to give it to Heavenly Petryk," I said. "A very attractive woman, wouldn't you agree?"

"Oh my God, she's like a movie star . . ."

"Bergeron delivers the skull to Heavenly, Heavenly pays the

three fifty, I get my half—I had better get my half—and what do you get? How much is Bergeron going to pay you?"

Max took his time answering.

"I'm a salaried employee," he said.

"Not even a bonus?"

Max shook his head.

"Hardly seems fair," I suggested.

Max didn't disagree. Instead, he took a long pull of his Molson before he asked, "What do you have in mind, old man?"

"Old man?"

"Well, you are old enough to be my father," he said. "And I call him 'old man.'"

Yeah, but is he also a zaddy like you are?

I waved the remark away with my fork.

"Are you averse to a little side hustle?" I asked.

"I won't go up against Louie. I mean, I'm not that dumb."

"I couldn't care less about Bergeron myself, only I made a deal with Heavenly Petryk and I intend to keep it. I intend to deliver the dinosaur to her."

"So, what are we talking about?"

This time I paused, taking a bite of chicken parmesan and a sip of ale.

"Dyson?" Max asked.

"Heavenly has already made it clear that she expects to have the skull delivered to her in the United States."

"So?"

"Who is going to smuggle it across the border?"

Max hesitated before he answered, "You and me?"

"Are we going to be paid extra for that?"

"I doubt it."

"So, Louie sits in his ivory tower pretending to be a man of commerce while we risk serious federal time if we're caught smuggling the *Ankylosaurus* into the States for free. I ask again—does that seem fair?"

Max shook his head.

"By the way, do you have any idea how we're going to do that?"

He shook his head some more.

"I do," I said.

"Tell me."

I did. Max's eyes grew wide; he even laughed a few times.

"That's why you left the message on the floor for the thieves to find," he said.

"That's why."

Max laughed some more.

"You're a smart old man," he said.

And a zaddy!

Max and I spent the next day just killing time. I went out of my way to be pleasant company to him; I even took him to see the Regina Pats play hockey at Brandt Centre. Only I didn't give his gun back.

Bergeron called—twice—and demanded a progress report. I told him if I had something to report, I'd call him. Next, he called Max, who pretended to be apologetic, yet gave him no more information than I did, at least not while I was standing there. After one call, Max tossed his phone onto the cushion of a sofa and announced, "I hate working for that guy. He's so belittling."

"Well," I told him, "if this works out, you'll have plenty of money to live on until you find a better gig."

Max seemed cheered by that.

I knew better, though, than to believe for a second that he and I had suddenly become best buds; that we were both on the same side. Instead, I vigilantly sought clues that would indicate that he and Bergeron were already hard at work plotting my demise, even listening at the door when Max went to the restroom. Once, I told Max that I was going to run down to Robin's Donuts not far from where we were staying. When I returned with a sack filled with Bismarks, Long Johns, and donut holes called Robin's Eggs, I noticed that his cell phone had been moved.

'Course, it wasn't one-sided. My real cell phone, not the burner which I purposely left behind, was in my pocket when I went to Robin's. I used it to call Nina and tell her that I missed her terribly. I also called Special Agent Linda Ambrose.

"I've been trying to get a hold of you for a couple of days," she told me.

"I've been incognito."

"We traced the phone number you sent me. It belongs to—"

"Let me guess—Milo Richardson?"

"If you already knew that—"

"I found out yesterday."

"You could have saved us a couple of man-hours."

"Sorry. Who's Milo Richardson?"

"He's thirty years old; owns an auto repair shop in Bloomington. He was working for someone else until last year and decided to go off on his own. Apparently, he's not doing well. On the other hand, he has no record whatsoever; not even a parking ticket."

Auto mechanic supports your theory on how the Ford F-150 was stolen, my inner voice told me.

"What else did you find out yesterday?" Ambrose asked. "Do you know where the *Ankylosaurus* skull is?"

"As a matter of fact . . ."

I could picture Ambrose shaking her head as I explained.

"You know, you could just call the Mounties and tell them where to find it," she said.

"Where's the fun in that? Besides, I don't know who stole it yet."

It was early Thursday morning when my burner phone rang.

"This is Dyson," I said.

Max was lying on his bed and watching curling on TV—Canada covers curling the way we cover the NBA. He gestured for me to put the call on speakerphone, which I did.

"What did you do?" a voice asked. I thought I recognized it.

"Is this Milo?" I asked. "Milo Richardson?"

"How do you know my name?"

"I take it you saw my message or you wouldn't be calling now."

"Where's my dinosaur?"

The question made me laugh. I mean, how many times have you heard someone ask that in a high, piercing voice?

"It's not funny," Milo said.

"Maybe just a little bit. Milo . . ."

"Who is this?"

"Didn't I tell you? My name is Dyson, Nick Dyson."

"What do you want?"

"I want to make a deal with you."

"For what?"

"For money, of course."

"We're not making any deals."

"Milo, Milo, Milo, may I remind you that I have the *Ankylosaurus* skull. You've got nothing."

I allowed that to sink in for a few beats.

"Still with me, Milo?" He didn't reply yet my cell phone claimed he was on the line. "Milo, there's a reason why I wrote my phone number on the floor of the storage unit."

"Tell me."

"I was exaggerating before when I said you had nothing. You do have something I want. A client."

"A client?"

"How much did McKenzie offer for the safe return of the skull?"

"How do you know about McKenzie?"

I watched Max while I answered. He was sitting on the edge

of the bed and leaning forward like it was the seventh game of the Stanley Cup finals.

"I was in Louie Bergeron's office when you and he had your argument . . ."

"You're working for Bergeron?" Milo asked.

"No, I'm not."

"But you said you were in his office during the auction . . ."

"Milo, this is strictly an independent business enterprise."

Apparently, he didn't know what to say to that.

"But, since you brought him up," I said, "I should tell you, Louie is very upset. You know what he did? Right after you hung up the phone, he contacted the Canadian Border Services Agency and told them, without revealing his name, of course, that an American named Milo Richardson was going to smuggle a stolen dinosaur fossil across the border into the U.S. Do you believe that?"

Max shook his head as if he didn't.

"That's why—my God, that's why we were delayed at the border," Milo said. "That's why the agents searched the truck. That's never happened to me before."

I had to smile. Some searches are made because the person crossing the border does something suspicious, smells like pot; has an iffy-looking passport. Sometimes it's because the agents decided that they were going to do a Level One search on every third vehicle that day or a Level Two on every tenth. Other times it's because they're looking for someone who matches a vague description on a BOLO that had been distributed. Milo had just been unlucky, and I leaned into it.

"Imagine what'll happen during your return trip," I said. "This is what comes from dealing with unscrupulous characters. Which brings us back to McKenzie. How much did he offer you? You said during your argument with Louie that you were going to contact him."

"None of your business."

"How 'bout I just hang up the phone and see if I can find this guy myself; make my own deal."

Milo answered with a defeated sigh—"Five hundred thousand dollars, payable with a cashier's check."

"Cashier's check? Seriously?"

"He said if we return the skull undamaged the owner won't prosecute."

"That's awfully trusting of you. Okay, here's the deal—we will return your dinosaur skull and help you smuggle it across the border. In return, you will give us half of the reward."

"No way."

"Like I said before—right now you got nothing."

"What do you have?"

I paused long enough to convince Milo that I was thinking it over.

"We could always contact McKenzie or one of the other bidders who got screwed over and make our own deal," I said.

"Except you're afraid that Bergeron will find out what you did and retaliate. That's why you're going to all the trouble of dealing with me instead of just taking off. You know what? Maybe I should give Bergeron a call myself; see if we can get back into his good graces."

Once again, I paused. Max was still watching me. He moved his hands as if he was impatient to hear my answer.

"Forty percent," I said.

Max shook his head.

"Twenty," Milo said.

Max shook it harder.

"A full third," I said. "Otherwise, we'll just hang on to the skull and see what happens. It's a seller's market, after all. I can wait three to five years. How 'bout you?"

I was leaning heavily on what Special Agent Ambrose said about Milo's failing business.

"Okay," he said.

"Okay?"

"Okay," Milo repeated.

I winked at Max. He was not pleased.

"Where are you?" I asked.

"Right now?" Milo said. "We're at StorageGuard outside Corinne."

"I will be there in about an hour."

"We'll be waiting."

"Oh, if I see a weapon of any kind, if I even suspect that someone has a weapon of any kind, I will wipe you off the face of the Earth. I've done it before."

"There's no need for that."

"Let's hope not."

I ended the call.

"Thirty-three percent?" Max asked.

I made a production of removing the Colt from my pocket and checking the load.

"No, we'll take it all." I slipped the piece back into my pocket. "It takes forever to cancel a cashier's check. We'll have the money in our pockets long before they can manage it. I know people."

"The same people that Bergeron knows?"

"There are others."

"Can I have my gun back?"

"Of course not."

SEVENTEEN

We took our own sweet time packing our bags, checking out of the motel, even grabbing breakfast at the London Belle before we left Regina.

"Keeping them waiting will remind them of who's in charge," I said.

Max excused himself to use the restroom.

"When you call Bergeron, tell him that we have the skull," I said. That caused Max to pause, his eyes wide with surprise. "Tell him that we intend to use these guys to smuggle it across the border. We'll let him know when and where as soon as we know."

"You really want me to . . ."

"We're stealing from Milo, not your boss. Oh, and have him ask Heavenly where she wants the skull delivered."

Max took his cell phone into the restroom. Apparently, it didn't occur to him that since I knew what he was doing, he could make the call at the table in front of me. I used the time to make my own call to Heavenly.

"Bergeron will contact you soon," I told her. "Give him whatever location that seems feasible."

"I will. McKenzie, I'm at Rickie's. Nina is standing next to me."

"Tell her I love her. Tell her I can't talk now; it would be too distracting."

I ended the call.

Sometimes you can be such a jerk.

My next call went to Special Agent Linda Ambrose.

"I'll be smuggling the *Ankylosaurus* across the border soon," I told her. "Somewhere in northern Minnesota."

"You'll be smuggling it?" she asked.

"Not me, exactly. I promised I wouldn't break any laws, remember?"

"You'll just bend them a little, right?"

"It could happen as early as today. By then I should also know who's responsible for the theft."

"I'll believe it when I see it."

I ended the call just as Max exited the restroom.

"What did Louie have to say?" I asked when he reached the table.

"He said to watch that old man like a hawk."

"It's bad enough that I have to hear it from you, but from Bergeron? I'm younger than he is."

"He pretends to be older because he claims his clients are more comfortable dealing with someone who projects a certain maturity. He's only about forty-two."

Well, crap!

There were three men standing around two vehicles in the gravel parking lot of StorageGuard Public Storage when we finally pulled in. One of the vehicles was a blue Ram 1500 pickup truck with the name RICHARDSON AUTO REPAIR printed on the door. The other was a black Chevy Bolt EV. I didn't recognize any of the men. I parked the Prius about twenty-five yards away from them.

The storage unit's lights were on even though it was just past ten in the morning. Because of the sun, I could see nothing but farmland and empty fields all around us. There was no one working the farms. The only sounds we heard were the ones we made ourselves; the only movement came from the few vehicles that passed us on the highway. It made me ask who would build a storage unit out there, although the answers seemed obvious. Someone who only wanted to pay five cents an acre for land and who didn't want any witnesses around when he robbed his own business.

Max and I moved toward the three men, making sure we were about five yards apart. Two of them appeared to be in their early to mid-thirties. The third was college age. I watched their hands. They were empty. At least for now.

"Are you Dyson?" one of them asked.

"I'm Dyson."

"Where's my dinosaur?"

"You mean *our* dinosaur, don't you?"

Max and I stopped just out of their reach in case someone decided to throw a punch. I spoke to the man who spoke to me.

"Are you Milo?"

"Yeah."

I gestured at the other two.

"And your friends?" I asked.

"You don't need to know who we are," the college kid said. He reminded me of that young good-looking actor who was in that limited TV series, you know the one. His face appeared as if he smiled a lot, although he wasn't smiling now.

"We're going to need some rules if we expect to pull this off to our mutual satisfaction," I said.

"Fuck your rules," the kid said.

Max moved to his left until he was facing the men from the side. The thirty-year-old who wasn't Milo turned toward him. I liked that he had to shield his eyes from the sun hovering behind Max's shoulder. It made me think that Max actually knew what he was doing.

"In the spirit of cooperation . . ."

Before I could finish, the kid reached behind his back, pulled out a revolver, took two steps forward and pointed the gun at my face, holding it with one hand. I forced myself to remain calm. Okay, that's a lie. I forced myself to *appear* calm. The truth is I was anxious; very anxious. Yet not as anxious as I would have been if the kid was standing five feet away. Instead, he was close to me. So close . . .

"Max," I said. "Kill this kid."

I could see the kid's eyes flick to his right as if he was desperate to see what Max was doing. That gave me enough time to shift my head out of the line of fire, bring my left hand up, grab the kid's wrist, and push the gun away. At the same time, I drove my knee hard into his groin. Twice.

The kid doubled over. I hit him in the jaw with my right elbow a couple of times just because. And yes, I practice this at Gracie's Power Academy, too. The kid would have crumpled to the ground, except I was still holding his wrist. I carefully removed the revolver from his hand and released his wrist. And he fell.

I looked for Milo. He hadn't moved except to raise his hands when I pointed the gun at him. The third man was on his knees, though, holding his face where Max and punched him.

I was trying to think of something pithy to say along the lines of "Can't we all just get along" except I was interrupted by a woman's cry.

"Please, don't hurt him," she said.

I turned to see a young woman standing in front of the Chevy Bolt, the passenger side door was open. She couldn't have been more than five feet tall; she couldn't have weighed more than a hundred pounds. Her hair was short and red. Her face was open; almost childlike.

I could barely hear myself think because my inner voice was screaming, *It's Winter, it's Winter, it's Winter. She knows you! Don't panic. Don't freak. You have the gun. You have the dinosaur.*

"And who's little girl are you?" I asked.

No, no, no, she's not a little girl. She's a woman. Treat her like a woman.

"Please don't hurt him anymore," Winter said.

She's not pointing and screaming your name. Doesn't she recognize you?

"Okay, I won't," I said.

There're three of them. And her.

"Thank you," Winter said.

And Max. Don't forget Max. If he finds out who you are, then so will Bergeron. That won't be good for Heavenly.

"What's your name?" I asked.

"Winter."

"Ms. Winter . . ."

"No, Winter is my first name. I'm Winter Billock."

"Ms. Billock, my name is Nick Dyson."

Winter bowed her head in recognition.

"Mr. Dyson," she said.

She's going along with this. Why is she going along with this?

I used the toe of my shoe to nudge the young man who was still clutching his groin and rolling about in pain.

"Brother?" I asked.

"Boyfriend."

I nudged him some more.

"I'm afraid he won't be of much use to you in the immediate future."

Winter shrugged as if she didn't care one way or the other. I looked down at the kid. I had a good idea who he was, but I was smart enough not to use his name.

"Hey, pal," I said. "Involving your girlfriend in a criminal enterprise like this, you must not think very highly of her."

I glanced at Winter to see if she received my message, only she didn't give me anything.

"Dyson?" Max asked. "What are we going to do about this?"

"Well, now that we've established a hierarchy . . . Milo, I'm disappointed in you."

Milo was still holding his hands in the air.

"It wasn't us; it was him," he said. "We told him to leave his gun in the car but he . . ."

"Who's the adult here?"

"You don't understand, it was all him. This entire thing was his idea."

"What thing? Screwing me over or—are you talking about the theft of the *Ankylosaurus* skull?"

"He thought we could make a lot of money stealing the skull and then selling it."

"Plus, he wanted to punish his girlfriend," Winter said.

"I thought you were his girlfriend."

"So did I."

"Winter, please," the young man said.

I gestured at Milo.

"Put your hands down."

He did. I called to the third man, who was no longer rubbing his face, yet was still on his knees.

"You. What's your name?"

"Matthew. Matt."

"What's your last name Matthew Matt?"

"Richardson."

I pointed at Milo.

"I take it you're related."

"Brothers."

I motioned again.

"Both of you, pick this kid up. Is he related, too?"

Milo and Matthew helped the young man to his feet.

"He's our cousin Jordan, Jordan Wall," Matthew said.

Yeah, that's what you thought. Now what? You have the Ank. You have the thieves. All you need now is the Royal Canadian Mounted Police. They have 911 in Canada, don't they? Except, what happens to Heavenly when Max and Bergeron discover who you really are? And what about Winter? Do you toss her on the pile, too? She might deserve it; why else is she here? Then again, she might not.

"Dyson," Max said. "What?"

"You're asking me what to do now?" I motioned at the two thirtysomethings. "I say we proceed as originally planned. I'm not suggesting that we forgive and forget what has taken place in the past fifteen minutes. I'm saying we learn from our mistakes and move on. There is, after all, a great deal of money to be earned if we can just cooperate. You'll get your share; not as much as you like, but then none of us get as much as we like. I'll get my share to make up for the severe trauma of having a gun pointed at me. And Max here will get his share for looking tall and menacing. What do you say?"

My speech sounded silly, of course, like something you might hear in a bad film noir or a Hallmark mystery. Yet it had its point. I was using it to deescalate the situation, to lighten the mood. I also wanted to send a message to everyone, especially Max, that they will all get their money. And I wanted Winter to believe that nothing bad was going to happen, at least not to her. The speech seemed to work, too. Jordan and the Richardsons appeared less frightened. Max's expression became less grim. And Winter—truth is, I couldn't read Winter.

Be careful, pal, my inner voice told me. *She hasn't blown your cover. That doesn't mean she won't the second you set down the gun. That doesn't mean she isn't involved in this up to her pretty eyebrows.*

"I'm perfectly willing to keep my end of the deal," I announced. "How 'bout you boys? And girl?"

They nodded like they were relieved.

"Where are we taking the skull?" I asked. "I can't help but notice that you have Minnesota license plates on your vehicles."

"Minnesota, yes," Milo said. "McKenzie says that's where we need to take it."

Winter didn't so much as flinch at the sound of my name.

"Where in Minnesota?" I asked.

"We haven't told him yet," Jordan said. I think he just wanted to contribute to the conversation.

"Good. We'll tell him where to pick it up *after* we get it there."

"But how are we going to get it there?" Milo pointed at his truck. "We can't use that and pretend it's auto parts like the last time. Not if, as you say, Bergeron ratted us out to the border patrol."

"That's how you smuggled it into Canada?" I asked.

Milo nodded.

"Well, you're right," I said. "That's not likely to work again. I mean you were damn lucky the first time."

I looked at Max who remained his usual silent self.

"Any suggestions?" I asked him.

"Hey, old man," he said. "I thought this was your show."

Really? He had to say that in front of the G-I-R-L?

"Does anyone have a laptop with internet service," I asked.

"I have one in the truck," Matthew said.

"Let's take a look at the Minnesota border."

While we moved to the Ram 1500, I decided to press my luck. After all, I still had the gun.

"Who is this McKenzie, anyway?" I asked. "Can we trust him?"

"We've never met," Wall said.

"I met him," Winter said. "He seems like a nice man. A friend told me he specializes in helping people."

"Like Andrew Cooke, the guy who's willing to pay to get the *Ankylosaurus* back," Jordan added.

"Well, maybe he can help you," I told Winter. "And me. And everyone else, too."

The sun made reading the PC difficult; I positioned it on the hood of the truck so that my shadow covered the screen. I used a couple of different map apps to study the border between Canada and the U.S. Suggestions were made while I did. Jordan wanted to drive to the Lake of the Woods, ferry the skull across the lake from the Canadian side to the Minnesota side on a boat, load it back onto the truck, and drive away.

"Do you have a boat?" I asked.

"We could steal one."

"I'm sure the border agents who diligently patrol the lake in their high-speed boats would be very happy if we tried that. They get so bored up there."

I was studying a satellite image of the area along the border roughly between Roseau and Warroad, Minnesota, when I had a thought.

"Milo, when you were on the phone with Bergeron, you said that the block holding the *Ankylosaurus* skull could be carried by two guys using moving straps," I reminded him.

"Yeah, yeah, like how they carry refrigerators and stoves into your house."

"Do you have any moving straps?"

"No."

"There must be a Home Depot or the Canadian equivalent around here somewhere."

"What are you thinking?"

"We'll carry it across the Slash."

"What's the Slash?" Winter wanted to know.

"Its official name is the Canadian-United States international border vista. Basically, it's a strip of land about as wide as a two-lane highway running along the forty-ninth parallel from Maine to Washington that has been completely cleared of trees, shrubs, whatever. You wander through the woods and come up to it; you know that's the border." I ran my finger across the satellite image. "That's what this line is."

"You can just walk across it?" Jordan asked.

"Yes, although we'll need to be careful. The two countries have assembled a collection of solar-powered motion-detecting security cameras known as the Slash CameraPole system. They watch for illegal activity around the clock. But here's the thing—the cameras are only placed along those sections of the Slash that are within hiking distance of major highways. Areas that are well away from populated areas are not monitored." I tapped the image. "Like right here."

Everyone moved forward to get a better view of the PC screen except for Max.

"What are we looking at?" Milo asked.

"This is Provincial Highway 12 in Manitoba, also known as Mom's Way, don't ask me why. This is a dirt road that runs from the highway due south. Notice the farm fields on both sides? I propose that we take this road as far as it goes, unload the *Ank*, and then you'll use the moving straps to carry it across the Slash. After you cross the border—this is the Lost River State Forest. After you cross the border you'll follow this strip—do you see it? It was cleared to make way for power lines. You follow it to here. It's a dirt road running east and west. Even if you're off course a little bit, sooner or later you'll reach this road. Right here"—I tapped the screen—"is where we'll pick you up. Look for our lights."

"How far is that?" Matthew asked.

"Three miles. Maybe a little more."

"Oh my God."

"It takes approximately one hour to hike two miles across unbroken, wooded terrain, double that because of the awkwardness of the load you're carrying and the fact that you'll be doing it at night. I estimate it'll take about three hours. More than enough time for the rest of us to get back on Highway 12, drive to the border crossing near Warroad, Minnesota, and work our way back to the pickup point."

"You keep saying 'you,'" Jordan said. "Who is you?"

"I'm an old man and far too decrepit to walk that far, just ask Max." Max smiled. "That leaves you and your cousins."

"No way," he said.

I ignored him and recorded the exact location of the pickup point on my cell phone using the decimal degree system that marked the exact latitude and longitude supplied by the map app.

"What are you doing?" Jordan asked.

"Making sure we can find you on that dirt road in the dark. It would be so sad if we got lost."

"This is crazy."

I glanced at my watch.

"It's a quarter past eleven," I said. "A half hour back to Regina to buy the straps. Seven and a half hours to drive to the spot on Mom's Way; we should get there just after sunset— Manitoba observes daylight savings time. Another three hours to carry the skull across the border. If everything goes according to plan, there's a joint in Warroad called Nomad Tavern that serves a decent pizza. We should be there well before last call."

"What about the skull?" Milo said.

"We'll pick it up on the way."

"Wait," Jordan said, "you want to do this now? Right now?"

"I suppose we could hang out for a couple of days; get to know each other better. What about you, Max? Do you feel like bonding?"

He growled his reply.

"And then what?" Jordan said.

"And then what, what?"

"After we smuggle . . ."

"After we smuggle the *Ankylosaurus* skull into Minnesota, you'll call McKenzie and tell him we want two cashier's checks made out to bearer, one for you and one for me. You guys good with that?"

I waved Jordan's gun for emphasis. Milo and Matthew Richardson both nodded.

"How 'bout you, Ms. Billock?"

"I just want it to end," she said.

EIGHTEEN

Regina did have a Home Depot located not far from the airport. We stopped there to pick up a "shoulder dolly," at least
that's what it was called on the box. We also bought a small
flashlight and a compass. Afterward, we circled back to the
airport where I dropped off the rental car. I rode with Jordan
and Winter in the backseat of the Chevy Bolt and Max hitched
a ride with the Richardson brothers in the four-door Ram 1500
where he could stretch out. Our new partners seemed surprised
when we swung off the CanAm Highway and returned to the
storage unit outside Corinne to retrieve the skull. They didn't
say anything, yet I knew what they were thinking—"If we had
only known . . ."

After strapping the block down in the back of the pickup, we
worked our way east across Canada, the long trip made longer
by the fact that we did it largely in silence. We paused in Glenboro, Manitoba, for gas, to use the restrooms, and load up on
fast food at the Glenboro Drive In, yet that was done mostly in
silence, too. While no one was looking, I sent the map coordinates and our ETA to Special Agent Linda Ambrose.

The closer we came to our final destination, the more anxious Jordan Wall seemed to appear. Several times he glanced at

Winter as if he wanted to say something yet didn't. Finally, he blurted out, "I'm sorry about all of this, I really am."

"I don't believe you."

"It's true."

"Then why am I here?"

"You know why you're here."

Winter's response was to move in her seat so that she was hard against the passenger door, as far away from Jordan as she could get and still be in the same car. She turned her head to look out the passenger window.

"I'm sorry," Jordan repeated.

Trouble in paradise, my inner voice concluded. *You might be able to use that.*

Once we merged onto Provincial Highway 12, I had Jordan take the lead. Using the map app on my phone, I directed him to the little-used dirt road—there was no signpost and we nearly missed it. By then the sun had set. I was relieved that we could see no lights except for our own.

We turned right onto the road and followed it slowly between the farm fields until it just stopped. Everyone except Winter vacated the vehicles and helped ease the block off the back of the pickup and into the two-person shoulder dolly worn by the Richardson brothers.

"It doesn't seem nearly as heavy as when we moved it by hand," Matthew said.

"Give it a couple of miles," I said.

I drew Jordan next to me and handed off the flashlight.

"Here's the compass," I told him. "This is north . . ."

"I know."

"This is the direction you'll be walking. See, it's almost straight south."

"I can figure it out."

"The Slash is about a mile from here. Cross it in a hurry."

"I get it," Jordan insisted.

I thought how much fun it would be to hit him again.

"All right, you're off," I said. "Try to use the flashlight as little as possible."

The trio found an opening in the trees, and with Jordan in the lead, disappeared into the forest. Max and I stood there and watched. Jordan was already using the flashlight more than I would have recommended.

"Well, old man?" Max said.

"So far, so good."

"If you say so."

"Do you want to drive the truck or the Chevy?"

Max answered by stepping to the Ram 1500 and climbing inside the cab.

"If either of us gets hung up at customs, the turnoff is at Highway 313 and 400th Street," I said. "After that . . ."

"I can read a map."

"All right."

I tapped the door a couple of times and went to the Chevy Bolt. Winter was still sitting on the passenger side, which suggested that I was supposed to drive. As I climbed in, Max started the pickup, turned it around, and started up the dirt road toward the highway. He drove like he was in a hurry.

Take note, my inner voice told me.

I started the Chevy, maneuvered it around the makeshift cul-de-sac, and started up the dirt road, myself. When we reached the highway, I hung a right and drove east. I could no longer see the pickup's taillights.

"So, Winter," I said. *"The time has come, the Walrus said, To talk of many things—"*

"Of shoes—and ships—and sealing-wax—Of cabbages— and kings—And why the sea is boiling hot—And whether pigs have wings. Do you know I have an English minor? I major in geology and minor in English. Some people think that's odd,

but I hope to write a lot of articles and research papers. McKenzie, you have no idea how happy I am to see you."

"Are you happy?"

Winter turned her head and studied my face as if she was surprised by the question.

"It looks bad, doesn't it?" she said. "It looks really, really bad my being here. That was Jordan's intention, to make me look bad."

Winter curled her small body and braced her feet against the dashboard just above the glove compartment. I didn't mind. It wasn't my car.

"Tell me more," I said.

"I didn't know what he had done, honest, honest to God, McKenzie, not until . . . until . . . the day you came to the science museum, and you spoke to Simon and me, remember? You gave us your card. Afterward, Jordan came by to pick me up, pick us up, me and Simon, and while we were driving back to the U, Simon told him about meeting you and about how you had informed us that Mr. Cooke was willing to buy back his *Ankylosaurus* skull from the people who stole it and Jordan—he didn't seem that interested until we dropped Simon off and suddenly he wanted to hear more, wanted to know who you were and how much Mr. Cooke was willing to pay and demanding, 'Give me his card, give me his card,' and McKenzie, I knew. Don't ask me how I knew, but I did.

"I asked, 'What did you do?' He told me. Not at first. I had to—I had to threaten him to make him confess. I had to promise I would never speak to him again unless he told me the truth. Finally, he admitted that he and his cousins stole the *Ankylosaurus* skull. He laughed about how much money they were going to make; over a million dollars he said. He also said that it was a way to get back at Angela, at Professor Bjork, for sleeping with him and then blowing him off.

"God, I hated her for that. You don't do that. Even if you

weren't a teacher and he was a student, you don't do that. Jordan belonged to me. I loved him. Only after I came to know her and like her and—McKenzie, I didn't know what to do and then I knew exactly what to do because Jordan—he told me what *not* to do. He told me to keep my mouth shut; told me not to tell anyone. I was debating who to call first—the police, Angela, you. That's when he swore, his left hand over his heart and his right hand in the air with three fingers extended like a Boy Scout, that if I revealed what they had done, he and his cousins would testify that I was involved; that it had been my idea all along."

Winter pounded the dashboard with her feet. Then she did it twice more.

"He reminded me that he only knew what was happening at the dig because I told him," Winter added. "Because I had called him or texted him every single night and gave him a detailed recap of what was happening. He said my cell phone records would prove that I had informed him of the plans to move the *Ankylosaurus* skull and skeleton to the Science Museum of Minnesota. That I had called him only hours before the theft to announce that the skull had been loaded on the back of that guy's pickup truck and was waiting for them to steal it. Only I didn't know, McKenzie. Please, you need to believe me. I didn't know that the three of them, Jordan and his cousins, were planning to hijack the skull when the moving people took it up the dirt road to where it met the highway near Powderville. I guess they were just waiting there. Only after I called Jordan and they knew the skull was on the truck, they changed their plans."

This means Nina's original theory about what happened that night was right. She's going to love hearing it, too.

"And they snuck into camp, and I saw them," Winter said. "I didn't know who they were, Jordan's cousins, I hadn't met them until later and they—they shot at me! Jordan's cousins shot at me!"

Winter pounded the dashboard with her feet again. She did it hard enough and often enough that I felt the entire vehicle shake.

"They shot at me!" she repeated. "Jordan claimed, 'We didn't know it was you, we didn't know it was you.' And then he said, 'We shot into the air.' And then he said—his voice got very low and he was smiling when he said, 'We shot into the air because we *did* know it was you and we wanted to give you an alibi.'"

She kicked the dashboard again, only she didn't put as much effort into it.

"That was Thursday," Winter said. "Last Thursday. I didn't know what to do. Jordan would threaten me and then he would tell me that it was all going to be fine, that Mr. Cooke would get his dinosaur back and his cousins would pay off their business loans and he would pay off his college debt and pay for grad school and even have a little left over for me, whatever that meant, and then he would threaten me again.

"Finally, Jordan told me on Tuesday that we were driving to Regina in Saskatchewan. When I asked why, he said because that's where the skull was hidden and my going there with them would prove to the authorities that I was involved in the theft from the very beginning which meant he could finally trust me to keep my mouth shut and that meant we could go back to the way things were before and McKenzie, something deep inside of me, some little piece, wanted to go back to the way things were before I learned the truth. When the two of us were happy. Only I can't—I can't sleep. After they shot at me, it was bad. I'd have trouble falling asleep and then I'd wake up in a sweat, but after a few nights it went away. This is worse.

"But now you're here. McKenzie, when I saw you get out of the car at the storage facility, my heart leapt. I nearly ran to you. I didn't because I was afraid that you would think that I was a part of all of this. At the same time, I didn't understand why you were there; we were supposed to be meeting a man named

Dyson. When you hit Jordan—I was glad you hit him, yet at the same time I didn't want to see him hurt. God, I've got it bad, don't I? Anyway, that's why I left the car and then you told me your name was Dyson . . . McKenzie, why are you here?"

"To recover the skull, of course," I said.

"To recover it without paying for it. To capture the thieves who stole it. McKenzie, how much trouble am I in?"

That depends, doesn't it? my inner voice told me. *Do you believe her? She sounds sincere; she sounds truthful, but do you believe her? Is she telling you this story because it's true or because she recognized the instant she saw you that the jig was up? The conversation between her and Jordan Wall earlier would seem to support her cause. Or they could have been talking about something entirely unrelated to this. Think about it. Is she a naïve young woman caught up in events not of her own making or a conniving bitch looking to cover her ass?*

"I don't know," I said aloud.

At the same time, I told myself not to let Winter out of my sight.

Max Love, on the other hand, had disappeared from my sight. He wasn't there when we passed through the U.S. Immigration and Customs Enforcement center just off Highway 313 after we crossed the border. Nor was he waiting for us at the intersection with 400th Street just one mile south.

I hung a right and followed 400th Street until it became a series of narrow, unnamed, seldom-traveled dirt roads that were cut through the thick forest. Most of them seemed to have been graded solely for ATVs; the car was jostled about even at a very slow speed and I heard and felt the floor of the Bolt hitting bottom and scraping hard earth. Finally, we arrived at the coordinates on my map app and found—nothing. The fact that Max wasn't waiting for us surprised me.

Several thoughts flashed in my brain like lightning bolts.

The first was that Max, despite his bravado, misread his map app and was now roaming aimlessly through the Lost River State Forest.

The second—Max and the Richardson boys cut a deal; they had plenty of time to talk it over while they drove here. Max told them to walk into the forest, wait for him and me to leave, and then he'd double back and pick them up where they were dropped off. Except, if they were going to cut Dyson out, I told myself, wouldn't they do it after they came across the border?

The third—it took a lot less time to get there than I had originally planned. According to my smartwatch, we were about ninety minutes early. Maybe Max stopped for a beer.

I went to the trunk and rummaged through the bags we had stored there for the guns I had hidden from the border patrol agents; the ones I had taken off of Max and Jordan Wall. I brought Max's .32 inside the Bolt with me.

Winter saw the gun. She said, "McKenzie," filling my name with unasked questions.

"It'll be fine," I told her. "And call me Dyson until all this is over."

"Yes, sorry, Dyson."

A bit of Henry Wadsworth Longfellow came to mind.

"Let us, then, be up and doing, With a heart for any fate; Still achieving, still pursuing, Learn to labor and to wait," I recited.

"I don't know who that is," Winter said.

And she's minoring in English? What are they teaching in schools these days?

The temperature had dropped to the mid-forties. I was fine, yet Winter was shivering, so I rolled up the Bolt's windows and turned on the heat. Again, there were no lights to be seen except for our own headlights and those shining in the night sky, which were spectacular.

Winter and I waited for what seemed longer than ninety minutes. Ninety-five minutes. One hundred minutes. I was starting to get anxious. Where was Max? Winter wondered aloud if paleontology was a good career choice, after all. One hundred and five minutes. Finally, I saw movement at the edge of the road. Winter must have seen it, too, because she seized my wrist.

"Is that . . . ?"

It was. About a hundred and thirty yards in front of us, Jordan and the Richardson brothers emerged from the forest. I couldn't make them out; the headlights of the Bolt barely reached that far. Yet I knew it wasn't a trio of bears because bears rarely carry a large rectangular box in a shoulder dolly.

I left the vehicle and started walking toward them.

They started walking toward me.

We were about thirty yards apart when a second pair of headlights flicked on behind me.

I spun toward the lights.

I heard the roar of a pickup truck as it sped along the road, scraping the side of the Bolt as it passed.

Max Love, I told myself.

He must have crept up behind us sometime during the past hour and three quarters.

I didn't hear him because I was sitting inside the Bolt with the windows rolled up and the engine running.

I didn't see him because his lights were off.

Why were his lights off?

Because he didn't want to be seen.

Until now.

This is not good.

My fight-or-flight reflex kicked in. I did neither. Instead, I moved to the very edge of the road, wishing I hadn't left Max's .32 in the car, telling myself I could run if I needed to; the forest would protect me.

The truck stopped just a few steps away from me. Its headlights covered Jordan and the Richardson brothers. They halted for a moment, and then started moving forward again until they were just ten yards in front of the Ram 1500's bumper.

"That was a lot harder than you said it was going to be," Jordan told me.

The doors to the pickup opened.

Doors, plural.

This is not good, this is not good, this is not good . . .

I could see everything from where I was standing by the headlights of the Chevy Bolt.

Max Love moved from the driver's side door to stand in front of the trio carrying the skull. He had a semiautomatic in his hand that I couldn't identify, although he wasn't pointing it at anyone.

"Don't move," he said.

The three men didn't. 'Course, they had nowhere to go, especially the Richardsons. They had lowered the *Ankylosaurus* skull to the ground yet were still attached to it by the shoulder dolly.

Louis Bergeron slid out of the passenger side door and stood staring at me.

He was followed from the rear passenger door by—*Are you kidding us?*—Noah Cloutier, the Toronto PI that Heavenly and I had messed up. His face was bruised; there was a bandage that suggested a doctor had used splints to repair his broken nose. Like Bergeron, he stood staring at me. Unlike Bergeron, he was smiling.

"Everyone relax." Bergeron pointed at me. "Especially you. This is what is going to happen. We're going to load the skull into the back of the truck, and we are going to drive away. And you're not going to do a thing about it."

"Wait. What? No," Jordan said. "This is our skull. Who are you?"

He seemed pleased to tell them—"Louis Bergeron. I'm the man you screwed over. Remember? I am very unhappy about that. Now, you will do as I command or there will be repercussions."

"Fuck that," Jordan said.

Max stepped forward and punched Jordan in the face as if he had been looking forward to the opportunity. The college boy collapsed to his knees.

You'd think he'd learn his lesson by now.

"Dyson, do something!" Milo shouted.

"Dyson?" Bergeron chuckled. "Yeah, the fearsome Nick Dyson. You deceived a lot of people. Me. Heavenly Petryk. I spoke to her this morning. She's even more upset than I am. You should know that she accepted responsibility for your outrageous behavior and promised to pay me her commission when I deliver the *Ankylosaurus* skull to her client as compensation for her naïveté."

Good for you, sweetie.

"McKenzie," Bergeron added. "I do not like being made to look a fool."

Oops.

"Neither do I," Max said.

Noah Cloutier continued to smile.

"McKenzie," he said, "did you think I wouldn't find out who you really were?"

Double oops.

"McKenzie?" Milo repeated. "Wait a minute. McKenzie? You're McKenzie? But you said—Winter said—Winter said she met McKenzie, met you."

"She did." Jordan was on his feet, again. "She said—where is she?"

"This is your fault," Milo told him. "You couldn't keep your big mouth shut. No, you had to tell her everything. And then you tried to blackmail her? Jesus."

"Where is Winter?"

"Halfway home, if she's smart." I spoke loud enough to be heard if she was still sitting inside the Chevy Bolt. I was hoping that she wasn't.

"Who's Winter?" Bergeron wanted to know.

"She's a loose end," Max said.

"Find her."

"McKenzie's a loose end, too," Noah said. There was a gun in his hand. He raised it.

"No, don't," Bergeron said.

Get inside the forest, I told myself. The forest is your friend. Darkness is your friend.

I leapt toward the trees.

A shot rang out. Only it didn't come from Noah.

As I hit the ground I saw a muzzle flash near the Bolt. Winter was standing there, holding Max's gun in her hand as if she had learned to shoot by watching bad 1980s TV cop shows.

I turned my head. She had missed Noah completely. But she hit Bergeron, who was now sprawled out on the dirt road. Noah did not return fire, choosing instead to fall to the ground and start crawling beneath the pickup truck. Max ducked against the front bumper and was cautiously looking around the corner of the Ram 1500 for a target.

I jumped to my feet and ran toward Winter. She was looking at the handgun as if she had never seen it before. I lowered my shoulder and literally scooped her up. I was surprised how light she was.

I ran forward, carrying her down the road; thinking I should get off the road. The headlights of the two vehicles were pointed the other way. Darkness soon engulfed us.

I saw it before I heard it, a large, armored SUV rumbling down the road, its high beams blazing; a searchlight on top. Suddenly, it was like we were standing inside Target Field where the Twins play ball.

The vehicle was followed by two more SUVs, the first with POLICE WARROAD printed on its door and the second tagged SHERIFF ROSEAU COUNTY.

I carried Winter into the woods to get out of their way. I couldn't help but notice two more vehicles joining the party from the opposite direction. All of the vehicles halted, surrounding the Chevy Bolt and Ram 1500 and the men standing near them.

A voice called out over a loudspeaker.

It was a female voice.

"FBI," it said.

JUST SO YOU KNOW

Louis Bergeron was DOA at the LifeCare Medical Center in Roseau. I was saddened to hear that. I don't think he wanted Noah Cloutier to shoot me. I don't think he wanted to shoot anyone. He was a man of commerce after all, and while much of what he did was immoral if not straight-up illegal, was he any worse than my Heavenly?

Heavenly was also upset, although she seemed to take a more cynical view.

"All for nothing," she said. "There was never anything on the table. It was all for nothing."

She hugged me and kissed me on the cheek and said, "See you around, Copper."

"Copper?" I asked.

"You'll always be a cop, McKenzie. Always."

She walked away and I wondered what I always wondered when she walked out of my life—Is this the last time I'll see her?

Noah Cloutier was charged with attempted murder. He vigorously denied that he tried to kill anyone; claimed that Winter Billock was the one who should be indicted. She wasn't. On the eve of his trial, though, Noah pled down to assault in the second degree and was sentenced to three years and a $10,000 fine.

Max Love, who everyone agreed never pointed his gun at anyone, also copped to assault in the second degree. He was sentenced to time served and kicked out of the country.

Jordan Wall and the Richardson brothers claimed that they shouldn't be charged with anything. They claimed they had a contract with Andrew Cooke stating that if they returned his dinosaur fossil, he would not prosecute them for its theft. It might have been an unwritten contract, but it was enforceable. That's when the assistant U.S. attorney explained that they were *not* being prosecuted for stealing the *Ankylosaurus* skull, which was a crime against an individual citizen. Oh, no. They were being charged with conspiracy against the United States, specifically violation of the National Stolen Property Act of 1934 as stated in 18 U.S. Code 2314—the transportation of goods known to be stolen across state lines and foreign borders.

Things became complicated after that with the defendants alleging entrapment by an "agent" of the Federal Bureau of Investigation, meaning me. Special Agent Linda Ambrose made it clear in depositions that the Bureau did not support much less condone my activities and absolutely nothing that I did was at their direction or with their permission or approval; quite the contrary. The defense attorneys suggested that the FBI's presence in the middle of the Lost River State Forest must have been a coincidence, then. Not only that, at the very least, they claimed I was guilty of conspiracy to transport stolen property across a foreign border—so, why wasn't I charged, too?

For a while, I thought I was in serious trouble. I was obliged to involve my attorney, G. K. Bonalay, who shook her head at me and said, "You just can't help yourself, can you?"

Fortunately, the court decided that I had not compelled the defendants to do anything, and their arguments were dismissed. Besides, during this back-and-forth it was determined, beyond a reasonable doubt, that while I might have kinda, sorta helped the defendants transport the stolen skull *into* the United States, the defendants most certainly smuggled it *out* of the country and hid it in the storage facility all by themselves. They went away for sixty months, which was a damn sight better than the ten years they could have served.

After the case was closed, Special Agents Brian Wilson and Linda Ambrose invited me to coffee at the Caribou in Brooklyn Center. I asked Ambrose why she had waited for the sound of a gunshot before swooping down on the smugglers.

"Unlike you, I'm a drama queen," she said. "Unlike you, I thrive on chaos."

I told her that I knew sarcasm when I heard it.

Brian told me that he was upset by the way events had transpired. I asked why.

"Because I know that the next time you take on one of these missions, you'll call Linda instead of me," he said.

Ambrose nearly choked on her latte.

"Please don't," she said. "Please, please, please, I'm begging you."

It seemed to me, though, that the person who suffered the most was Winter Billock. She killed a man. She did it to save my life, yet that did little to still her nightmares. We managed to get her into therapy and that seemed to help. And yes, I paid for it. At first, she resisted. That's when I told her the story of the woman on a white horse who had also saved my life and what I was happy to do for her in return. She and Angela Bjork became close after that. "It's like we're members of an exclusive club," Winter told me. While she continued to blame herself, no one else involved in the dig held her responsible for Jordan Wall's actions. It didn't hurt that she was also constantly being supported and comforted by a young man—what was his name? Oh, yeah. Simon Stevens.

Unfortunately, Andrew Cooke passed long before his *Anky-losaurus* could be restored and put on display. Shortly after he learned that the skull had been recovered, he died in his sleep. The cause was cardiac arrhythmia. I was told that if you have to die, there is no better way to go. I attended his funeral. Megan Cooke-Jackson delivered the eulogy. She said that because of the love of his family and the recovery of his dinosaur, her grandfather died happy. She was reading the eulogy from a sheet of paper. Halfway through, she broke down. Kevin Jackson stepped up, took his wife in his arms, and finished reading the eulogy. I was moved almost to tears. So was Dr. David Seeley who was standing not too far away from me, only not for the same reasons.

Megan and Kevin were holding hands when the Science Museum of Minnesota held a black-tie gala to display the nearly complete skeleton of the *Acheroraptor* a week after Thanksgiving Day. The museum staff, as well as other prominent members of the paleontology community, all sang praises to Cooke and announced that the dig sponsored in southeastern Montana will now and forever be known as the Andrew Cooke Creek.

Once again, I found myself wondering what it was with dinosaurs and creeks.

Nearly everyone who was at the dig that summer was at the gala. Professor Ashley DeLuca kissed my cheek and then brushed the lipstick stain away, which made Nina laugh. She was there with her granduncle who shook my hand and said he was grateful that I had recovered the skull.

"Otherwise, I would have had to step in," Martin DeLuca said.

Angela vigorously hugged me, hugged Nina, and then hugged both of us at the same time.

"You people," she said.

We took that as a compliment.

Professor Gary Phillips bought Nina and me a drink. He

didn't chat with us very long, though. He was too intent on dancing with Angela who waved at Winter who was dancing with Simon next to Megan and Kevin.

"Ah, to be young and in love," I said.

Nina punched me in the arm.

"Are you saying we're not young?" she wanted to know.

Not long after, I entered into a conversation with Dr. Weston Hegarty and Dr. Nicholas Larsen. They both praised my investigative skills. I told them that Nina had figured it out long ago and all I did was prove her theory.

"Like a peer review of a paper," Dr. Hegarty suggested.

"Exactly," I said.

Nina seemed very pleased by that.

"I must say," Dr. Larsen told us, "After you came to my office, I was wondering if you knew what you were doing."

I pretended it was a joke and said, "So did I."

Dr. Hegarty asked if I was working on any other investigations.

"I was told that there are some people at the U who are using their positions of power to extort sexual favors from their staff," I said.

I was staring directly into Dr. Larsen's eyes when I said it.

Dr. Hegarty saw me looking into Larsen's eyes.

"Is that right?" he said. "I've heard rumors but so far they've been unsubstantiated."

"It might be something worth looking into. I haven't decided yet."

By the time the spring term began in January at the University of Minnesota, Angela Bjork had been made an assistant professor and Ashley DeLuca was promoted to associate professor. Both were praised for their discovery and study of the *Ankylosaurus*, although I suspect the fear of lawsuits and bad publicity might have added to their advancement.

The evening of the gala, though, it was all smiles and warm

wishes. A photograph of Andrew Cooke, taken a couple of years before he passed, was placed next to the *Acheroraptor* display. He looked happy.

Apparently, I did, too, because while we were dancing Nina kissed me like she meant it and said, "You know what? You are a zaddy."

ABOUT THE AUTHOR

Renée Valois

DAVID HOUSEWRIGHT has won the Edgar Award and is the three-time winner of the Minnesota Book Award for his crime fiction. He is a past president of the Private Eye Writers of America. He lives in St. Paul, Minnesota.